RECONSTRUCTING SOLDIERS

RECONSTRUCTING SOLDIERS

An Occupational Therapist in WWI

Margaret Drake

iUniverse, Inc.
New York Lincoln Shanghai

RECONSTRUCTING SOLDIERS

An Occupational Therapist in WWI

iUniverse, Inc.

For information address:
iUniverse, Inc.
2021 Pine Lake Road, Suite 100
Lincoln, NE 68512
www.iuniverse.com

The characters are fictional. None of the main characters are based on real persons, present or past. Famous personalities from history and specifically from occupational therapy history are depicted as accurately as possible from what we know of them today.

ISBN: 0-595-28723-9

Printed in the United States of America

Contents

Acknowledgements

Using history as a backdrop means many facts must be verified. It is possible to find some information on the Internet. I want to thank my 97 year old step-mother Jessie N. Williams and her 107 year old sister Letitia N. Lawson for their help with details of clothing and technology of the WWI era. Both of these women remember that era well. I thank my oldest sister Jean who proofed my first chapters. When I had specific questions, specialists who know their own field were more accurate and quicker than the Internet. I have used a number of such experts. Dr. Alan Sabrosky gave much information about soldiers in WWI. Dr. Julius Cruse verified several "history of medicine" facts. Lt. Col. JoAnn Bienvenu shared information about women in the service in WWI. Imke Streuding, my friend, consulted with me about European cuisine. Dr. Cyndi Scott shared physical therapy documents which describe reconstruction aide uniforms and embarking from Ellis Island. Neva Greenwald suggested resources, both people and documents. My OT colleagues at UMC listened uncritically to my ruminations about my heroine. Carol Tubbs MA, OTR/L, with her superb English skill proofread the whole manuscript.

Chapter 1

Humble Beginnings

"What to do? Which road should I take for my future?" Lorena spoke mostly to herself but her landlady's daughter named Elsie, with whom she shared the room, lay on the other side of the bed. Elsie grunted her response from her half-asleep state. Elsie was not interested in a future without her Fred. She had not enjoyed school and was bored by Lorena's discussion of her own conflicts about her future education. Lorena, on the other hand, spent a great deal of time reflecting on her past as well as her future education. All her college years, she had been on scholarship. Did she want to continue to always feel like the poor child at the table? She lay on her back in her iron bed. She felt alone, though Elsie lay only inches away. Her thoughts flew back over her route to this place near William Penn College. Her parents had allowed her to continue her education at the academy though her ten brothers and sisters had all had to stop their schooling after a few years at the country school.

The wonderful development that pushed Lorena into further education occurred because of the intercession of Miss Colben, the London, Kentucky town librarian. She and Miss Colben had become acquainted during the hours Lorena spent studying. The three room house of Lorena's parents, in the country village a few miles from London, had been too noisy and crowded to allow for serious study so Lorena had spent her Saturdays in the new Public Library when she could get away from work responsibilities. She would finish her daily chores, which included feeding the chickens and gathering the eggs, wiping up spots of tobacco juice in the corner of the kitchen where Pa missed the spittoon. Then she would clean herself up as well as she could in the wash basin outside of the back shed. By the time local people were heading toward town for their Saturday shopping, with their teams hitched to farm wagons, Lorena would be standing by the road signaling for a ride to town. Pa and Ma usually came in later. Pa was a late starter, which was probably why he had never been able to keep a job and advance enough to keep his large family from struggling for necessities. If she waited for Pa and Ma, she would not get to town until noon. And then they would usually want to send her off on an errand since she was their star child. Whenever an especially delicate situation with merchants came up, they relied on Lorena's ambassadorial skills to help the family.

She had discovered hitchhiking when she was seven-years-old when her older brother Charles took her with him one Saturday. He lay in the ditch and got her to flag down a neighbor because he knew that girls were more likely to get rides than boys. Then when a neighbor would stop, Charles jumped up and trailed her as she got into the neighbor's wagon. Often, after that first exciting trip on top of firewood, to be sold to town-dwellers, she'd wheedle her brother into taking her along. By age nine, she was hitch-hiking a ride by herself. She was usually able to get to the library a short time after the 9 AM opening. During the next five years, she and Miss Colben had become something of an institution in London, Kentucky.

At first, Miss Colben had seemed to be annoyed by her constant questioning. "Where are the books about mining?" How can I find out about Jane Addams and the Women's Peace Party?" Why can't Negroes come into this library?" Gradually, Miss Colben came to look forward to Lorena's Saturday visits. With small steps their relationship moved into solid trust and devotion. Other library users came to expect to see the two of them sitting, talking together behind Miss Colben's desk. While other girls talked about their fiancés, Lorena could only think of time spent discussing national and world news with Miss Colben as worthwhile. The middle-aged librarian came to cherish the bright-minded young woman.

Miss Colben remembered the sacrifices she herself had made in order to avoid being forced into the trap of marriage and motherhood. Despite the fact that she was sometimes lonely, she usually did not regret her choice to remain single. The one gift she could give to Lorena besides their friendship was to encourage her to further her education so she could manage to live without relying upon a husband's support. In this second decade of the twentieth century, married women were virtually the property of their husbands.

Miss Colben had gone to her friend, a wealthy widow in town, to ask for money to pay Lorena's academy fees. The woman had agreed to pay her travel and living expenses at Vermillion Grove Quaker Academy in Illinois if Lorena would work to get the money to pay her tuition. The widow believed that women who took some financial responsibility for themselves while they were young, were less likely to succumb to the security of being taken care of by a husband. Fortunately, the Vermillion Grove Academy gave her a scholarship for her tuition.

Lorena had been thrilled when she saw ahead a new life of study and satisfying her curiosity. Previous to Miss Colben's intercession for her, she had faced the same life she saw for so many other young women; working at home helping Ma and Pa, or being hired as a hired girl for one of the more substantial families, or marrying one of these local lads and start raising babies. This last alternative was the most horrifying. She's seen her sisters, one by one, fall into this trap. All but one of her five sisters had married her local swain and now even Margaret, who was younger than Lorena, was about to have a baby. The thought of such a life was deadening. No, the alternative of attending Vermillion Academy in Illinois had been her lifesaver. In fact, there were times during her early teens when the thought of repeating her mother's life of hard work and subjugation to Pa's whims, had made her think of killing herself.

The widow who agreed to finance Lorena's academy living expenses had insisted that she attend the school run by the Quakers. This had not been what Miss Colben, who was a Presbyterian, had in mind, but at least Lorena would get an education, and not be condemned to a life of breeding and allowing her bright, challenging mind to slowly congeal into acceptance.

Despite her job working in the library at the Quaker academy, she had done so well academically, that the faculty had assisted her in finding scholarship money to pay for four year at William Penn College in Oskaloosa, Iowa, another Quaker school. She had embraced this further opportunity to avoid a life of married drudgery. She had been lucky to find a boarding house on the north side of Oskaloosa, only three blocks from the Penn campus. She was able to work for part of her room and board and thus use the money sent by the wealthy London widow for her tuition. It worked out well. She helped Mrs. Cooper, her landlady, cook meals and do laundry for the other boarders. She still had time to study for her classes. During this time at college, she had been exposed to a new way of looking at the world. Mrs. Cooper rented her other two bedrooms only to females. A faculty member from the college had occupied a room during one year. Twins from Chicago, who were students at Penn, had shared one room for two years because their parents knew Mrs. Cooper. She had learned a great deal from these women from other places and other classes. There had been a few male students in a few classes. However, most were seminary students. Lorena could not see herself as a minister's wife and consequently did not respond to any attempts by these men to be come more closely acquainted. Self-searching about her repulsion by this idea often surfaced when she watched the other female students coquettishly responding to the seminary students.

Now, in 1915, three and a half years after she came to Penn, one of her professors was giving her an opportunity to accompany her during her semester break on a trip to Chicago to visit the famous Hull House. Jane Addams had been Lorena's heroine for some time. Now, she would get a chance to visit the famous woman's shrine. However, she knew that her professor, Miss Ring, had another agenda.

"Lorena, do you know about settlement houses? My classmate from Claverack College, Eleanor Clark Slagle, has started a program to educate occupational therapists. Hull House, seemed a perfect place to do this according to her."

Lorena glibly repeated what she had learned in her modern history class. "Hull House is a pioneering effort by a group of modern social reformers. Immigrants and poor people are taught to help them better themselves."

"Oh, my dear, it is much more than that," said Miss Ring. "These women who started Hull House, have worked to reduce the ill effects of child labor, to regulate working conditions for women and generally to force Chicago factory owners to observe safety requirements for their workers."

Less glibly, Lorena replied, "Yes, I do remember Professor Wooler mentioning these ideas in his lecture on social reform." Lorena had not realized that Miss Ring was so socially conscious. However, she had been aware that Miss Ring was trying to steer her toward the new profession Mrs. Slagle was involved in starting, this occupational therapy.

Lorena rolled over and covered her head with her pillow hoping to shut out the sound of Elsie gritting her teeth in her sleep. She continued to ruminate about her future. If she took that road, studying occupational therapy, which she and Miss Ring had discussed at length, she would again be in the situation of the poor sister suffering the indulgence of her richer associates. Lorena had seen advertisements on the society pages of the *Chicago Tribune*. She could see that the advertisements had pictures of rich women. Lorena may have gone to school with some rich women, but she herself, had always had to struggle to get money for her education. She had no difficulty getting good grades in her classes. The only trouble was paying the extra school fees for special events. But she resolved not to be drawn into something she did not want to do as a career. She would look with realistic skepticism at this "opportunity."

"Ah well," she murmured to herself as she drifted toward sleep, "My bag is packed and I'll just go and enjoy the train ride."

Chapter 2

Chicago

She met Miss Ring at the train station next morning. Although it was only 7:30 a.m., Lorena had already done one third of a day's work.

By 5 a. m. she had been out feeding the hens and gathering the eggs to be cooked for breakfast. Mrs. Cooper had a hen house in the back yard. Lorena had started heating up the cook-stove before she went to the hen house. She ground some fresh pork for sausage patties, which she put on to fry as well as cornmeal to boil for cornmeal mush. The smell of boiling coffee mixed with the smell of frying food. Meanwhile, she boiled some eggs to take with them on the train. She had heard how expensive food in the dining car was. Also, she sliced some bread and cheese for their meal after the boarded the train from Des Moines to Chicago.

After serving the meal to the other three boarders, and Mrs. Cooper and Elsie, she gathered up the dishes and left them for Elsie. She had bargained with Elsie that if she would do the breakfast dishes for her this morning, Lorena would let her wear her new brown corduroy skirt she had made before the Christmas holidays.

Except for two summer trips back home to London, Kentucky, this was the first time Lorena had left Oskaloosa since she arrived in August of 1911. Her agreement was that she would be excused from her laundry and cooking chores for the duration of this Chicago trip if she would do all the cooking, cleaning and laundry while Mrs. Cooper and Elsie went to Ottumwa for two weeks next month. Mrs. Cooper's other daughter expected her first baby then.

These compromises and sacrifices went through her mind as she sat shivering alone on the bench outside the small train station watching Miss Ring approach. They would take the "mixed" train to Des Moines where they would catch a regular passenger train straight to Chicago. A "mixed" train carried both passengers and freight. At this time of year, they shared the trip with bins of shelled corn and stock cars of cattle and hogs. The seats for the few passengers were wooden benches along the wall of the passenger caboose. A big wood burning heat-stove occupied the middle of the car. As they rode along through the winter farmland, Lorena could feel a draft on the back of her legs where the wind came through the cracks between the floor and the wall. She squeezed her leather valise under the edge of the bench trying to block the draft. Her face felt scorched by the heat from the stove.

After a two-hour wait in Des Moines, the two women boarded the passenger train headed east. As they left the outskirts of Des Moines, Lorena spread out the lunch she had prepared for the two of them on half of the small table they shared with the couple in the seat across from them. She started to peel the boiled egg for Miss Ring, but the teacher took the egg from her hand, protesting that since Lorena had prepared the lunch, the least she could do was peel her own egg. The slices of brown wheat bread, which was left over from yesterday's noontime meal, were still soft enough to taste good with the slices of farmers' cheese. Lorena had been afraid that milk might sour, so instead she had included two pint-fruit-jars full of tap water to accompany their train meal. She promised Mrs. Cooper that she would bring the empty fruit jars back to the boarding house, as they would be needed when canning started in July.

Lorena had always enjoyed watching other people. As soon as she and Miss Ring were settled in seats side-by-side together facing forward in the direction the train was going, Lorena entertained herself and Miss Ring with fantasies about their various fellow passengers. There was a tall, well dressed man in a dark business suit and matching hat carrying a leather case whom she fantasized was on his way to Chicago to work in the new radio industry. There was the jolly woman wearing too many ruffles for her full figure, whom Lorena thought was a prostitute. She could not say this to Miss Ring, so she told a fantasy that she was a simple farm girl on her way to meet her future husband, a farm boy who had gotten a job in the Chicago stockyards. There was a sad elderly man and woman dressed in black and speaking another language sitting across from Miss Ring and Lorena facing backward in the direction from which they had come. Their clothing was slightly different from other passengers, perhaps more conservative and also more worn. Lorena imagined that they were foreign travelers who had come from Europe to visit their children whom they found dead here in this new land. Lorena's fertile brain kept silently inventing stories of other's lives long after she knew Miss Ring was tired of her inventions. It was a way to pass the time as the train passed through the plowed fields of the former prairie that had so few years before been only grass. The simple stark farm buildings pierced the landscape. Farm odors occasionally overwhelmed the atmosphere as the train passed near livestock feedlots. Even the cold air could not disguise the odor of animal feces.

As the train approached the outskirts of Chicago, clusters of houses of similar size and style passed by the windows. Suddenly they were passing through the city. The change from the clean country and suburban landscape to dirty street and back walls of tenements was drastic.

Miss Ring had written to make arrangements to be met by Mrs. Slagle. The women had not seen each other for over five years. Miss Ring had begun to wonder aloud whether she would recognize her classmate as the train began to slow down. The Chicago train platform held more people both standing and rushing than Lorena had ever seen together in one place before. The two women clutched their valises as they crowded with the other passengers toward the door. At last they were on solid ground and Miss Ring scanned the faces on the platform. Suddenly she began to move rapidly toward a small, dignified woman who ran toward her without losing any of her dignity. As they neared one another, they both stopped, looked at each other, laid their hands on each other's shoulders before embracing. Mrs. Slagle had a calm, square face with well-spaced blue-gray eyes. Miss Ring was struggling to keep tears from her eyes and voice as she turned to introduce Miss Slagle and Lorena. The calm composure of Mrs. Slagle appealed to Lorena who disliked the feeling of frenzy that frenetic people produce in those around them. They shook hands gravely as Miss Ring told Mrs. Slagle that Lorena was her favorite student. This was news to Lorena though later she reflected that she should have known that since teachers do not take less favored students on two hundred-mile trips.

Mrs. Slagle had brought a young Irish immigrant boy with her to help with the luggage. The boy, named Colin O'Donnell, picked up the bags and led the way through the throng of passengers and those greeting or saying good-bye to them. He deftly avoided hitting their luggage against other luggage or limbs. He led them straight to the nearby station for the "L" electric train to the Congress Street Line. Again, he made sure the ladies were all seated and he stood nearby the door guarding the bags. Lorena judged him to be about sixteen years old though it was hard to tell. Later, she learned that he was one of the children who had worked in the clothing industry until the child labor law was enforced. He had been orphaned at age five. The custom was to allow business men to become the guardian of such children. Often greedy men would assume responsibility for many such orphans and then use them as virtual slave labor until Ms. Julia Lathrop, the social worker and reformer, put an end to this practice. When Colin was liberated from his enforced ten hour per day servitude at age twelve, he had already aged so he looked older than his years.

They got off the electric train at Racine Street and Colin carried their valises four blocks to West Lexington Street. Mrs. Slagle led them to her apartment in this area called the Near West Side. She had the young man put their valises on the elevator with the three women. She said goodbye to Colin and pushed the iron elevator gates together before pushing the *up* button. Mrs. Slagle lived in an apartment house in which the street level was filled with shops. Her apartment on the fourth floor had windows looking down unto the busy street below. She showed Miss Ring and Lorena the bedroom, which they would share, which looked South out across the busy street into Arrigo Park. There was still some afternoon sun slanting into their bedroom.

Immediately after they had refreshed themselves in the bathroom at the end of the hall in the apartment, Mrs. Slagle called them into the formal dining room for dinner. A young Scandinavian girl, Lena, whose exact country of origin Lorena was unable to identify, served the supper of what Mrs. Slagle called New England boiled dinner with wholesome brown bread and butter.

The two old friends dominated the conversation at the meal as they brought each other up to date on their lives. Miss Ring told how she had come to take the job at Penn College and why she had not married the young man they had both known in college. This story of his death during the sinking of the Maine in Havana Harbor was something Lorena had never known before. She realized her teacher was allowing their relationship to advance to a different plane by letting her hear it. Mrs. Slagle listened and nodded.

Eventually, their hostess began to tell of her career during the past decade. She told of the founding Hull House by Jane Addams and her colleagues in 1889, of the Chicago School of Civics and Philanthropy at Hull House in 1908, of the Henry B. Flavill School of Occupations this year in 1915. Her own involvement with these events had not occurred until she registered to take the course in occupations in the summer of 1911. She had visited in the Eastern Illinois Asylum for the Insane in Kankakee. The patients she saw there seemed to benefit so much from the housekeeping, carpet making and sewing that she observed. The following summer she had taught the occupations course by herself. She had been working in the Phipps Clinic at Johns Hopkins Hospital in Baltimore before she was persuaded to come back to Chicago to be director of the instructional program in occupational therapy. Her full-time job as the head of occupational therapy for the Illinois State Mental Hospitals and her new position as the director of the Flavill School of Occupations hardly left her time for a husband. Mrs. Slagle, whom Miss Ring familiarly called Eleanor, was so eloquent when she described how patients improved their health while doing occupations. She believed her work was as important as that of the doctors. Satisfying occupation was so important in healing. Mrs. Slagle's passion for her work was contagious. Lorena felt it must be wonderful to see people's lives change because of the time they spent in therapy.

After the two women had apparently caught up on their most recent life changes, the conversation topic changed to the war in Europe and what should the USA do. Lorena had not thought too much about whether the USA should join with France and England against the Germans. She listened carefully as Mrs. Slagle discussed the consequences of not throwing our strength with the other countries fighting the "Hun". Miss Ring, whom Eleanor Slagle called Rosetta, echoed the excuses she heard from the local Oskaloosa newspaper, about the US's need to protect themselves and not get involved with distant wars. The suffragists trying to be allowed to vote was a topic that interested Lorena but seemed to tongue-tie the two older women. It seemed as if neither wanted the other to know her feelings on this issue. They discussed the $10 per week wages of the workers in the neighborhood around Hull House and the cost of a loaf of bread at 6 cents and a gallon of milk at 36 cents. Mrs. Slagle, who continued to respond to that formal appellation from Lorena, despite their two hours together, gave her opinion that people could not live adequately on such wages. She further described the work of Jane Addams and Julia Lathrop to teach immigrants how to better themselves. Miss Ring gave no opinion on the wages as her life on the campus of the small college seldom brought her in contact with such problems. Because Lorena had struggled and squeezed her money for school, she could sympathize with people who struggled to buy the milk and bread.

As the Scandinavian servant served the dessert, Mrs. Slagle described the course of study for the occupational therapy curriculum she was embarking upon at the Henry B. Flavill School of Occupations. "This course of study will be five months long. There will be classes on medicine, psychology, physiology and sociology, physical recreation and arts and crafts. There will also be lectures on the principles of management, organization and administration."

Her interest and passion for her work caused the listening Lorena to eat the Apple Betty with sweet cream almost without tasting it. Lorena felt excited and inspired by the conviction with which Mrs. Slagle spoke. She forgot her resolve not to be drawn into something she did not know about. Mrs. Slagle was so convincing that this new "occupational therapy" was an important way to contribute to patient health, that Lorena began to harbor thoughts of joining the new profession. The woman envisioned "occupational therapy" as an independent medical specialty. Being part of a new profession was a rather titillating idea for Lorena.

There were twin beds in the room Lorena shared with Miss Rosetta Ring. Now each time Lorena thought of Miss Ring, she mentally added her given name Rosetta, though she did not say it aloud. Each bed had small shaded electric lamp clipped to the headboard. Lorena was grateful for this private light because she felt she would not be able to sleep for some time. The trip, the city of Chicago, the dinner conversation, had provided her with so much to think about, to scan back over in her mind, that she knew she would need to read her textbook on 19th century British poets in order to calm her mind for sleep. She decided to attempt to help calm herself by taking a hot bath. It was wonderful to have hot water straight out of the tap. Mrs. Slagle had shown them, which towels on the wooden towel rack in the bathroom were for their use. When she returned to the bedroom, Miss Ring was breathing loudly and regularly.

She was right. Lorena heard the hall clock strike two before she slept.

Chapter 3

Sampling Chicago

Next morning, Miss Ring had to awaken Lorena because she was making up for the lost sleep of the previous evening. She usually was in bed by ten o'clock and asleep almost as soon as her head was on the pillow. Miss Ring told Lorena it was eight o'clock and the servant Lena had called them for breakfast. Lorena leapt out of bed, grabbed her comb and went toward the bathroom. She was glad she had taken a bath last night. After relieving herself, she combed her hair and rushed back to the bedroom to put on her plain brown school dress which Miss Ring had approved for her time in Chicago.

When she joined the two women in the dining room, she wondered as she ate the hearty breakfast of coffee, milk, muffins, butter, apple butter, hard boiled eggs and sausage, what Lena's servant quarters were like. What time did Lena have to get up to cook breakfast and how late did she have to stay up to wash the dishes? Lorena wondered how different Lena's life was from her own. They both earned their living by cleaning up after and taking care of others.

Mrs. Slagle, Miss Ring and Lorena all arose together from the breakfast table leaving their cloth napkins beside their soiled china plates and cups.

Mrs. Slagle reminded them, "The sunshine outside the window is deceptive. At this time in the windy city, you will need your coats."

Lorena looked forward to the time when she could choose her own coat in a fabric and color she liked. But now, she would have to be satisfied with the gray wool felt coat which had seen her through four winters in Oskaloosa. There were several torn and worn places, which Lorena had cleverly concealed with black braid. But it was getting harder and harder to conceal the worn spots on the elbows. In another two months, she would graduate from Penn College and hopefully find a job. Despite her current trip to explore the new profession "occupational therapy" she continued to think of herself as "almost done" with school.

The three women turned east out of the entrance to Mrs. Slagle's building. It was an eight block walk to Hull House on the corner of Halstead Street and Polk Street. Lorena walked behind the two women, as they still seemed to have so much to say to each other. Now it was Miss Ring's turn to tell about the music club she had organized with the girls on campus.

Obviously, most people who lived in this Near West Side district were workers. The apartment houses had an air of work and regret. There were still a few larger residences between the tenements. Lorena heard several conversations in languages she did not understand. They walked on Polk Street to Racine Avenue where they took a slight jog and continued east past Sheridan Park and into the back of Hull House which was connected to a number of other big buildings. Mrs. Slagle pointed out the Butler Art Gallery and the Children's Building.

The first order of business after they went up the steps to the back door was to go to Miss Addams "octagon" study for introductions. Eleanor Slagle said, "You are lucky. Miss Addams is in her study as she is so often traveling and giving speeches."

In her dark dress and white collar, Miss Addams looked every bit someone you would not want to cross. Her firm mouth, hair pulled back into a loose bun confirmed her no-nonsense attitude. But her welcoming smile contradicted all the messages given by her hair and clothing. This was a woman who loved people.

After the brief introduction and shaking of hands, Miss Addams assigned a young Russian immigrant woman, Ludmila, to take Lorena on a tour of the Settlement House complex while she invited Miss Ring and Mrs. Slagle to sit down for a discussion about occupational therapy. The tour took nearly two hours. Lorena wanted to examine every room, every display case in the museum. After a tour of the main building, the Labor Museum, The Art Building and the Children's Building, Ludmila took Lorena to the coffee shop where she found Miss Ring and Mrs. Slagle enjoying a sandwich. Ludmila led her to the cafeteria line to choose a sandwich of her own.

The next day, Mrs. Slagle needed to resume her work preparing for the occupational therapy classes. She instructed Miss Ring and Lorena in how to find their way by trolley to the Lake Avenue shopping area and recommended the luncheon at the Blackstone Hotel at Michigan Avenue and Balboa. After so many years in the small city of Oskaloosa, where the tallest building was four stories, Chicago was extremely exciting for both women. There were so many well-dressed people shopping on Lake Avenue. It was still cold enough for both men and women to show off their furs. Miss Ring was frightened enough of the bordello and gambling sections of the city, that she guided Lorena away from several interesting side trips. Even the newspaper in Oskaloosa had articles about "white slavery" in Chicago. The female students not uncommonly whispered stories they heard about kidnapped women and what happened to them in Chicago. One recent story was about a 16 year old girl from Des Moines, who had to earn money for her widowed mother and her brothers and sisters, was promised at good job in Chicago. When she got to Chicago, the couple who had persuaded her to come gave her some new clothes, then told her she would have to work to pay for the clothes. The way they proposed she work to pay for the clothes was to work in their bordello.

In the shops in the Lake Avenue shopping district, Lorena saw lovely outfits in the display windows. One she particularly wished she could afford was a ladies' two piece house dress in brown broadcloth with sprays of small white flowers printed on it. It had a plain waist with full-length bishop sleeves and a front closing. The full-length skirt had seven gores and gathers across the back of the waist. She wondered if it had pockets. Lorena studied the dress on the mannequin in the window hoping she could reproduce it when she had free time to sew in summer. She wondered what it would be like to just walk into such a shop and ask to be shown such merchandise knowing that if she found something that caught her fancy, she could pay for it. But she had usually just avoided such shops knowing that she would feel embarrassed by not being able to afford anything she asked to see. In Oskaloosa, once she had accompanied a classmate from a prominent Dubuque, Iowa banking family into an expensive dressmaker's shop. She had been horrified by her classmate's plan to buy a certain dress on credit and then return it after she had worn it to the college President's tea. She left the shop and waited outside in the rain rather than be involved in such chicanery. She felt her facial expression could not help but expose her classmate's unfair purpose. She knew the dressmaker would have spent hours of labor on the lovely frock. Her own background of hard work and effort for every small privilege or luxury caused her to be repelled by such exploitive behavior. Her classmate had defended herself, after she joined Lorena under her umbrella in the street, by saying, nobody would ever know it had been worn. She would take it back in as good a state as she had borrowed it. The girl from Dubuque thought of it as borrowing, not stealing. Lorena had asked her classmate what her parents would think of such a scheme. The young woman said she had learned how to do this from her mother.

They walked down State Street to Marshall Fields & Company department store on their way to Michigan Avenue and Balboa Street. They passed the elegant ironwork doors of the Carson Pirie Scott Building. Lorena felt she had to see what was inside the exquisitely formed lacy metal work. Though they were foot-weary now, they still wandered through two floors of elegantly displayed merchandise in Louis Sullivan's store.

At luncheon in the dining room of the Blackstone Hotel, Lorena told Miss Ring of the incident when her classmate took out the dress intending to return it without identifying where the student was from. Miss Ring listened in silence as she too, had lusted after the beautiful dresses she had seen in the shop windows and on display in the stores. However, Miss Ring, who was probably near forty years old, knew that her day of frolicking in filmy frocks was an opportunity lost. Both women knew that they could not purchase anything larger than a handkerchief, or they would not be able to close their valises.

They had persuaded the jacketed waiter to seat them in a corner partially hidden by a large potted palm. While it was not unheard of for women unaccompanied by a male escort to dine out, it was unusual. Women without male companions knew they would be stared at if not accosted and solicited for lewd encounters. It was better to be as inconspicuous as possible.

During luncheon, Lorena was as talkative as she had been quiet at the meals at Mrs. Slagle's table. It was as if she and Miss Ring had reversed roles. Lorena talked and Miss Ring listened. Lorena shared some of the things she had seen as they walked on Chicago streets, things she knew Miss Ring hadn't seen because of her anxiety about avoiding danger. "Did you see the small girl with puppies in a wooden box, which she was trying to sell from her mother's vegetable stall," she questioned. Without waiting for the answer, she went on, "Did you see the Chinese man carrying a heavy laundry sack. Professor Wooler discussed Sun-Yat-Sen, the revolutionary hero of China. This is the first real Chinese person I have ever seen." She paused for Miss Ring's response to such novelties. The woman simply nodded so Lorena went on, "On another corner, I saw a policeman take an envelope from a man dressed in a derby hat. He wore a checkered vest and bright green jacket and matching slacks. I wonder if that was one of the famous "pay-offs" Chicago is famous for."

Miss Ring listened to these wonderings without comment. Finally, they called for their bill and were astounded that they owed $1.10 apiece. Fortunately they already had their tickets for the return trip to Des Moines. However, they still had to buy their tickets from Des Moines to Oskaloosa. Lorena confided that she would have only enough money left to buy the Oskaloosa ticket but no food to eat on the trip.

Miss Ring reassured, "You will not have to go hungry on the train. Mrs. Slagle's Scandinavian helper will probably pack food for us to take on the train."

CHAPTER 4

THE DECISION

School was over. Lorena was the proud possessor of a Baccalaureate of Liberal Arts. During the commencement ceremony, she had been taken by surprise at receiving an award for Diligent Scholarship and Self-Improvement. The faculty members had decided that this young woman who had worked so hard to be able to pay for her baccalaureate education needed special recognition. She had come to the campus from a distant place and had adapted well. Her grades were not the highest at Penn College, but she had worked harder than most of the girls who were supported by their families. The opaque sheep skin certificate of recognition was packed along with her baccalaureate in the bottom of her trunk with other treasures. Though she had not decided exactly when she would leave Oskaloosa, she had begun to prepare for her exit into the adult world of work. Retrieving her trunk from the attic of the boarding house had been a symbolic act of preparation. It sat now at the foot of the double bed causing the bedroom to be very crowded.

Since returning from the eye-opening trip to Chicago and Hull House, Lorena had thought a great deal about the ideas of Mrs. Slagle. Work did heal people. Certainly, she had felt better about her own loneliness in this boarding house when she put her mind to her work.

Being the only one of her family to complete high school and now college, she knew she could not return to live with them as they would never allow her to be who she had become. There would be constant attempts to pull her down to their level. She had completely given up any idea of returning to Kentucky.

The easiest route for Lorena would be to take a teaching job right here in Iowa. The State Department of Education in Des Moines offered help to new college graduates in finding placement in schools. Teaching is a noble profession, Lorena reminded herself during her regular dialogues with her inner voice. Also, she had become the acquaintance, if not friends with many Illinois and Iowa girls who would be glad to introduce her to their local school superintendents. But teaching did not hold the excitement of working in a hospital or settlement house.

She weighed the merits of the two professions when she awoke in the morning, and before she slipped into sleep at night. Teaching was hard work but a proven profession in which women could work independently. Occupational therapy was a big risk. It was so new, not really even known yet to most nurses, let alone to doctors. It would require continuation of her education and a move to the big city of Chicago. She would not receive any salary until after she completed the five-month course of study and found a job. What would she use for money to live on in expensive Chicago? Perhaps, since occupational therapy was so new, she would not find a job immediately after she completed the course and might have to again take some work such as seamstress or laundress. However, the idea of guiding patients in renewing their ability to live and work, drew her toward occupational therapy. It was a daily dialogue she had had with herself for the past month. Occasionally, she had had a moment alone with Miss Ring so that she could discuss her vocational confusion with her teacher. Miss Ring wisely listened and offered no advice.

But she needed to make a decision. Commencement had been one week ago and she had had two letters, one from the Kentucky widow asking what her future plans were and one from Mrs. Slagle asking what her future plans were. What were her future plans? This was a decision she could no longer put off. Mrs. Slagle informed her that the next five-month course of classes in occupational therapy started in one month. The widow did not ask directly but subtly implied that it was time for her to begin to contribute to the world. And there had been no bank draft included in the letter, for the first time.

Lorena thought about the crafts that she had learned in her homemaking classes at the academy. It was a long time since she had been at the academy so she felt somewhat unsure, but she had learned tatting, knitting, crocheting, china painting, butter sculpture, tole painting, in addition to her long-time skill in dressmaking which she had learned from her mother and sisters. At Penn College she also had taken a painting and drawing class. She enjoyed these artistic attempts but felt she was not particularly gifted in art. No opportunities to learn woodworking had presented themselves. Mrs. Slagle had mentioned how important knowledge of woodworking would be in the occupational therapy curriculum. She had reassured Lorena that basic skills would be taught during the five months course.

As she ruminated over this choice, she packed her textbooks in the bottom of the trunk on top of her award and baccalaureate degree. The small shelf beside the clothing hooks on the wall of the bedroom was empty now except for a package of writing paper and an inkwell. Because there was no room for a desk or writing table in this cramped bedroom, Lorena had done all her letter writing as well as homework and studying on the dining room table after the boarders' dishes were removed and washed. Lorena picked up her ink well and a sheet of paper, a pen and went into the dining room to write to Mrs. Slagle.

June 1, 1915

Dear Mrs. Slagle,

Again I thank you for your hospitality to Miss Ring and me when we visited Chicago. The ideas you discussed about occupational therapy training have been turning over and over in my mind. I think I would like working with disabled people. Now that I have graduated from Penn College with a Baccalaureate in Liberal Arts, I wonder if you think I am qualified to study occupational therapy. I must leave Oskaloosa soon to begin a teaching job unless I enroll in your courses. I would still need to earn money for my living expenses during the five months of the occupational therapy program. Do you think the people at Hull House would help me find a job so I could attend the occupational therapy classes, too?

I await your reply.

With admiration,

Lorena Longley

She folded the paper so that it made its own envelope and walked to the post office to mail it. She conjectured that it would take two days for Mrs. Slagle to receive it and, if Mrs. Slagle answered immediately, two days for her to receive a reply. As she dropped the stamped letter through the post office slot, Lorena internally remarked to herself "I release it to God. If I do not hear from her in one week, I will take the train to Des Moines and go to the Education Department."

CHAPTER 5

THE LETTER: JUNE 1915

The week passed slowly. Each day, Lorena asked Mrs. Cooper if she could go to the Post Office to pick up the mail. Each day, she was disappointed because there was no letter from Chicago for her. Her trunk was packed and she washed out her clothes by hand each night so that she would have all her clothes clean if she had to go to Chicago. If she had the opportunity to go to Chicago, she did not know where she would live. Miss Ring had suggested a women's hotel she had heard about but for which she did not have the address. Lorena could contact the Quakers when she got to the city, as there were quite a few who lived there. She felt somewhat ill at ease about contacting Quakers since she had never joined the denomination during her four years at Penn College. No one pressured her to join, but she knew that the Quaker members of the faculty and administration were always eager for students to join. On several occasions she had attended the Quaker meeting with Quaker classmates at the College Avenue Friends Meeting-House. It was across the street from Old Main Building. There she had heard prayers for changing of hearts. She recognized "changing of hearts" as a euphemism for becoming a Quaker. She had never been able to bring herself to join because she did not feel in her heart that she could honestly say she believed in her "inner light" or in some of the other ideas they so frequently mentioned.

Two days later, at the post office, she received a most positive response from Mrs. Slagle. She put the other letters for the boarding house in her cloth bag and tore her letter open immediately.

Dear Miss Longley,

It was a pleasant surprise to receive your inquiry about our new occupational therapy courses. It has been my custom to seek students for our new profession among women who are slightly older than you. However, because I became acquainted with you during your recent visit to Chicago with Miss Rosetta Ring, I feel you have the necessary character required to work with disabled people. Your past experiences in securing a good education while supporting yourself, was described to me by Miss Ring. You appear to have the necessary fortitude to undertake this demanding work. I invite you to join us in this noble endeavor of being a pioneer in getting people back to work after they are ill or injured.

The occupational therapy course will start in three weeks on the first Monday of the month. It would be helpful if you could arrive the week before and bring your grade record from Penn College. Because you have already stayed in my home, I invite you to stay with me again until you are able to find an appropriate residence for females. Some women who are coming for the courses will stay at Hull House but I know that they have very few rooms for students in occupational therapy. If you will please let me know when you will arrive, I will send Colin to meet your train. Lena can let you into my apartment. Please affirm as quickly as possible whether or not you will join us for this first course.

Sincerely,

Mrs. Eleanor Clarke Slagle.

Lorena sped back to the boarding house after she sent a telegram to Mrs. Slagle accepting her offer. She told Mrs. Cooper that she would be leaving at the end of the week. That was just two more days away. Meanwhile she had many things to do. She would need to say goodbye to Miss Ring and two other teachers whom she felt had been especially kind to this poor scholarship student from Kentucky. She wanted to get their addresses. She wanted to walk over the Penn campus one more time just for memory sake. The things she felt she needed to do before she left Oskaloosa were not the kind of things that kept a body together, just the sort of things that kept a soul together. She had not ordered a school annual because she felt she could not afford it. However, now there were several left over and a classmate had told her she could probably get one for half price of twenty-five cents. She wanted one of those picture books to remember these four important years of her life even though she had frequently felt she was outside looking in at the girls who lived in the dormitory. Also, there had been some commemorative spoons for sale. Lorena wondered if they were also half price.

The next day, she paid one of the other boarders to take her trunk to the train station for shipping to Chicago. She realized it would not be on the same train with her but they would keep it for her in the baggage room in Union Station. She would leave the next day on the morning mixed train, the same one she had used when she and Miss Ring went last month, no it was two months ago. Time had gone so fast that she wasn't sure it was that long ago. It would be easier for her to travel without her trunk since she would be traveling alone this time. She would not have to worry about luggage, except for her valise that she could store under her seat. After she got to Union Station, Colin could help her figure out whether to take the trunk to Mrs. Slagle's or to leave it at Union Station until she found a women's residence.

For breakfast on her last day, Mrs. Cooper and Elsie surprised Lorena by having her breakfast all ready for her when she came into the kitchen to get the egg bucket to gather the eggs. They had not said anything to her about not doing her regular tasks on her last morning. She had had no expectation of the lessening of her workload just because it would be her last time. It was a pleasant surprise that showed her how much they appreciated her now that she was leaving. Appreciative words had seldom been spoken in this boarding house except by herself, she thought. They ushered her on through the kitchen and to the dining room table to Mrs. Cooper's usual place at the head. This, indeed, was an unusual honor. The breakfast of eggs, biscuits and sausage gravy with a few early blackberries rolling around on the plate would fuel Lorena at least for the trip to Des Moines. The food almost tasted different, perhaps more delicious, since she had not cooked it herself. She brought her soiled dishes to the kitchen and Elsie took them from her hands not allowing her to do any kitchen work. Lorena hugged her, perhaps for the first time ever. Then she went out the back door to complete her final toilette before bringing her valise down to the front door. Then Mrs. Cooper placed a clean lard bucket full of dried apples, cheese sandwiches and boiled eggs beside her valise. Lorena promised to send her address as soon as she was settled. Mrs. Cooper had already rented her room to a widow whose husband had been killed in a farm accident. This woman had a job working in the kitchen at Penn College.

During the ride from Oskaloosa to Des Moines, Lorena learned a lesson she remembered the rest of her life. In her usual attitude of curiosity, she looked at each person who got on to the train meeting their eyes and nodding pleasantly. A large man, probably thirty, smelling of alcohol met her eye and laboriously navigated himself toward her bench. He slid down on the bench beside her, flooding the air about her with the reek of stale alcohol and cigar breath. He had leaned against her, possibly by accident but possibly by plan. She picked her valise up off the floor and moved across the car to the only other vacant seat beside a pious looking gentleman in a black suit. It seemed all the passengers in the car had viewed the incident and she felt their silent approval of her quick decision to move. This lesson coupled with the stories of kidnapped young women in Chicago was enough to cause her to draw her limbs into her body and keep her eyes down for the remainder of the trip including the change of trains in Des Moines. When she boarded the Chicago bound passenger car, she quickly sought the seat beside a stout middle aged woman with a bag of vegetables between her knees on the floor. She seemed like a farm-woman as her hair was slightly greasy and pulled sharply back into a knot on her neck and tied with a frayed scrap of cloth. Her long cotton feed sack dress hung loosely over her large breasts. She had a shawl of faded pink over her shoulders. Her front tooth was missing when she warmly smiled at Lorena and asked, "Where are you going and why? I am Greta Andersen." This started a conversation that lasted all the way to the Mississippi River Bridge at Davenport. Then both women seemed talked out and fell asleep until they heard the conductor call out "Chicago Union Station."

CHAPTER 6

BACK TO CHICAGO

It was six in the morning when this milk train that had seemed to stop at every small city arrived. They had picked up some dairy products at each of the towns on the last sixty miles of the trip. Lorena had awakened about an hour before they arrived in Chicago to see out the window a man wheeling a large cart full of milk cans past the passenger car toward the freight cars at the rear. As she dozed the last miles, she heard other milk cans clanging as they were loaded.

Union Station felt like an old friend since she had been here so recently. She bade her farm-woman friend good-bye, promising to visit her daughter whom she had discovered lived here in the city in a women's residence for factory workers. The daughter's name was Lena Andersen. She worked as a knitter in a sweater factory. Lorena had already declined to follow Greta to her daughter's residence to see if they had a room for her there. She chose instead, to go straight to Hull House. She felt that the people at Hull House were probably more likely to be able to help her find a room close-by so she could spend her time studying and learning, not traveling. She had not had time to let Mrs. Slagle know to send Colin and she felt uncomfortable staying in Mrs. Slagle's apartment. Lorena confirmed the arrival of her black rectangular trunk in the baggage room the day before.

She decided to walk and carry her valise with her to Hull House. It was such a glorious June morning and it was only a dozen blocks. By the time she reached the front door, it was eight o'clock. She was hungry, having eaten last evening when she shared her food with Greta Anderson, who reciprocated and shared fresh radishes and carrots with her. That nourishment had long ago ceased nourishing. Lorena smelled the breakfast and followed her nose into the dining hall first. She loaded a plate with oatmeal and sugar, hotcakes, butter and syrup. Never had coffee smelled so good. She turned with her tray and saw a table with a tall slender female figure seated alone. Something about the woman made Lorena think that perhaps she might be another of the new potential occupational therapists. Lorena walked toward the table holding her valise in her left hand and balancing the tray against her midriff with her right, trying not to spill the coffee. The woman raised her eyes to Lorena's face as she approached. She had an open welcoming look in her posture and expression. Lorena asked, "May I eat my breakfast here with you?"

Thus began a long acquaintanceship that matured into a secure friendship over the next weeks. Carolyn Spence-Warren was the recent widow of a wharf owner and manager from Cincinnati. The couple had had one child, a little girl who had died in the same boating accident which took her husband. This latter information, Lorena did not learn until days later. Yes, indeed, she was an aspiring occupational therapy student. Though Carolyn did not give her age, Lorena judged her to be in her early thirties.

Other parts of Carolyn's story unfolded during the following weeks. Carolyn had returned to her birthplace in Chicago after her husband and daughter's deaths. She was living in her own childhood room in her parent's home on Calumet Street near Washington Park. Her brother had become involved in a clothing business in the garment district. He had been invited by Miss Addams to attend a program given at the Hull House auditorium because of his business's proximity. Gradually he built a friendship with Miss Addams, though their approaches to solving city problems were quite different. When Carolyn returned to Chicago as a sorrowing widow, he had brought her to Hull House to try to take her mind off her grief. It had been partially successful. While volunteering as an English language tutor, she had met Mrs. Slagle who recruited her to study occupational therapy. Lorena became aware that Carolyn's family and upbringing were quite different from her own humble beginnings.

In the cafeteria, the two women conversed about recent news stories. They discussed the sinking of the *Lusitania* and the resignation of Secretary of State William Jennings Bryan. Carolyn invited Lorena to visit her parent's home by taking the "L" and getting off at the 51st Street Station.

Because of her own privileged background, Carolyn was unaware of any specific "women's residence." She knew they existed but had never personally known anyone who lived in one. The two women carried their empty dishes and tray to the "clean-up" table where they scraped and stacked their plates. Because Lorena had only been in this building once before, she welcomed Carolyn's offer to take her to the office where she might learn about the proximity of "women's residences." They parted at the office door and Lorena entered a room with two desks, a potted palm and a file storage cabinet. She explained her reason for coming here to a young woman who spoke with an unfamiliar accent. "There a woman's hotel. Go by Throop and Filmore Streets," she said. "Here, you write um down." She held out a sheet with a list of addresses and pointed to one. Lorena wrote the address on the back of her ticket stub.

Lorena asked, "May I leave my valise here while I go to look at the woman's hotel to make sure it is a safe place to live?"

The young woman apparently was embarrassed to speak more but nodded in agreement and reached for the valise. Lorena thanked her and set off on foot. It was a ten-block walk through an area of tenement-houses and alleys. She heard at least five different languages spoken during her walk. She had studied German at William Penn College and was thus able to recognize that language. The Yiddish that she heard sounded somewhat like German. But the other languages were nothing she had ever heard before. She recognized a nurse standing on the porch of one house and she wondered if it were a hospital.

The two story "women's' hotel had formerly been a residence for female medical students at the Women's Medical College on Wolcott Street. It had recently been opened to other kinds of women in healthcare. It was equally as dingy as other buildings in the neighborhood. The woodwork around the windows had at one time been painted yellow but now it was faded to a uniform dirty cream color along with the previous ivory wood siding. There was a covered porch across the front of the building with a door in the center and a large window on either side. Lorena grasped the brass doorknob and turned. The door needed to be tugged open. Obviously, the building had settled some and the door no longer fit the space. She saw before her a long unlit hallway with a stairway rising on the left side. Dozens of closed doors were on either side of the hallway. The first door had a small, carved wooden sign with *concierge* incised into it. While this was not a word commonly used by Lorena, she knew what it meant. She knocked and it was fifteen seconds before she heard heavy footsteps approach the door.

Before her stood a middle aged woman in a dark blue gingham housedress. She was neither thin nor fat, however, her flesh had settled around her waist. The belt on her dress emphasized this section of her body. She was shaped like a lumpy apple. However, her cheeks did not fit in with the apple picture, as her angular face was pasty in the way of people who seldom go outside. Her grim expression gave the message that she was used to setting rules and enforcing them.

Lorena almost unconsciously politely bent her knees in almost a curtsy. She was not accustomed to curtsying but somehow, this grim woman's demeanor caused her to do so, she reflected and then said, "Madam, I was sent from Hull House to ask if you had any vacant rooms." Lorena realized she had made a mistake in mentioning Hull House, as the woman's face grew even more forbidding. She muttered under her breath in a language Lorena could not understand.

Then in broken English she replied, "We only rent rooms to women who are quiet and clean." Lorena wondered if she looked as if she were dirty and noisy.

"Madam, I am going to study in some new classes taught at Hull House. I would like to rent a room for about 5 months. Is that possible?" As an after thought Lorena added, "I have a college diploma."

The woman's face became slightly more respectful but still scowling enough to scare off a timid person. Lorena's background had made her more brave than timid in most situations. She pushed her own need by saying "I lived in the same rooming house in Oskaloosa, Iowa for four years. I can get Mrs. Cooper to write a reference letter for me if you would like."

By now, the 'concierge' was almost obsequious. "Na, come on in. There is an empty room upstairs at the back." She took a huge ring of keys off the desk by the door and led Lorena up the gloomy stairs. The upstairs was slightly less gloomy perhaps because there was a window at each end of the hall and a large open area toward the middle of the hall where it opened into a sort of sitting room alcove on the east side. They walked past this wide section of the hall and stopped before the last door on the left. The "concierge" bent her head over the ring of keys and read some numbers painted on them finally identifying the correct key. Then she fitted it into the box lock on the outside of the door. This door did not swing open easily but required lifting and pushing at the same time.

The room was surprisingly bright. Because it was the last room on the west side of the building, it had windows on both the west and north. This made it more cheery than the other rooms, Lorena felt sure. The pink calico curtains were tied back but could be released to cover the windows. The walls were painted a soft pinky-ivory. There were old water stains near the northwest corner of the ceiling. Lorena asked, "Does the roof leak?" as she pointed to the spot on the ceiling.

The woman said somewhat defensively, "Fixed, Yah, Yah, but not painted yet."

There was an ivory color iron bedstead against the west window, a dry sink with a basin and pitcher against the south wall. It had some drawers. A small railroad desk and matching chair sat under the north window. Lorena looked down into the back yard and saw almost no green growing things. Instead she saw the roof of one of the rear wooden shanties that she discovered were so common in this section of the city. That explained why there was no grass in the backyard. There was one electric light bulb with a switch string hanging from the ceiling and one place to plug in something electric on the south wall. These seemed like marvelous improvements over what she had in Mrs. Cooper's house. The electric wires to both the light fixture and to the round wall plug were prominently mounted with large metal staples holding them in place on the wall and ceiling. There were six clothing hooks mounted on a painted board on the east wall near the door. Lorena asked the price and was shocked to learn that I was $3 a week. She would hate asking the wealthy widow for this kind of financial support but if she had to, she would. She felt sure she would be unable to find anything closer or cheaper or safer. Then the concierge led Lorena to the toilet and shower room. It was a square room the same size as the bedrooms with four white porcelain sinks mounted against the north wall and a row of toilet stalls with no doors on the south. There was one large iron bathtub with claw feet near the frosted glass window. Lorena thought she could be happy here.

They went back down to the concierge's room near the front door. The woman pointed out a parlor with a piano near the front door on the across hall, the only room where male visitors were allowed. Lorena explained, "I would like to rent the room for the next 5 months, if possible."

The woman stepped inside her own room, opened the desk and brought out a receipt register. She took the proffered $3 and told Lorena that the rent was due each Saturday. She recited a litany of rules—no men visitors except in the parlor, no overnight guests, no cooking in the bedrooms, lights out at eleven o'clock at night except Friday and Saturday when lights could stay on until midnight. Any food kept in the room must be in tins so it would not attract rats and mice. No more than two baths per week. Then she handed Lorena a key and a receipt for the three dollars.

Lorena walked back to Hull House. By now, the street was bustling with people, buyers, sellers, unsupervised children, and horses pulling wagons of produce and goods. She avoided small piles of dog droppings on the sidewalk. She retrieved her valise and asked the woman if she knew Colin. The young woman said she did and that if Lorena would wait a minute she would find him so he could bring her trunk. They would allow her to borrow a wheelbarrow from Hull House for Colin to carry the trunk to her boarding house.

By mid-afternoon, Lorena was settled in her new home. She did not even remove her clothes before lying down on the bed to sleep. The sleep on the train had apparently not been restful. She relaxed for the first time that day. When she awoke, it was beginning to get dark outside. Lorena realized she must have slept five hours or more. She got up and turned on the bulb hanging from the ceiling and began to unpack her trunk. When it was almost empty, she pushed it over near the bed so she could use it as a bedside table. Inside were still packed in tissue paper, her black silk dress to be worn only at funerals and special occasions. There had only been two funerals while she lived in Oskaloosa, one of the other boarders who was an elderly woman who died and a male classmate during her second year who left school to go to a tuberculosis sanatorium and died there. Since both funerals were held in Oskaloosa, she had attended them wearing her black silk. She had struggled with the silk sewing it herself during her freshman year. It was a very plain shirtwaist, no ruffles, lace or tucks. But it was the only dressy dress she owned so she treated it with special care. She realized that as she had unpacked and handled her few possessions, that she had envisioned with each the last time she had used them or worn them. It was almost as if she was allowing each item to say good-bye to the old life and introducing it to the new life she would share with them.

CHAPTER 7

BECOMING PART OF HULL HOUSE

It was time to start the course of study to be trained as an occupational therapist. As she entered the classroom where they would be meeting in Hull House, she felt somewhat nervous. The other twelve women who sat in the room with her waiting for the arrival of Mrs. Slagle all looked more sophisticated, like they had more money than she did. However, this self-comparison did not last long. Mrs. Slagle walked purposefully into the room and stood at the lectern at the front. The lectern had been built for a taller person. The students could see her face but not her shoulders. She spent the first hour explaining what she hoped for this new profession. She laid a heavy load of responsibility on this class of thirteen women to carry forward her ideas. "Habit training" was what most patients needed, she thought. She referred to the educational ideas of Professor John Dewey who had become so well known here in the Chicago area. She spoke about how efficient "learning by doing" had proven to be. Then she said they would begin to practice this by going to the workshop and beginning to make simple looms for weaving. But first, she would join them in riding the "L" to a lumber store to choose wood. Lorena wondered if she would have to spend any of her valuable hoard of coins to buy wood. When they arrived at the end of the line and walked on the wooden boardwalk to the lumberyard, she discovered that Mrs. Slagle had used her influence to get the lumberyard owner to donate the wood for the class. In her position as head of occupational therapy for Illinois State Mental Hospitals, she had purchased enough from this lumber merchant, that she was able to persuade him to donate the wood to the Henry B. Flavill School of Occupational Therapy. The troop of women carrying boards of wood made quite a picture as they boarded the "L" for the return trip. That afternoon, they stored their wood in the carpentry shop along with supplies for baskets and pottery. Some students organized another room with tables and cupboards for needlework, weaving and rug hooking. In the room in which they had started their morning lecture, they stored materials for bookbinding, kindergarten work, block printing, and watercolor painting.

The next day, their classes started in earnest, with a morning lecture by Mrs. Slagle on the history of occupations, on the new psychology described by Sigmund Freud, the German neurologist. The afternoon was spent with Mr. Hans Meyers, a carpenter of German birth whom Mrs. Slagle has engaged to teach the woodworking portion of the curriculum. His heavy Rhineland German accent made it somewhat difficult to follow his verbal instructions, but he made it admirably clear by his practical demonstration of each step. By the end of the second afternoon, three of the students had completed the basic frame for a simple Turkish knotting loom. Tomorrow, they would hammer nails into the frame for the weft and warp. This kind of work was so much more precise than any handwork Lorena had done previously in her life. She had been too busy with books, pencil and paper to learn any craft but sewing clothes and the simple ones taught a Vermillion Grove Academy. Or she had been too busy earning her keep to learn luxury hobbies like weaving and embroidery.

It was almost impossible not to compare herself with her wealthier classmates. Several of them had learned china painting in their finishing schools. However, they did not know much about cooking and baking as they had had cooks to do that drudgery work. Broom making was new to everyone in the class. Mrs. Slagle, with Miss Adams help had engaged an Italian widow to demonstrate this useful occupation. Again, her accent was so difficult to understand that her demonstration was mandatory in order to comprehend the method. Each student produced one lovely broom. Lorena took hers to her room and gave it a good sweep.

Thus progressed their education into this new profession. Each week, they completed at least one craft project. An Irish woman taught spinning. A Danish woman taught Swedish weaving. An Italian woman taught the beautiful Italian linen cut-work. And the wonders of the human body gradually unfolded to these women students. Several of them were or had been mothers like Carolyn and lost a child. Over the weeks, these thirteen women came to know each other's stories in some measure of detail. Gradually, Lorena came to feel she was an indispensable member of this group despite her differences of heritage.

Most afternoons, each student returned to her own home to study alone because Chicago after dark was not a safe place for respectable women to be traveling without a male escort. However, some evenings, there were lectures and discussions held at Hull House that Mrs. Slagle encouraged them to attend. On these occasions, Mrs. Slagle made sure that a strong adult male escorted each of the women students who did not live in Hull House residences or have a family vehicle picking her up after an evening event, to her own residence. There were lectures on German literature, progressive education, industrial history, human progress over the centuries, and on city gardening. One evening, Miss Addams invited Mayor Wm. Hale Thompson to speak to the members of the neighborhood about his plans to assist this community by cleaning up the streets and to explain why he had snubbed the Morals Squad. This was followed by a lively discussion that continued the following day between class members.

Usually after evening events, young Colin, the Irish youth that Lorena had met in the train station on her first visit to Chicago, accompanied her to the women's hotel. Lorena always felt guilty that she did not have money to give him because she knew he was struggling since he was no longer able to earn money from factory work. On these occasions, she usually asked him to wait on the front porch, since male visitors were prohibited except in the parlor, while she ran up to her room and brought back some store-bought cookies or buns to give to him. She felt this was a paltry reward but it was the only thing she could afford at this time. Inwardly, she promised herself that when she had a real job, she would reward Colin for the many times he had helped her. If she had asked him to come in and wait in the parlor at that hour, she expected the concierge would suspect her of trying to sneak a man into her room.

On these walks back to the women's residence, she had discovered that Colin was sleeping in the basement of a gambling house in exchange for helping wash out the beer steins from the night before. Sometimes the bartender would give him leftover food from the kitchen situated behind the bar. However, most of his meals were taken in the Hull House dining where Miss Addams had made an arrangement with the cook. This erratic life did not make him look any less stressed or any younger than he had when she met him three months ago. By now he was 13 years old but could still pass for 16 or 17. Miss Addams persuaded him not to pass himself off as being legally old enough to work. She parented him as she did so many others in the surrounding neighborhood.

Colin was enrolled in classes in Hull House. He would go on Sunday over to the Mid North Side to St. Andrews Catholic Church on the corner of Addison and Paulina. Religion was one of the topics he discussed with Lorena as they walked down Taylor Avenue. There was less traffic there than on Fillmore Street. Colin described how the monks had taken him into an orphanage when his parents died in the typhoid epidemic, and enrolled him in a Jesuit school. "I realized that the monks expected me to eventually become a monk myself. I could never accept this vision of my future. Eventually at age 11, I ran away from the monastery boarding school. It was after being after being physically punished for making a mistake in Latin class." Lorena nodded sympathetically to encourage him to tell her more.

He obliged her. "I lived hard on the streets for a few summer weeks until I met a street recruiter for a businessman. He took me to work in a clothing factory. When the government inspectors discovered that I was too young to legally work in the shoe factory, I was fired. I was afraid of being forced into a similar situation again. I did not want others to be in control of my life. I fled rather than join one of the groups of boys being sent to live on farms in Iowa. Another fellow I met on the street, told me about a place to sleep in the basement of the gambling house. Two other boys were also sleeping in the basement." He sighed with earnestness as he realized how hard this tale must seem to Lorena. "I learned of the wonders of Hull House from the other boys. I found my way there and sneaked inside fearing I might be thrown out. But there were so many other people just like me at the settlement house, I was quickly accepted and included. Miss Addams enrolled me in classes. My days were spent in Hull House. My nights were spent in the gambling house basement where my mornings were spent washing glasses. I prefer the freedom of this life compared to the strict Jesuits." He paused and considered before discussing his current ponderings, but eventually he went on. "My exposure to the variety of immigrants from around Europe made me further doubt the religious ideas expressed by the Jesuits. There are just too many different ways to describe God. Why should one be more right than the other?" These were weighty ideas for such a youth thought Lorena.

By age 13, he was big enough to repel most physical threats that could be made. His physical build was almost that of a grown man. The professional haircuts given by German barber who came to Hull House once a week immensely improved the look of his dark brown mop. Lorena kept this last thought to herself.

To Lorena, Colin became something like a younger brother. Despite her relief at not being dragged down into a life of hopelessness by her family, she still missed their comradeship during the past 7 years. Colin temporarily filled this void in some way. She gave him advice. It was apparent that he worshiped her but she was enough older that there was no question of real romance. Because he lost his parents at such a young age, there was no trace of the Irish brogue in his speech.

Chapter 8

Goodbye to Chicago and Colin

Near the end of the five-month course of study to become an occupational therapist, Lorena began to think about how she would earn money using her new skills. Part of their instructional program had been to visit several of the Illinois State Mental Hospitals. The class of occupational therapy students had made one field trip to visit the occupational therapy shop that Mrs. Slagle had started there. It was the first time Lorena had seen severely mentally disturbed people. Lincoln and Oskaloosa had had their share of alcoholics but none as severely disturbed as the patients at Kankakee State Hospital. Or at least Lorena had never seen them on the streets. However, the patients that came to the Kankakee OT Shop were not the most severely disturbed. The most severely disturbed were locked in wards and seldom allowed out into the other departments like Occupational Therapy and Industrial Therapy.

Each student had been assigned one of the patients to sit with during the students' visit. Lorena had had an interesting conversation with the man she was assigned to, who was working on a tooled leather holster. He told her that during the Garment Worker's Strike in September 1910, he had been among the people who marched in the streets for improved working conditions. His job had been a materials carrier pushing handcarts full of large bolts of cloth to the cutters. One day as he marched in the rain, he began to hear voices in his own head telling him to kill his boss. He had no weapon so he followed his boss home one evening as he left the shop and tried to choke him. He had been arrested and spent a month in jail before his new wife was able to persuade the jailers to send him to Kankakee. He had episodes when he would hear the voices again, but usually, he felt almost normal. He told his story in a monotone without meeting Lorena's eyes. None-the-less, his story touched Lorena. She realized she could work with a man such as this during his lucid times. She was curious about what his life in the hospital was like when he was not in the OT Shop. He did not tell her and she was afraid to ask.

Living in a big city such as Chicago was so exciting; Lorena could not envision herself returning either to a small city like Oskaloosa or London. When Mrs. Slagle reported that she was going to take the job at Johns Hopkins Hospital in Maryland, Lorena wondered if there might now be a place for her in the Illinois State Hospitals. When she questioned Mrs. Slagle about this possibility, she received encouragement.

One evening on the walk along Taylor Street, she discussed with Colin the possibility of a job in the State Hospital at Kankakee. Colin asked her to describe it to him. "It was quite a beautiful place and close enough to Chicago that I could come into the city by train on Saturday evening after work or on Sundays," she began. "The four limestone pillars at the front gate of the hospital frame the view of the clock tower of the main building. The buildings still look quite fresh and the trees and shrubs are mature enough to make the grounds lush in late summer. No doubt in winter, it will be grimmer."

As they walked she continued "If I were offered the job there, I would be allowed to live in the nurses' dormitory. That would be an advantage financially. Most of my classmates wanted to find employment in the city of Chicago because they hoped to go on living in their own homes." Lorena's situation as a single woman made her more willing to live on the State Hospital campus 60 miles from Union Station. She waited for Colin's reply to all this information.

Colin listened to her, quietly acknowledging that he had heard by simply nodding. Except at Hull House, he seldom saw "good" women as few of them came to the gambling house. The ones he saw there were mostly prostitutes who took men into the small bedrooms off the hallway, which led from the front door with the guard, then up the stairway to the large room with the bar and gambling tables. By the time he got up to the kitchen to wash the glasses in the morning, there weren't even many of them around.

He would miss Lorena if she moved 60 miles away. Finally he spoke, sharing this feeling of impending loss with her. "I'll miss you terrible" he said while keeping his eyes on the ground. Suddenly Lorena was aware that there was more than a brotherly longing in Colin's voice.

"I'll come into Hull House on Sundays" she said. "We could meet there for the Sunday afternoon lectures. And if I really do take that job, after I'm settled, you can take the train out to visit me." She made sure she had Colin's postal address.

When Lorena finally sat down in her room at the women's hotel, she felt a little sad. This pleasant room had given her the privacy that she had never had either at home, at the Academy where she slept in a dormitory with a dozen girls, or at Mrs. Cooper's boarding house. Here she could scatter her few possessions around without worrying about annoying anyone. During the five months of occupational therapy training, her possessions had multiplied. She now had an oak chair she had built and caned. Two-nested reed baskets sat beside the black trunk. She had woven a honey colored table runner which she had draped over the marble top of the dry sink and set the ceramic pitcher and bowl on it. The broom sat in the corner. The unfinished tablecloth she started embroidering was draped over the ivory rods of the bed headboard. An intaglio wood carving plaque of a bird was propped against the wall on the railroad desk beside an unframed watercolor of Lake Michigan. A ceramic bowl sat on a tatted coaster on the trunk. Mrs. Slagle had cautioned the students to care for their projects, as they would be good samples to carry with them to show their patients.

Tomorrow, each student was instructed to choose three of their crafts to bring back to Hull House for an arts and crafts show in one room of the Butler Art Gallery. Lorena fell to sleep trying to decide which of her projects she would carry back with her tomorrow.

Chapter 9

Beginning Work

The view through the sandstone front gateposts of Illinois Eastern Hospital for the Insane was grimmer here in the first week in December. The porter trudged in front between the pull bars of the platform trolley, which held Lorena's valise and trunk. His nose appeared red, perhaps from the cold wind, perhaps from drinking. He knew where to lead her when she said she would be living in the nurses' dormitory.

The room that Lorena would share with three nurses at Illinois Eastern Hospital for the Insane Nursing Dormitory was spacious. Mrs. Slagle had assisted her in getting the job in the OT Shop as well as getting assigned to this dorm-room. The imposing dormitory housemother, Mrs. Segal, escorted Lorena to the door to her room on the third floor then left her there. The door opened in the middle of the north wall of the room off the hallway. There were two large south windows with flowered draperies. Only one nurse was in the room when Lorena arrived and she was asleep. Lorena's bed was in one corner facing the windows. She knew this because there was a stack of bed linen, a towel and wash rag lying on the bare blue and white striped ticking of the mattress. The bed had a small round oak table beside it and a chest of drawers at the end. She tiptoed to the bed and put her valise on it. Then she returned to the front hallway to retrieve her trunk. A bedraggled looking nurse was coming in the front door and asked if Lorena would like assistance carrying the trunk up the three flights of stairs to her room. She quickly accepted the offer of help. The nurse grabbed the leather handle at her end of the trunk and trudged up the central stairway almost dragging Lorena along with her. She did not speak until they were in the third floor hallway. "You must be the new girl assigned to sleep in our room because that's the only empty bed up here." She pushed open the door and continued to nearly drag Lorena into the room. They put the trunk down beside the round table. Then she held out her hand and introduced herself. "I am Edna May Fagan. Welcome to Kankakee. Supper will be in a few minutes if you'd like to go down with me. I'd better wake Connie up so she can eat before she goes back to work." Connie had slept right through Lorena's entire arrival including bringing the trunk into the room. Edna May went over and shook Connie's shoulder. "Supper time" she sang out as she turned around and removed her nurse's hat. She shook out her dusty brown curls and took the brush to them.

Connie shook her head of tumbled red hair off the pillow and eyed Edna May blearily. She spoke no words but hurumphed and slowly swung her legs over the edge of the high hospital style bed. While they waited for Connie to get out of her cotton flannel nightgown and into her uniform, Lorena began to fold the flat white cotton sheets over the corners of her bed. Meanwhile, as Connie dressed, Edna May introduced Lorena to her and explained that she would be rooming with them. When they were all ready, Edna May led the way to the bathroom to wash their hands, down the hall to the stairway to the front hall and through the dining room door. The dining room held three large oval oak dining tables with eight chairs surrounding each. This first sitting for supper began at 5 p.m. Edna May explained the meal requirements, and as important, the customs. Brown haired Edna May led their way to the table closest to the kitchen door, explaining that this table always got served first. The nurses and other therapists like occupational therapy who lived in the nurses' dorm ate in two shifts, breakfast at 5 and 7 a.m., dinner at 11 a.m. and 12 noon, and supper at 5 p.m. and 6 p.m. Some nurses ate with the patients in their wards if they were on duty and unable to attend the two sittings offered in this dining room. Soon, other young women filled up the table near the kitchen door and the kitchen door swung open to show Lena, Mrs. Slagle's former servant. She wore a brown uniform with a ruffled white apron, waitress cap and collar. She and Lorena exchanged a smile of recognition. She put down a basket of sliced bread and a pitcher of milk. Each place at the table was already set with a plate, knife, fork, spoon and glass. Lena returned with a platter of meatloaf, and a bowl of mashed potatoes. Each of the other tables also had their own serving girl. When all the food choices were on the table, they included a big serving dish of cooked sliced carrots, another of garden lettuce and yet another of sweet cucumber pickles. There must be a hot house here if there was December lettuce. Lorena ate with gusto since she had only had cold meals in her room except when she ate at Hull House for the past five months. It was always such a treat to have a regular meal at which she was not the servant as she had been at Mrs. Coopers for so many years. She intended to speak to Lena and find out how she came here but not until the meal was over as she could see Lena had important kitchen responsibilities.

Suddenly the door to the hallway opened and Mrs. Segal, the housemother entered and looked over the 24 girls seated at the tables. The eating went on somewhat more quietly. Edna May explained in an undertone, "Mrs. Segal checks the girls at each meal to see that we are either in our uniforms or in appropriate street dress. There are no casual clothes here even at breakfast or on weekends."

Mrs. Segal wore a black wool broadcloth shirtwaist. Connie said softly, "Mrs. Segal has worn black dresses for the full two years she's been here. Her widowhood is unrelenting."

Edna May went on, "Mrs. Segal has a bedroom off the other side of the front hallway. None of the girls here have been allowed inside." Mrs. Segal's octagonal glasses gave her an owlish look. The bun into which her hair was combed was tight and unforgiving. After her obvious judging eye surveyed each one present, she turned and left the dining room. The noise level rose a whole decibel after her departure.

Lorena noticed that all the young women at the table near the kitchen door waited until Connie, who ate slowly, finished her meal, before excusing themselves en masse and arising to leave the dining room. Lorena dawdled a moment so she could speak to Lena who came out of the kitchen to clear off the dirty dishes. Connie did not wait for her but left to go to her nursing work in a cottage. Edna May waited for her near the hall door. Lena's broken English was difficult to decipher but after two repetitions, Lorena understood that Mrs. Slagle had helped Lena get this job in the nurse's dorm dining room. After a hasty goodbye and promise to talk soon, Lorena joined Edna May to return to their dormitory room.

By now it was nearly six o'clock on an early December evening. Lorena had spent a long day first, packing the last of her possessions into her trunk and valise, and then getting her trunk to the station with Colin's help. She had waited thirty minutes for the train to start its two-hour ride to Kankakee, then engaging a porter to bring her trunk and valise by platform wagon to the Illinois Eastern Hospital for the Insane. Lorena's box of craft samples that she had made during her five months in occupational therapy was being stored at Hull House until she had the opportunity to bring them here. She wanted to see exactly what space she would be assigned before bringing bulky things like a chair and a loom to the ward.

She unpacked her valise into the wardrobe at the end of the room between the feet of the two beds. Gratefully, she got into her own flannel nightgown and crawled under the two wool blankets.

Chapter 10

First Day on the Job

The noise of Edna May getting into her starched nurse's uniform awoke Lorena next morning. She found it hard to believe that she had slept ten hours straight. The silver painted radiators under the windows had kept the room warm. Now it was time to go to the occupational therapy shop and learn about her new responsibilities. She had not received a uniform so supposed she would just wear her brown corduroy skirt and ivory shirtwaist blouse. She looked forward to the day when she could afford to buy a new coat. The gray wool melton coat she had worn for the last four years at William Penn College was definitely threadbare. She had repaired the cuffs twice by covering them with wide velvet ribbon binding. That was worn bare and needed replacement again. But she picked up the old coat and followed Edna May down to the dining room for breakfast.

Here was Lena again, serving the pancakes and fried eggs at the table near the kitchen. Lorena wondered where she slept. There was a tub of creamery butter and a quart pitcher of maple syrup. The coffee was hot and the cream was thick. Conversation at the table was more subdued. Either the girls were exhausted from a night's work or they needed the coffee to awaken them. Connie returned too late to join them at the table by the kitchen. She looked tired and rumpled. The starched uniform she had put on last night looked slept in. Mrs. Segal made her appearance and inspection just before Edna May and Lorena arose from the table. Somehow, each time the woman appeared the mood in the dining room changed. This time it was even more somber after her departure. Lorena tucked this bit of observation in the back of her mind to ponder later. Now it was time to start her new career.

Edna May pointed out the route to the administration building and then went off toward the side door of the big front building.

Lorena went to the woman seated at the desk near the front door to ask where she should go first. She was directed to another woman inside an office off the central hall. The woman had her write her name and the date in the large employee ledger. There was a column beside the date for her wages but the woman said to leave it empty. Then she asked Lorena if she knew how to get to the Occupational Therapy Shop. Lorena thought she remembered from the student trip how to get there but asked the woman to tell her the route anyway. She was directed out through the back and into another building. Lorena was glad she had not bothered to remove her coat. A blast of wind from between the four-story buildings met her as she pushed open the back door to the administration building. The OT Shop was in the basement of the building behind the administration building. When Mrs. Slagle was working at Kankakee, she had also trained her new supervisor, Mrs. Radicky. Mrs. Radicky had come by train into Chicago to interview her for this position as occupational therapist. Mrs. Radicky was another widow but she did not have the dour countenance of Mrs. Segal. In the main OT Shop room, she sat at her yellow oak desk, which faced the wall. There was a large bulletin board on the wall above her desk with Christmas watercolor pictures on it. The large basement room was open with one area screened off from the rest by a latticed wood panel set into wooden support-feet. There were round worktables scattered between the supporting pillars in one half of the long room. The other half of the room was filled with floor looms, table looms, warping frames and shelved full of spools and balls of yarn in a glorious spectrum of colors. The narrow basement windows inside their window wells, added a muted morning light to that of the conical glass fixtures handing from the ceiling.

Mrs. Radicky was obviously expecting Lorena and complimented her on her timely appearance. "It will be about half an hour before the nurses bring the patients to the OT Shop. This is Mr. Wiggins," she said indicating a man who was also in the OT Shop. "His responsibility is Industrial Therapy."

Lorena did not query him about what he considered to be the division of labor between them though she wondered in her own mind. Mrs. Radicky gave Lorena a note to take to the uniform supply room in yet another building, to get fitted for her three uniforms issued to each new employee. She put her coat back on and followed Mrs. Radicky's instructions.

The wind blasted her again as she felt the wind sweep between the buildings. She shielded her face from the bitter air with her arm. The wind pushed against the door as she went back into the administration building. She walked the length of the building and down a staircase to a large room with many shelves of different colored uniforms. Another woman led her behind the counter and asked her to stand in front of her chair as she measured Lorena's waist, hips and breasts. Then she measured her arm length and waist to hem length. She showed Lorena the blue and white cloth that was designated for the OT staff uniforms. The first uniform would be ready at the end of the day. She was given a white hat that was slightly different from those of the nurse. The other two uniforms would be ready in two days. Meanwhile, she would wear a black smock lent to her by Mrs. Radicky. Back into the cold.

The first group of patients had arrived from the women's recuperative unit. They were seated around the round tables with four women at each of the four tables. Mrs. Radicky called out to the women, "Ladies, I want to introduce to you our new occupational therapist, Miss Longley." Some of the women obediently raised their eyes and greeted her while others simply went on with their work as if they had not heard.

Most of the women were at different stages of completion of woven baskets. One table had only two women working at Turkish Knotting. Each woman propped a small wooden knotting frame against the table and rested it on their knees. A few of the women looked as if they were wearing their own clothing but the remainder wore full length body smocks of coarse dark blue cloth. Lorena remembered seeing a rack of similar smocks in the uniform room she had just left. Not one of the women looked up from her work as Lorena walked across to hang her coat on an empty hook on the row of hooks against the wall.

Mrs. Radicky was at one table demonstrating a weave to one patient. A very large red faced woman whom Lorena assumed to be the attendant sat in a large wooden chair against the wall and seemed to be reading a book. Wash tubs with reed soaking in water stood near the basin in one corner. A length of rubber hose was affixed to the faucet. However, no water seemed to be running into the tubs as they were already full to within three inches of the tops of the tubs. Several bricks held the reed under the water. Lorena went to see what Mrs. Radicky was demonstrating. The four women at that table watched intently as the head occupational therapist wove the wet reed through the spokes. As she worked, she talked to the women about the importance of careful handwork. One of the women drummed her fingers on the table as she watched. Another women tapped her foot against the table leg, however the sturdiness of the oak worktable kept it from jiggling. Mrs. Radicky ignored these obviously agitated behaviors and introduced Lorena. She then instructed one of the women to go to the wash tubs and bring some more reed back to the table after letting the water drain off. Each woman had the beginning of a basket sitting before her. While the patient was getting the new reed, Mrs. Radicky looked up at Lorena and instructed her to go to the table where the two women were doing Turkish knotting and to check their work. Lorena walked to the Turkish Knotting table and sat in one of the empty chairs. She introduced herself to the women and said she was the new occupational therapist. A row of small piles of short pieces of wool yarn of various colors lay between the two women. A woman wearing one of the hospital smocks looked across the table and replied "My name is Eugenia. I am just learning to make these rugs. Maybe if I ever get out of here, I can make rugs to sell." Her dull hair was cut short about the bottoms of her ear lobes. The other woman was wearing what appeared to be her own clothing, a white long sleeved shirtwaist and a black sateen skirt. Her hair was clean and piled upon her head with tortoise hairpins. She looked up and smiled pleasantly at Lorena who judged her to be about 35 years of age. Though Lorena felt great curiosity about why these two women were in Kankakee Hospital for the Insane, she restrained herself from questioning them. Rather, she commented upon their work and asked what their names were and how they had decided upon their carpet design.

The shorthaired woman wearing the hospital smock stopped her work and said, "My name is Mildred Bowen and I should not be in this hospital since I am not sick. I am here because my husband has a new girlfriend and he doesn't want me around. He tricked me into coming here and now he won't let me out." Lorena was at a loss about how to respond to this dramatic statement.

The other woman quietly continued her work and waited until the first woman had ceased her protestation of her wrongful hospitalization. Then she said in a slightly accented voice, "My name is Latrice and my family lives in Louisiana." Then she stopped talking and went on with her rug-hooking. Lorena felt such pressure to ask questions of the two women, especially Latrice, but she remembered Mrs. Slagle's particular reminders about not prying into patients' private business until you knew them better.

She stayed seated with the women until Mrs. Radicky summoned her with a crooked finger and asked her to accompany one of the women to the restroom. She whispered to Lorena, "This woman has 'The Curse' and there are rags in the restroom cupboard so she can change her pad." Mrs. Radicky slipped a key off her key ring and handed it to Lorena with a cautionary reminder, "Do not lay the key down anywhere. Go out into the hallway and turn right into the little alcove. You will find the restroom door there."

The woman with "The Curse" was from neither the Turkish knotting table, nor from the table where Mrs. Radicky was working. Lorena wondered why Mrs. Radicky had not asked the red-faced attendant to accompany the patient instead of herself. Later, Mrs. Radicky would tell her about the attendant's bad temper and how she humiliated the patients whenever she was asked to assist them. It was just better to ignore the woman since any disturbance of her apparent reading meant retribution for the patients.

The patient, wearing a hospital smock, stood by the OT Shop door and waited for Lorena to come to her. Docilely she followed Lorena as she discovered where the restroom door and lock were. Inside the square restroom were two stalls built around toilets. A large wooden cupboard with floor to ceiling doors was against the wall opposite the toilets. In a corner was a tiny hand-washing basin. Lorena turned her back to the woman in the stall behind her to allow her some privacy despite having been told in the OT classes never turn your back on a psychiatric patient. She used this opportunity to open each of the cupboard doors to discover the pile of clean rags for absorption of women's menstrual flow. When she turned around, the woman had pulled up the blue hospital smock and dropped her bloomers around her feet. The bloody rag had fallen from between her legs unto the floor. Lorena handed her a clean rag to replace it. The woman replaced the rag, dropped the edge of the smock and started to simply walk toward the door. Lorena spoke firmly but calmly "Pick up the old rag and put it in that waste can." The woman took a moment before she slowed, stopped and like an automaton, turned and followed Lorena's instruction. Again the patient started for the door. Lorena said, "You must wash your hands." Lorena walked to the corner basin and turned on the water.

The woman stopped, looked at her hands and said "But they are not dirty."

Thus began Lorena's job as a teacher of healthy living skills. She explained to the woman about invisible germs on her hands especially after touching her genital area. The woman listened in amazement. The lesson continued through washing and drying her hands on a towel hung on a wall roller and on into the OT Shop where she listened raptly to Lorena until she returned to her basketry.

The morning passed quickly. Lorena began to learn a few first names of the patients. The women stopped and put their unfinished work on the shelves against the wall when Mrs. Radicky called out the time. After all the women had retrieved their coats from the wall hooks, the red-faced woman led them out into the hallway and up the stairs toward the December weather.

Mrs. Radicky asked "Please help me move the tubs of water and reed behind the screen because the men in the afternoon will not be making baskets. Some of them are so easily distracted; I want to remove anything which will divert their attention away from their own work." Between them, the two women tugged the tubs out of the way.

Mr. Wiggins returned through a door in the other end of the OT Shop. The three therapists put on their coats and went together through the cold wind of the field between the building to the dining hall for hospital workers. After they were seated together with their food, Lorena asked Mr. Wiggins, "How did you spend this morning?"

The man was a robust middle aged man with a shiny pate. He explained "I was in the wood shop teaching several men on the bicycle saw. Another man was on the peddle lathe and several were using hand tools. They are making projects for Christmas gifts for relatives."

Lorena asked, "May I be allowed to observe in the wood shop?" Mr. Wiggins gave her an appraising look and slowly nodded in the affirmative. The two older therapists began to discuss the patients and their work. Lorena quietly ate the bread and rather watery New England boiled dinner off the heavy hospital crockery, while observing the variety of workers who took their meal in this drafty dining room.

There was one table of noisy younger men in rough canvas overalls whom she judged to be agricultural workers. There were a number of young women in the uniforms Lorena now recognized as nurses. The obsequious young women who acted as waitresses wore the same uniform that Lena wore in the nurses' dining room, a ruffled white apron over a brown uniform and a similar cap. However, these young women appeared to possibly be patients rather than employees by the slow way in which they responded to requests and commands. There was a responsiveness missing that the dormitory waitresses had. Lorena realized it would take her some time to be able to tell who hospital workers were and who patients were.

CHAPTER 11

MALE PATIENTS

The afternoon session was for male patients from the rehabilitation ward. Mrs. Radicky has explained during lunch, that these men were considered to be almost ready for discharge from the asylum. Lorena confided to Mrs. Radicky that she still felt very uncertain about measuring the warping threads on the warping board, however, she felt confident of all other parts of weaving. In the moments before the patients arrived with their keeper, Mrs. Radicky showed Lorena the status of the work on each loom. She promised to supervise all the warping herself until Lorena felt confident of her capability to do it without help.

Two keepers arrived with twenty-five male patients. Ten of the patients went through the same door through which Mr. Wiggins had gone. One of the keepers went with these men. The other went to the chair by the wall and turned the chair around so he could rest his chin on the back of the chair.

Each of the patients seemed to know which loom was his and went straight to work as soon as they had shaken the snow off their coats and hung them up.

Mrs. Radicky had suggested that Lorena walk around and introduce herself to each of the patients and to ask them about their weaving. "Be sure to introduce yourself as Miss Longley" she reminded Lorena. "We must always remember to have patients use our family name as it reminds them of our authority here."

Lorena was aware that the men were watching her covertly while they worked on their looms. She decided to go to the far side of the room and begin there so she would be far enough away to not be nervous because Mrs. Radicky was listening.

The patient on the big eight-harness loom near the door to the woodworking room slowed the back and forth thrust of the shuttle as she drew near. The cloth he was weaving was a traditional American two-color pattern with lots of small squares. The warping was cream colored and the weft threads were leaf green. When she stood by the harness bar and faced him, he stopped completely and looked up at her. She introduced herself as Mrs. Radicky had reminded her and asked his name. His Eastern European accent made it difficult to understand him so she asked him to repeat his name. He said his name in Greek was Nikolai Papadapolis but that she could call him Nick. Lorena asked him how long he had been working on the weaving and he replied "One week. Mrs. Radicky, she show me." He seemed embarrassed and suddenly looked toward the other side of the loom and began to talk to himself in a language Lorena could not understand. Lorena remembered the description of hallucinations from the lectures on abnormal psychology and decided that that was what Nick was doing. Since she did not know how to respond to this behavior, she moved on to the next weaver who was at a four-harness table loom.

The slender patient at the table loom continued on with his weaving as she stood what she considered to be a safe distance away. She again introduced herself, "I am Miss Longley. Please tell me about your weaving." The piece was about 12 inches in width and beautifully and tightly woven. It had a cream colored warp and bright blue weft. The design in the middle of the strip of cloth was a six-pointed star about five inches in width repeated every 12 inches.

Before he could answer her previous question, Lorena remembered to ask his name. He blurted out "My name is Irwin Segal. Do you like my design?" He spoke in clear Mid-West English.

Lorena replied "The weaving is very neatly done. The six-pointed star comes out clearly from the background. This is an unusual design. Where did you find it?"

Irwin completely stopped his weaving and lowered his voice so it was not audible to the other patients. "Do you like it? This is a Jewish design. I am making it for the rabbi who comes to visit me each week. I drew the design myself. Mrs. Radicky helped me make the design into a weaving. Do you like it?" he repeated.

Lorena could hear the pathetic yearning in this last question and reassured him as she had been taught in occupational therapy training as well as responding to her own impulse to make him feel good about his work. He rewarded her with a generous smile. She moved on to the next loom, which was another eight-harness floor loom. Gradually she made her way around to meet each of the weavers before Mrs. Radicky called for a short tea break.

A man from the dining hall had come into the clinic with a large steaming teakettle of hot tea. Each patient went to the sideboard type cupboard against the wall near the pillars, which divided the weaving from the empty tables, which had held basketry in the morning. The open shelves on the top of the sideboard held ceramic cups, a sugar bowl and some spoons. The men made a line and Mrs. Radicky poured a cup of tea for each man as he passed the cupboard. The keeper was last in line and then he went back to his seat against the wall. Lorena realized how tall Irwin Segal was despite his slender frame. The men stood as they drank the tea and then replaced their ceramic cups on the sideboard. They returned to their weaving, each man at his own pace. Mrs. Radicky told Lorena how each man had made his own cup when they had done ceramics. Lorena looked carefully at the cups and decided they must have been poured in slip-molds as they were too uniform to be hand built. The blue-green glaze on each was a different pattern. Lorena spoke so she was sure all the men could hear, "What nice cups they are." She saw several grateful glances though no one spoke in response.

The rest of the afternoon went quickly as Lorena tried to maintain the balance between dignity, warmth and friendliness. She was aware that her comparative youth made her a more attractive helper than Mrs. Radicky. However, Mrs. Radicky did not seem to mind that the men paid Lorena more attention. As long as their behavior was pleasant and dignified, she saw no problem. Maintaining dignity seemed to be an important part of successful relationships here at Kankakee Asylum.

At 3:30 p.m. exactly, Mrs. Radicky raised her voice and announced to the men, "Stop as soon as you have finished the particular sequence of the design you are working on." By four o'clock, the men were gone and she and Mrs. Radicky cleaned up the whole room, sweeping the floor, wiping the tables and emptying all the waste paper baskets into a large metal barrel near the woodworking room door. Then Mrs. Radicky put on her coat "Come, Lorena. I live in a small house just near the hospital grounds. I walk home and stop off at the small meat market on my way. If you'll walk with me for a bit, we can discuss the occupations of the weavers while we are walking. My route is on the way where you turn off toward the nursing dormitory." As they walked, Lorena felt suddenly tired as she realized her first day in the OT Shop was finished. Mrs. Radicky told her about several of the male patients as they walked but she did not mention Irwin.

Back in the nurses' dormitory, she lay on her bed and fell asleep, waking only when Edna May burst in the door and said, "Let's go down for supper."

As they hungrily ate the meat loaf and mashed potatoes with gravy, Mrs. Segal entered and did her inspection. At that moment Lorena made the connection in her mind of the patient Irwin Segal and Mrs. Segal, the housemother. She waited until they were in their dormitory room to ask Edna May and Connie if they were any connection between the two. Before she answered, Edna May faced the wall as she undressed and put on her long flannel gown. The room was cold. Apparently, the furnace had not been stoked to heat the boiler for the radiators. She looked over her shoulder at Lorena as she told what she knew. "Irwin was brought here in the spring last year. I had just started working on the admissions ward when he came. He was brought by the Jewish rabbi. The next week, Mrs. Pauley, the housemother in the nurses' dorm was told she was being transferred to another state hospital. Apparently they made it attractive for her to move because she did not make a fuss. In fact, she came into the dining room during supper and announced it and said she would miss the girls. Most of the girls liked her a great deal and were sad to lose her. She said the new housemother would come before she left so she could show her what to do." Edna May bent over to pull on some warm socks before she went on. Her voice showed her fatigue as it got lower. Lorena hoped she would be able to continue the story, which she did more slowly. "The girls had a farewell party for Mrs. Pauley and Mrs. Segal arrived during the party in the parlor. She was so serious that she immediately put a damper on the girls' fun. She seemed to be offended that the girls were sad to say goodbye to Mrs. Pauley though she said nothing. She just looked stern and critical. The party ended soon after she arrived. I recognized then that Mrs. Segal and Irwin's faces looked similar in some way and that they might be related but I never mentioned it to anybody till now. I also know that on weekends, sometimes I've seen them walking together on the grounds. They seem to try to walk far away from the nurses' dorm. But I just figured it was none of my business since Irwin was such a nice patient. I never could understand why the rabbi brought him." By now, Edna May had pulled down the covers on her bed, put her body between the two sheets, pulled the hem of her flannel gown over her stockinged toes and pulled the top sheet and comforter up to her chin. She stretched out an arm and grasped the book that was lying on her bedside table. In the fading light, she turned her attention to her book.

Lorena felt the cut off by Edna May of the conversation and wished it had not ended. However, she took the message and sank into her own thought. She decided to try to warm herself in this chilly room by remembering those she missed. It would have been nice to discuss her work with Colin. She realized how much she has relied on that boy.

Chapter 12

Christmas at the Asylum: 1915

The first weeks at Illinois Eastern Hospital for the Insane at Kankakee passed so quickly. Lorena was surprised and dismayed the day before Christmas when she received a letter from her sister Margaret in Kentucky telling that her mother had died. She had been in bed with pneumonia for several days before she died. The funeral had been held on December 16. Lorena felt the sadness of her mother's diminished life. However, she had been away from the travail of the rural poverty of the family in Kentucky for so long that she felt little strong emotion. It was as if the news were about a stranger. She wondered if she were simply numbed by her mother's death. She felt slightly ashamed that she felt no more than she did. However, she did wonder who would take care of Pa now and asked about this in the letter on black bordered paper that she borrowed from Edna May that she returned to Margaret.

In the week before Christmas, while the patients were making Christmas designs on letter paper, she had joined them in their work since no particular help seemed to be needed. That evening, she used the few sheets she had decorated in pen and watercolor of holiday scenes, to write a letter to Carolyn Spence and one to Colin.

On Christmas Day, she joined some nurses and nursing students as they went from ward to ward and cottage to cottage singing Christmas Carols for the patients. They had had a few practice sessions around the piano in the front parlor of the nurses' dormitory. There was a big fir tree covered with popcorn strings and ribbons in the corner of the parlor. Most of the patient cottages also had a Christmas tree in the dayroom, which was also decorated with popcorn and homemade decorations. Some of the tree decorations, Lorena recognized as projects the patients had done in occupational therapy. One morning the week before their caroling event, the group of women occupational therapy patients had stitched sachets from red cloth. First each woman drew a small design on paper and traced it onto her 6 inch square of red cloth and then embroidered it before stitching it together and stuffing a small hand-full of lavender blossoms saved from the summer garden inside. A gold ribbon hanger was stitched to the top of each sachet. They were tree decorations as well as gifts. Some of the women had stitched the name of the recipient on the sachet. The mood of the women that morning as they made the sachets was certainly more lively than usual. Some of the women had chosen to give their sachets to their favorite attendant, some to their relatives who would hopefully visit them near the Christmas holiday. Several of the women occupational therapy patients lived in the same cottage on the hospital campus. Their tree was especially pretty. Lorena felt a surge of pride as she viewed it. She complimented them on their handiwork as some patients she recognized clustered around her. She realized she felt completely at ease with these women though there had been several times during the preceding weeks when she had observed and mentally noted some of their strange behaviors. None of these behaviors had frightened her though. Mentally she compared this with her feelings of more heightened vigilance when she was with the male patients. When they entered one of the male cottages, several of the male patients with whom she had worked surrounded her, all talking at once. She was glad the nurses were with her, as they seemed less constrained here in the cottage than they did in the OT Shop with Mrs. Radicky nearby. Irwin did not appear though Lorena remembered that he had said he lived in this particular cottage. She did not know much about the Jewish religion.

By the dinnertime, they were all famished. The noontime fare was especially nice. There was sliced glazed ham, jellied tomato aspic, ham and cornstarch gravy, sweet potato casserole, fresh white yeast roles with honey butter, raspberry jam, baked creamed corn, three kinds of pickles and apple cider to drink. Each table had some pine boughs with pinecones arranged in the center. What a feast! The carol singers were ready for it.

After the noontime dinner, the denizens of the nursing dorm who were not working on the wards, assembled around the Christmas tree in the parlor. Some of the girls had been together for several years. They exchanged more intimate or elaborate gifts that suited the level of intimacy of their relationships.

Lorena was surprised and pleased that her roommates of only a few weeks had small gifts for her, a hand sewn collar edged in lace for her non-uniform dress, some special taffy sent by Edna May's mother, and an embroidered circular doily for the oak table beside her bed from Connie. She wondered aloud when Connie had had time to work on it without her seeing it. There was even a ceramic teacup with her name painted on it that Mrs. Radicky had somehow made and placed under the tree in the Nursing Dormitory without Lorena knowing it. She felt overwhelmed with a feeling of acceptance and belonging that she had not felt since she left Miss Colben and the library in Kentucky.

After all the gifts had been unwrapped, the girls smoothed out the wrapping paper to save for another holiday. The paper that was too tattered to save was wadded and put into the big fireplace, which was burning warmly with a large pine log. The girls took turns warming their backsides at the fireplace as each girl showed off her gifts. Then the room was cleared of any residue of their party before the girls departed for their rooms.

Lorena lay back fully clothed on her bed with her hands clasped behind her head and thought about her family in Kentucky. This first Christmas without her mother living, though far away, would be sad. Their holiday preparations had always been meager due to lack of money but Mother had always made the day seem special by cooking traditional holiday foods. They had not had Christmas trees because their small three-room house was so crowded, there was no space. However, the church always had a Christmas tree as did the one room country school. The school children would go out and cut a tree off the property of the farmer whose land was next to the acre and a half upon which the school stood. Even while Lorena had been away from home, she was always warmed by the memory of what Christmas in Kentucky would be if she were there. Somehow with her mother's death in her mind, she felt unable to conjure up those images.

CHAPTER 13

TOGETHER WITH OTs IN CHICAGO

Lorena had little time for thoughts of events outside the hospital during that winter. In early April when the weather had warmed up from its usual frigid mien, Mrs. Radicky did tell her that that she had had a letter from another occupational therapist in Chicago informing her that there would be a meeting at Hull House. She encouraged Lorena to attend. A Canadian occupational therapist would speak about the war effort since Canada was already receiving injured soldiers back from the war in France. Lorena kept this in the back of her mind.

She was seldom able to get time away from the OT Shop between 8:30 a.m. when the first group arrived and four o'clock in the afternoon when the afternoon group left. Sometimes in the evening after supper, she would walk to the main building where the library was situated and read the *Chicago Sun* to learn of the events in Europe. She often had the library to herself.

Different patients would take her attention at different times. At meals and bedtime she asked the nurses she lived and ate with about the different patients. The patients who came to the OT Shop were all patients who had begun their recovery and the doctors and nurses felt they could be trusted to walk the distance from their cottage to the OT Shop. Connie worked in one of the cottages where patients were sent when they were being rehabilitated. Poor Edna May had to work on one of the wards in the big building where long-term sick patients were kept that were not expected to ever leave the hospital. Edna May had some entertaining stories to tell about her patients but none of her extremely ill patients were allowed to come to the OT Shop. They were the screamers and the ones who sat in the corner facing the wall picking at their clothes. Edna May had to remind them to go to the toilet and to help them change their clothing when they forgot.

Lorena decided she would try to attend the meeting of occupational therapists at Hull House if she could get Mrs. Radicky to allow her to leave early on Friday. Because Mrs. Radicky had encouraged her to attend, she felt sure she would give her the needed permission. She planned that she could take the train, perhaps stay with Carolyn Spence and be there in time on Saturday morning for the opening lecture. She was feeling very isolated working out here more than an hour away from her new occupational therapy friends in Chicago. Mrs. Radicky was a pleasant person to work with. The nurses she roomed with were also friendly and supportive but none of them had attended occupational therapy classes. A letter to Carolyn secured a quick reply. She would love to have Lorena come and stay with her at the family home on Calumet Street near Washington Square. Her own new job two days a week in the new Cabrini Hospital was interesting. She was working with Italian immigrants who had been injured on their job in the stockyards. Carolyn also planned to attend the lectures by the Canadian occupational therapist.

Lorena mailed another letter to tell Carolyn what time she estimated she would arrive. She also wrote to Colin in care of Hull House, asking him to meet her at the train. She was not sure he would even get the letter. He had responded to her Christmas letter but the envelope had had no return address. She hoped he would receive it if she used the same address she had used at Christmas.

On the Friday afternoon in March, she pushed against the north wind as she clutched the collar of her melton coat with one mittened hand, her valise with the other and lowered her head to keep the wind from making her eyes water as she headed for the Kankakee railroad station. She saw little of her surroundings as she shielded her face with her collar. She had to remove her mittens to find the money in her pocket to pay for the train ticket.

Because the weather was so bitterly cold, the train was not full. It seemed that most people must have decided to forego the pleasures of the city for the warmth of their firesides this Friday evening. Lorena was able to have a pair of seats all to herself. She put the valise in the one near the aisle to keep anyone from sitting there next to her. She was the only woman traveling alone in this car.

It was dark outside when she got to Union Station, however, the station itself was ablaze inside. Carolyn had given her instruction on how to take the "L" and where to get off for the walk to Calumet Street. As she stepped off, valise in one hand and mittens in her other, she expected to walk out and climb the stairs to the "L" station. There was Colin, whom she had not seen for almost four months. He had grown up and begun to fill out. His face had changed and become more rugged. There was the whisper of a mustache across his upper lip. She thought he must be 14 by now but he looked as if he were her own age, 23. How could someone so much younger look so mature she wondered? He held out his arms inviting a hug, which she gave with vigor. Suddenly, he gripped her around her waist and back and swung her around. She was glad the platform was not crowded or her feet might have hit someone. Finally, he set her down. Lorena realized it was something he had done to show her his strength. She also realized it was not a brotherly act. Colin was almost a man. She realized she must maintain a certain rectitude with him lest his youthful enthusiasm cause him to be misled in his thoughts about her.

She realized that he felt her stiffen and pull away. It was with chagrin that she allowed this to happen and did not explain to him that she must keep her distance. Colin turned and picked up her valise and led her out the door toward the "L" station. He accompanied her all the way to Carolyn's front door and waited until it opened to Carolyn's smiling face before lifting his wool cap and saluting the two women. He said "I'll be back on Sunday at two in the afternoon to accompany you back to Union Station." And with that he disappeared into the darkness back toward the Washington Square "L" station.

The next morning in at Hull House, the classroom was packed with mostly females. Carolyn led her houseguest to two empty seats near the front. They removed their coats and hung them over the chairs to indicate that the seats were taken. Lorena recognized several of her classmates from the classes last year. It was so renergizing to hug them and ask about their work. Then about half an hour after the announced time for the lecture, Mrs. Slagle stood before the group and asked for silence. Despite her small stature, she carried such an aura of authority; the room immediately quieted. She wore a brown silk dress with decorative buttons and an over jacket. Her hair was nicely coifed with tortoise shell combs to hold it in place. She discussed the war in France and Belgium and how some Canadian soldiers had been on the battlefront. She then introduced the speaker, Thomas Kidner, an elegant man of slightly above medium height with a thin crop of light hair on his oblong head. Mr. Kidner told several stories of young Canadian soldiers who had been injured in France and how the reconstruction aides had helped them start back to living again. The audience was so quiet; it was obvious that they were enthralled by his stories. He continued talking for over an hour. Then Mrs. Slagle walked to his side at the podium and announced that tea and cookies were served in the room next door. Those with specific questions could bring their tea back to this room and ask Mr. Kidner then. She then took Mr. Kidner's arm and led him out the door first and into the room with the refreshments.

The group reassembled teacups in hand after half an hour. Again, Mrs. Slagle called for the attention of the group. Before she allowed Mr. Kidner to take possession of the podium, she told the group of two new books that she had just learned had been published about occupational therapy. An East Coast colleague had sent her copies. She held up a copy of each of the books and said she would put them on the table under the window for those present to examine. Always the teacher, she had written the titles and authors' names on the chalkboard;

- *The Work of Our Hands: A Study of Occupations for Invalids* New York: Moffat, Yard and Company by Herbert J. Hall & Mertice M.C. Buck (1915)

- *The Untroubled Mind* by Herbert J. Hall (1915) Boston Houghton Mifflin.

Lorena got out her pencil and copied the titles and authors names on her notepaper. She would request Mrs. Radicky to purchase these two books for the medical library at the Asylum.

It was such a pleasure to be together with this group of women who were pioneering so many new projects. Lorena had thought pioneers finished with the last century. When the lecture and discussion were over, she and Carolyn walked to a teashop near the "L" station to prolong the pleasure of the day. Several other occupational therapists joined them there. They took up several small round tables where discussion of materials and ways of organizing supplies went on. They also wondered what it was like to work with soldiers, especially the drastically wounded. Finally, as night fell, they said their good-byes while getting each other's addresses so they could keep in touch. It had been a thoroughly invigorating day, Lorena told Carolyn as they climbed the steps of the elevated train station.

CHAPTER 14

COLIN

Next morning, Sunday, after a sumptuous breakfast prepared by the Spence family cook, Lorena accompanied Carolyn and her parents to the Church of the Good Shepherd. The wind off Lake Michigan was bitingly cold. Lorena was again wearing the old gray melton coat so she felt the wind less than if she had been wearing a prettier wrap such as the indigo shawl she had crocheted in the evenings in the nurse's dorm. It was in her valise. She had never been in a Congregational church before. The music was familiar and the sermon was palatable. After service they walked back to the house on Calumet Street for dinner before Lorena had to leave to catch her train to Kankakee. The weekend had been so enriching, that she felt nourished enough to face the isolation of working in Kankakee again.

Promptly at 2 p.m. there was a knock on the door signaling that Colin had arrived to accompany her back to Union Station. He swung her valise as they walked toward the "L". The "L" was not crowded so he sat down beside her as they sped toward Union Station. Lorena was aware of his very maleness and it surprised her since she now worked with many male patients. Seldom did she experience this awareness of a male being so close by. In the beginning of the trip, Colin seemed to demonstrate his awareness of her closeness by his silence and seeming shyness unlike their old carefree talk. He finally blurted out that he thought of going to Canada to join their army. Lorena replied in amazement, "You aren't old enough to join anybody's army."

His expression was defensive as he explained, "Army life would probably be better than how I live now."

Lorena said "Colin, I must express my reservations about the Canadian army as a career choice. You are so intelligent. There are many other things you could do where you wouldn't have to lie or risk your life." His facial expression was a combination of pleasure and chagrin as her disapproval of his plan.

By the time they arrived at her railroad platform, they had almost achieved their former level of intimacy. However, Lorena was aware that never again could she think of Colin as a child. She promised to write to him and he to her. They spoke of how they missed their former talks. Then he lifted her valise inside the railroad car door and held out his hand to assist her in ascending the steps. He swung himself up behind her and followed her still carrying the valise. He put it into the rack over her window seat and bent down to shake her hand suddenly kissing her cheek before exiting just as the wheels began to turn. Lorena waved until she could no longer see him before turning her attention to the widening scenes in the window. The kiss even on the cheek had been disturbing from a boy so young, even though he looked so much older.

Much of the trip she pondered about what she should do about Colin. Should she further discourage him from going to Canada and lying about his age? He had had so little in his life; perhaps army life would not seem like depravation. Perhaps it would be the family he had never had. Then she thought of some of the patients Mr. Kidner had described and shuddered to think of young Colin's body being so destroyed.

Next she thought about the occupational therapists that Mr. Kidner had described and wondered what it would be like to work with men whose bodies had severe injuries and burned lungs from poison gas. Would she be able to stand to look at men her own age that had lost legs, parts of their face or had burn scars on their face and neck? Perhaps working with the patients in the Asylum was the best place for her. She had always avoided stories in fiction or history that described mayhem too graphically. In fact she had found it very difficult to sit still to listen to Mr. Kidner describe the patients the occupational therapists were working with from the war in France. When she heard of bodily injury, it was as if her own body felt the same pain. To avoid experiencing such pain, she usually avoided listening to such stories. For example in London, Kentucky, there had been an old man who lived near her parents' home who had been a soldier in the Civil War. He often told horrifying stories to the neighborhood children. After the first time, she always had an excuse to keep her from having to listen to his painful stories.

Lorena thought of a song that she had recently heard one of the nurses playing from some sheet music on the piano, "I Didn't Raise My Boy to be a Soldier." Some of the nurses had been singing it while one of them played the score. Then a day later one of the nurses said that former President Teddy Roosevelt had scorned the song. The sheet music disappeared from the piano and the song was heard no more in the parlor.

One thing she resolved after the weekend in Chicago was to read the newspapers more regularly. She felt she needed to know more about that war in France. It had seemed so far away until Mr. Kidner spoke about the patients his occupational therapists worked with and then Colin, 14-year-old Colin talked about joining the Canadian army.

At the first opportunity, Lorena wrote a letter to Colin addressed to Hull House since she did not trust that he would receive the letter if she sent it to the gambling house. She realized that she should have been writing to him all these months that she had been in Kankakee. The Christmas letter had not been enough. He was a lonely young man. Perhaps he would not now be thinking of traveling to Toronto to join a foreign army, if she had been a more regular core-spondent. These guilty feelings involved her as she saw the outskirts of Kankakee through the somewhat dusty railcar window.

CHAPTER 15

IRWIN

Irwin Segal began to show so much improvement. He came to occupational therapy only occasionally as the month of May arrived. He had been assigned to a work crew for the spring planting. On the few occasions when he did come to occupational therapy, it was because it was raining outside and they could not work in the gardens. He began to initiate conversations with Mrs. Radicky, Lorena and even with some of the other male patients near his worktable. Also, he often sought out Mr. Wiggins to allow him to work in the woodworking room. Lorena asked, "To what do you attribute your improvement?"

He paused before he told her, "Just getting assigned to work with the spring planting crew had helped me so much. All that digging and bending over the flowerbeds and the vegetable patch felt good. I never think about committing suicide when I'm working hard."

One rainy day on a whim, while Irwin was working on lacing a leather holster for his trowel, Lorena remarked, "I saw you walking with the nursing dormitory housemother on the grounds."

He replied, "Mrs. Segal is my step-mother. My father, a kosher butcher, who owned several butcher shops, married her to take care of us when Mother died. After my father died when I was nineteen, I became so sad, that she had the rabbi bring me to the Asylum."

Lorena wanted to ask what "kosher" meant but she just nodded in an encouraging way to try to get him to keep on talking. She was successful as he went on,

"She and I never got along very well. I was ten years old when Mother died and eleven when Father married my stepmother. She was an old maid that worked in a weaving factory. Somebody at the temple arranged for the two of them to meet each other. After the wedding, she always made me take care of my five younger brothers and sisters. I could never go off and play by myself or with my friends. I got plenty of punishment from her for not watching them carefully enough. Father was always gone so much because of all his shops; even though he loved me, he was never around when I needed him."

Lorena encouraged his narrative by sitting down across the table from him. "When Father died two years ago, I felt like dying myself. I was expected to take over the butcher shops. He had been teaching me how to be a kosher butcher. I just couldn't manage the shops properly. We had to close one shop. I tried to drown myself in Lake Michigan but some sailors on one of the boats pulled me out. Mrs. Segal, I've never called her 'Mother,' she went to see the rabbi and he is the one who brought me here."

There was a long pause as he was apparently waiting for Lorena to respond. Feeling this obligation, she made a stab at giving a non-committal reply. "That must have been a difficult thing for both of you."

"At first, I was angry because I thought I would just be better off dead but the rabbi talked with me about abandoning my brother and sisters. My father and stepmother never had any children. Even though she was not kind to me, she still expected to act like my mother. When I came here, she went to one of my father's friends at the temple and got him to help her get a job here. She sent the other children to my father's sister in Evanston. They have come to visit me once since I've been here." Warmth crept into his voice when he talked about his brothers and sisters.

This was the most he had ever said in her presence. Lorena was not quite sure how to answer him. He seemed so normal unlike many of the other patients whose illness was written on their faces, in their posture, in their uncombed hair and stained clothing. Except for a moustache and short beard, his face was clean-shaven. Many of the other male patients were perennially in need of a shave and a hair cut. She simply nodded her agreement with all that he had said. Then she thought to ask "Has Dr. Goodner said anything about your future here?"

Irwin looked thoughtful "He says he thinks I am ready to leave now but he wants me to try to find some other work, not butchering. My uncle has been managing the butcher shop while I am in the State Hospital. Dr. Goodner thinks that perhaps I could finish my high school work. I dropped out of school to work in the butcher shop with Father. Dr. Goodner even thinks that perhaps I might be able to go to college if I finish my high school diploma. What do you think?"

It was difficult to reconcile this talkative young man with the morose man she had encountered when she first came to Kankakee. She wondered how she could help him make this decision. Her first impulse was to write to Hull House and ask where a young Jewish man might go to attend high school. But for the time being she just reassured Irwin that he was doing some good thinking as she moved on to other patients.

That evening, she took out her writing paper and went down to the parlor and wrote to Miss Addams at Hull House. She realized as she wrote it that Miss Addams was so busy, that she probably would get a staff member to answer her letter. However, Lorena could not think of the name of another person at Hull House to whom she could address the letter about Irwin's education.

May 10, 1916

Dear Miss Addams,

I hope you can remember me. I was one of Mrs. Slagle's students in the first occupational therapy class. I am writing because I need your advice. There is a Jewish patient here at the Kankakee State Hospital who is about to be discharged. He is considering going to high school. Could you recommend an appropriate school for him. I know you are very busy but it will be so helpful if he can succeed.

Thank you.

Sincerely,

Lorena Longley

She posted the letter in the mailbox in the Clock Tower Building.

A few weeks later, people at the hospital were all surprised when Superintendent R. A. Goodner announced that he had another position and would be leaving Kankakee. For a week after, there was apprehension in every conversation about who would take his place. He had only been superintendent a few months. Gossips wondered if he had had some sort of scandal. However, the general anxiety was quickly dispersed when it was announced that Dr. Eugene Cohn would be taking over in his place. Lorena felt especially badly for Irwin, as he seemed to have built quite a good relationship with Dr. Goodner.

The next rainy day, when Irwin appeared in Occupational Therapy, Lorena waited for an opportunity to open a conversation with him to discover his response to Dr. Goodner's departure.

This day Irwin assisted another male patient in learning how to tool a picture unto a leather book cover. When he got up to go and get a new lacing needle, Lorena walked toward him and accompanied him back to his table. "I suppose you have had a chance to say good-bye to Dr. Goodner" she said. Irwin's face contorted slightly before he was able to return it to a mask-like immobility. He just shook his head "No.". Lorena vowed to speak to Dr. Goodner and ask him to make it a point to say good-bye to Irwin Segal.

Two days later she had a reply directly from Miss Addams.

May 13, 1916

Dear Miss Longley,

Of course, I remember you. You came to us from Penn College. The work you are doing is important. After discussing your question with several others here, we recommend that the best place for your patient would be the Jewish Training School on Chicago's West Side. It has been mostly industrial training for immigrants, but they have begun to offer high school classes. From your description I believe that he would be happiest there. There is a dormitory for male students in that neighborhood. If he will come to Hull House, we can direct him to a safe clean place to live.

How are you enjoying your work there?

Best Wishes,

Jane Addams

Lorena felt gratified that Miss Addams took the time from her busy schedule to answer personally. The last line of the letter, did it mean, Lorena asked herself, that Miss Addams wanted to continue their correspondence? The idea that the great reformer would want to keep in contact with her was indeed gratifying. Lorena knew Irwin had enough relatives in the city that finding a place to live would not be a big problem for him. She put the letter aside to answer later and went to find Irwin even though it was evening. At this time of year, there was plenty of evening light to walk across the hospital grounds alone. Irwin had been moved to a cottage that was further from the main building, a cottage in which were housed the "almost" well. With the help of the nurse on duty, she found Irwin seated on a bench reading behind the cottage. He looked up as she approached and moved to make a place for her on the bench. She explained her presence by first telling him that she had taken the liberty of writing to Miss Addams about him. He looked surprised so she said, "It is part of my duty as an occupational therapist to assist my patients to do the best they can and I felt schooling was probably the best thing you could do for yourself." She did not want him to think that he was receiving any special attention, even though he was. He looked so humbly pleased that she pulled Miss Addams letter from her apron pocket, opened it and passed it to Irwin to read.

After several quiet moments in which Irwin read and reread the part about the Jewish Training School, he met Lorena's gaze and said he would think about this new information. Lorena asked him if she could do anything to assist him in making his decision or plans and Irwin arose from the bench and said that he would need time to think about this and to write to his uncle. He was not dismissive in manner but it was obvious to Lorena that her task here was finished. She arose as well and walked around to the front of the two-story cottage toward the path to the nursing dormitory.

Chapter 16

Letters: Fall 1916

Summer came and went. Lorena realized she was approaching the anniversary of having been employed at Kankakee State Hospital for almost a year. Was this a time for a celebration? Those years at the Quaker college, where boisterous events were discouraged, had apparently influenced her more than she realized. She felt that perhaps such an anniversary was not sufficient reason to celebrate when men were dying on the Front in Europe. Nonetheless, she mentioned this upcoming anniversary of her employment to Mrs. Radicky who hugged her and said how much she had added to the occupational therapy program. The two women had gotten along remarkably well despite the generation difference in their age. However, Mrs. Radicky did not say anything about celebrating.

From a West Side Chicago address, Lorena received a letter from Irwin Segal telling her that he was living with his uncle, the butcher who oversaw his father's shop and his wife in their apartment, and attending classes at the Jewish Training School. He was thoroughly enjoying his studies. The exuberance that his words expressed were so unlike the somber young man she had met last December. Though she answered the letter, she felt that Irwin had probably closed the door on his life at Kankakee, with this letter. Irwin's stepmother continued in her job as dormitory housemother. Lorena realized that Irwin had been gone at least a month before she had gotten that letter. She wondered why Mrs. Segal stayed on in her position since she apparently had come to the hospital to be close to her dead husband's oldest son. This is a question she knew would not be answered as

Mrs. Segal continued her "off putting" behavior so none of the nurses and other workers who lived in the dorm felt like asking her anything personal.

Several of the nurses, whom she had gotten to know, had become engaged and married. During her ten months here, she had attended the weddings of two of them. One wedding was here in Kankakee and Connie's had been in Chicago, which had required her to make another trip into the city. She had tried to contact Colin before she went but had received no answer from him. In fact her letter came back as undeliverable so she decided she would try to find him after the wedding and before she took the train back to Kankakee. That had been an unsuccessful adventure. The other boys at the gambling house said he had left two weeks before to take a train to Toronto, Canada to join the Canadian Army so he could go and fight in France. They told her of how Colin had taken some of his hard-earned dollars to buy a forged Canadian passport, which had put his age as 18 years. Lorena was horrified but was unable to think of anything that she could do to prevent his enlistment. This situation made the headlines about the war in France that she had been reading take on more importance.

She did not want to miss her train back to Kankakee so she left the boys at the gambling hall resolving to try to find Colin. When she got into the nursing dorm, Edna May was the only one of the nurse friends left now that Connie was gone. Edna May sat and listened to her as she wept and told of the youth who had decided to become a man by joining the Canadian Army.

At the end of the first week in December, Edna May helped her to celebrate her year's anniversary of working as an occupational therapist. Mrs. Radicky gave Lorena the afternoon off and the two young women had a late noon meal in the hotel restaurant near Courthouse Square. Afterward, they explored the Christmas displays, which were just being put up in the Kankakee retail establishments. It was a wonderful afternoon.

When they returned to the nursing dormitory in the evening, there was a letter with a foreign stamp on her bedside table. She turned the envelope over and recognized Colin's handwriting. He had left the O' off his name and just wrote Colin Donnell in the address. His address was a series of numbers and abbreviations, which Lorena did not understand. She simply held the envelope a few moments before taking her nail file to slit the envelope. The letter read as follows;

November 26, 1916

Dearest Lorena,

I am to board a ship for France tomorrow. For the past six weeks I have been in training to work on an artillery team with the Canadian Army in Europe. I wanted you to know what happened to me. We had no writing paper at the training camp so I could not send you a letter. I think of you often and wish you could send me a memento of yourself for me to keep close beside me while I am at the Front. A curl of your hair or a handkerchief would be fine. The boys on my artillery team are jolly fellows. They are a little older and they all have girlfriends. They have told me about these girls and it makes me feel lonely for our conversations. It would be so nice to hold something from you in my hands and also wonderful for me to be able to show them something from you. I cannot give you any more information than I have already written or the censors will cut it out of my letter. Please write soon to the address I put on the back of the envelope. It should reach me even at the Front.

Affectionately

Colin Donnell

Lorena realized that he had not used the "O'" before the Donnell in his name. She wondered what that was about. But without an explanation she could not make conjectures however, his reference to the censors was a warning to her for her own reply.

She was dismayed that he wanted to impress his fellow soldiers by insinuating that she was his girlfriend. On the other hand, would she be unsupportive of him if she denied him this small request. If he died in France, she would never forgive herself for not sending him something for comfort. After ruminating on this dilemma and discussing it with Edna May, she finally cut one of her tresses and folded it inside a paper upon which she had written a short letter. She mailed it to the return address Colin had written on his envelope.

Chapter 17

Headlines and Letters: Early 1917

She made herself pay more attention to the news from France. Each day before she headed for the nurses' dormitory, she stopped into the main building at the hospital and went to the library to read the newspaper.

Headline Monday January 12, 1917

WILSON'S NOTE REJECTED

The Allies responded to President Wilson's "Note to the Belligerent Nations" for protection of neutral nations by asserting that they are not the offenders in this war which will soon have been going on three years.

On January 20, 1917 she received another letter from Colin.

December 23, 1917

My Dear Lorena,

I realize that you will not receive this before Christmas but I shall be thinking of you then. We arrived at the port of Le Havre after a very rough twelve-day crossing. Most of the men, including me, were seasick much of the time. There was a small library on the boat. Many of the men do not read so I had it pretty much to myself. We had two alarms when the crew of the ship thought they sighted German U-boats, which would surely have attacked a troop ship. They were mistaken sightings. Nonetheless, we had several life preserver and life boat drills.

I received the letter from you with the lock of your hair yesterday, which you wrote December 8th. I appreciate it and have placed the letter folded around it in my breast pocket over my heart. It makes me feel close to you as well as protected from bullets. However, we have not seen any bullets yet here. In fact the bullets and guns have not been issued as we are still in barracks awaiting transport to the front. It is better than being on the ship and feeling seasick but there is no place to be alone so I can think of you and remember our conversations. I am writing this while sitting on the side of my bunk which is why my penmanship is not the best. The food is OK but seeing it dipped out of the big vats makes it seem less appetizing. I have been out for walks outside the army quarters three times. It is too cold here near the North Atlantic for much outdoor exercise. I shall look for your next letter.

With affection,

Colin Donnell

Headline Monday February 2, 1917

GERMANY THREATENS SEA WARFARE

Germany announced today that she will no longer abide by the rules of international law against attacking merchant ships. Ships near Great Britain are in jeopardy of being attacked by German U-boats. Last year the United States government declared it would sever diplomatic relations with Germany if she attacked passenger or freight vessels. Germany is attempting to blockade Great Britain to end the war. The communication was delivered to the State Department by Count von Bernstorff yesterday afternoon at 4 p.m. Germany has between 300 and 500 submarines.

Headline Thursday, March 1, 1917

PACIFISTS VISIT THE PRESIDENT

This afternoon, a number of prominent pacifists met in conference with President Wilson. They includes Jane Addams of Chicago's Hull House, economist and sociologist from Wellesley College Professor Emily Balch, politician and statesman William Jennings Bryan, North Carolina Republican representative Joseph Cannon, Illinois politician William E. Hull, liberal reformer Amos Pinchot 2nd, crusader and author of the book *Understanding Germany* Max Eastman, journalist Paul Kellogg and organizer of public health nurses Lillian Wald. None of the conferees would discuss what went on during the conference. However, Mr. Bryan did say that President Wilson hoped to keep the country out of the war.

It thrilled Lorena to see the name of someone whom she had met personally mentioned in the newspaper. Though she had talked with Miss Addams, she did not feel she really knew her. Miss Addams was too busy with her work in trying to educate immigrants and persuade the Chicago city government to keep the city clean and safe, to allow someone like Lorena to get close to her. However, she still felt a bond to the reformer.

Letter from Colin, posted February 14,1917 received March 2.

Valentine's Day, 1917

My dear Lorena,

Thinking of our friendship is what keeps me sane. The weather here is terrible. It is so cold that I can hardly write this letter even though we have a small camp stove in our trench and the trench is covered. We work long hours digging more tunnels or working on roads where there is no firing going on. We play cards mostly and talk in our free time. We work so hard that I am usually asleep when I am not working. I have a gun now but I hope I do not have to use it.

The food is filling. I have had my first taste of hard tack. It tastes something like I imagine sawdust does. We have tin plates to eat stew from when we can get to the camp mess hall. Occasionally there is firing and when that happens we stay in the trench and eat hard tack and canned rations.

I want to tell you much more but we have been warned that the censors will black out anything that could tell the enemy anything if they got our letters. So I will sign off by saying I am thinking of you on this Valentine's Day.

With affection,

Colin Donnell

Headline Friday March 16, 1917

CZAR ABDICATES: REVOLUTION IN RUSSIA

The Emperor Nicholas of Russia abdicated and his younger brother Grand Duke Michael was named Regent in his place. He is under guard at the Palace at Tzarskoe-Selo. Some ministers have been killed and some are under arrest. They supposedly were the pro-German ministers. Prince Lvoff was named President of the Council and Premier. President of the Duma informed the Imperial Council of the grave situation. The Emperor hurried to the capitol but the new government was already in place. The Empress reportedly has fled the capitol. There is a shortage of bread. Some bread shops were looted. Workers at munitions factories have gone on strike. They have marched in the streets. Troops were ordered to fire on the marchers and refused. The police replaced them and did fire on the people marching in Petrograd. Soldiers and workers took over the Duma after the Czar's abdication. The British government is glad Russia joined the democracies of the world against Germany.

Headline Monday, March 19, 1917

U-BOATS SINK 3 AMERICAN SHIPS

The City of Memphis left Cardiff, Wales on Saturday. The Stars and Strips were painted on both sides of the ship. Despite this visible sign that it was a neutral ship, the U-boat commander fired a warning shot, then order by megaphone that the crew had fifteen minutes to abandon ship. The fifty-seven men of the steamer filled the five boats before the U-boat sent a torpedo smashing into the US ship. Some of the boats got separated and have not yet landed. Those that did land after spending the night at sea, were suffering from exposure. The other two ships were the Illinois and the Vigilancia.

Headline Tuesday April 3, 1917

PRESIDENT WILSON CALLS FOR WAR

Because of the German attacks on clearly marked hospital ships, on ships with German government "safe passage" papers, the President has called for Americans to join their European allies against Germany. He declares that Germany has made war against all nations. He calls for 500,000 men to join the armed forces. He says we must help supply our friends who are already at war with materials. We can no longer remain neutral. The president says, "The world must be made safe for democracy." The President was cheered, as he has never been before in the Capitol. The War Resolution is before Congress now.

Headline, Thursday, April 5, 1917

SENATE ADOPTS DECLARATION OF WAR

By a vote of 82 in favor and 6 opposed, the Senate voted to join the ten other nations in their war with Germany. The debate went on for 13 hours. The House is expected to adopt the same resolution tomorrow. The six who opposed the Senate vote were from both Democrat and Republican parties.

Headline Friday, April 6, 1917

HOUSE VOTES FOR WAR 373 TO 50

At 3:12 AM this morning, the House of Representatives voted to adopt the resolution already passed Wednesday by the Senate. The United States entry into the War will begin this afternoon with the President's signature. One hundred speeches were made before the vote. Representative Jeanette Rankin of Montana broke into tears as she said "I want to stand by my country but I cannot vote for war. I vote no." This was her maiden speech in the Congress. Applause from the gallery and the floor followed this statement.

On April 9, 1917, the Monday after Easter, Lorena received another letter from Colin. He had posted the letter on March 26.

March 25, 1917

My dear Lorena,

It had remained quite cold until this last week. The wind that we feel when we stick our heads up out of the trenches has a warmth that I feared I might never feel again. There have been a few men who have been killed by the Germans because they were not careful when they stuck their heads up. Now I expect with this warmer weather, the trench will be muddy again. It is a balance to judge which is worse, the cold of the winter or the mud of the spring. They are issuing us new knee high rubber boots. We are able to see German spy balloons sailing over our trenches. We try to shoot them but they are usually to high and beyond the range of our guns. The Canadian soldiers often ask me why the Americans have not come into the war yet. I have no good answer for them. We seldom get to see newspapers. The Young Men's Christian Association has sent a box of books for our trench to keep us entertained while we wait for the war to start again. It is difficult to read after dark as a light in the trench shows the Germans just where to send a shell.

There are a few men here who have been through several battles. They try to tell us what to expect. I wish I could tell you more but the censors are strict.

Affectionately,

Colin Donnell

Somewhere in France

This was the last letter that Lorena had from Colin for many months. Two days later, the newspaper told of the Canadian divisions' capture of the Vimy Ridge in France. There were costly losses as the infantry attacked the heavily fortified Hill 145. After two days fighting, they were successful. Lorena looked on the map and found Vimy. She realized that undoubtedly, her Colin was in that fight. She realized it was the first time she had ever thought of him as "her Colin." It slightly embarrassed her, even to herself, to think in this fashion. However, her next thoughts were about his safety and survival. The article in the newspaper went on to describe the fierceness of the battle and the 3500 dead out of the Canadian 10,500 casualties in this Allied victory.

Chapter 18

America Prepares for War

Recruitment posters began to appear everywhere Lorena went; in the post office, in the library, in the railroad station, in the window of the grocery market, even on the mayor's new car. Those of the army and the navy competed by the attractiveness of the young men that were pictured.

A great controversy went on in newspapers and among friends, about whether or not men should be conscripted or whether they should be allowed to volunteer. Over the meals in the nursing dormitory, most of the women said they thought the men they knew were so patriotic that conscription would not be necessary. Lorena had been living in the nursing dormitory for almost a year and a half. She had heard so many discussions of different topics at the different tables with nursing staff from different shifts. The commonest topics seemed to be boyfriends' proclivities, clothing for weekends away from the hospital, and now, the immanence of war. All of the women knew of men who were enlisting. Edna May's brother had just joined the navy. Edna May had taken a few days off to go into Chicago to spend time with him before he boarded the train for his navy training. Lorena missed her grievously, as the two women had become bosom friends during their year and a half sharing the big bedroom with others that frequently changed. Other staff nurses had come and gone from the nursing dormitory and from their bedroom. Each was treated with warmth and acceptance but the friendship of the two longest occupants of the bedroom had deepened into an almost sisterly love. Lorena had finally brought herself to share Colin's letters with Edna May. At first she had feared that Edna May might judge her badly because of Colin's youth, but she had explained that she felt a sisterly concern for Colin even though he seemed to have more mature desires of their friendship.

Through the grapevine of the nurses, Lorena began to hear of opportunities for women to do patriotic work. Several nurses had left the Kankakee State Hospital to train at Walter Reed Hospital. Apparently the Walter Reed Army Hospital was in a frenzy of building to hopefully accommodate all the war casualties they expected now that American boys would be filling trenches and stretchers in France. Lorena listened to the excited conversations of the nurses about their plans to try to get placed in the first aid stations near the front lines. One of the women's magazines had a tale told by an American nurse who had joined the British Red Cross Brigade and worked in the first aide stations in France. Her story had included some frightening bits but for the most part, it seemed like a romantic adventure. The author of this article had emphasized the excitement of helping badly wounded men rather than the drudgery of scrubbing bloody floors and folding baskets of fresh bandages. She had seldom hinted at the corpses that all the nurses knew must accompany this frontline work. One had only to read the newspaper to know that many men were killed daily.

On July 20, 1917 the drawing to select men to be drafted began. Very shortly there after all the newspapers began to report the daily count of dead and wounded.

Lorena was dismayed when Edna May began to talk of trying to join the nursing corps. She hid her feelings of anxiety and sadness at the thought of parting from the woman who had become the best friend she could remember in her life, except Miss Colben in the library in Kentucky. She enjoyed Mrs. Radicky's company but Mrs. Radicky was her supervisor and also was almost twice her age. There were so many things she could not share with the older woman that she had shared with Edna May. She had never told Mrs. Radicky about Colin or about the more private conversations with Irwin before he left. The thought of losing this confidante was not pleasant though she tried to keep these feelings from Edna May as she considered war work. The war fever among almost all the nurses under forty years of age was to join up to nurse in one of the branches of the services. It became infectious. Lorena wondered if there was any place in war work for occupational therapists.

In October, she received a notice of another occupational therapy get-together in Chicago. This one was to discuss the National Society for the Promotion of

Occupational Therapy, which had been formed the spring of 1917. Again, the meeting was conveniently scheduled for Saturday. She mailed a letter to her classmate Carolyn Spence-Warren. She craved contact with other occupational therapists. Within the week, she had a reply with an invitation to stay at her home while attending the meeting. It felt so good to be invited to be in that warm, family atmosphere. Lorena missed the feeling of a "household" here in the nursing dormitory and on the psychiatric wards. In the OT Shop itself, she never felt coldness or loneliness as she and Mrs. Radicky kept the place decorated for whatever season it was. The OT Shop always felt more like a welcoming classroom than a big institutional room. Lorena decorated her part of the dorm-room she shared with the nurses but she did not try to impose her penchant for bright colors and patterns on her roommates. They accepted her artistic touches to the windows and an occasional table decoration. She had a few gifts made by patients that she had placed on a bookshelf that she had found discarded in a ward hallway and had moved to the nursing dormitory on an OT Shop cart. It made her quarter of the large dorm room a little crowded but she felt an attachment to each gift from the patients and could not discard them as had been suggested by one nurse roommate. Fortunately, that roommate did not stay long.

The last Friday of October was cold and windy as she boarded the train for Chicago. The fields through which the train went were somberly brown. A few farmers were out working but the threatening sky did not encourage harvest. Because she was familiar with all the travel routes to get to Carolyn's home, she was able to relax and not anticipate the next step of her journey. She knew a warm house, clean bed and hot meal awaited her when she arrived in Calumet Street. There were some soldiers on the train apparently returning from furloughs. Their presence put her in a mood to contemplate the possibility of joining Edna May if she left the hospital to do war work.

CHAPTER 19

RECONSTRUCTION AIDES

Because of Miss Addams opposition to the war, the meeting could not be held in Hull House. Instead, the meeting was held at Palmer House on the corner of State Street and Monroe. Entering the meeting room and seeing her classmates from two years ago caused a surge of positive emotions as she remembered the esprit de corps. that the women students had developed. She saw several of her former classmates in the room along with many others she did not know. The room must have held at least twenty women. Lorena barely had time to greet her former classmates before Mrs. Slagle strode in and stood with her erect posture near the front. There was an ornate podium from which to speak. On the table in front of the podium lay a book titled *War Work for Women*.

After a few moments of friendly chatter while the women continued to greet each other, Mrs. Slagle rapped on the table and asked for their attention. She waited until there was absolute silence. Then she began to speak of the need for occupational therapists to help maimed and injured men become productive citizens again when they returned to the United States from France. She went even further and explained how the Medical Department of the Army would need experienced occupational therapists to teach rehabilitation techniques to the many artists and craftswomen who would be recruited to work in hospitals both in France and in the United States. The injured men would need to be retrained for new roles in civilian life, particularly the ones who had amputations or had shell shock. Mrs. Slagle went on to say that she hoped that her former students would consider this opportunity to serve their country. At this time, there was no firm plan for this restorative effort, but since she knew it would take some time for women to make decisions, she wanted to put the idea to them today. Some women would need to discuss the possibilities about which she spoke with their families and employers. Her own contribution would be to direct the war emergency school at the Henry B. Favill School of Occupations at the Chicago School of Civics and Philanthropy. What she did not say was that the Army medical people had been trying to get her to move to Washington to direct rehabilitation work there. She discussed her current work as the new superintendent of occupational therapy for all the Illinois State Hospitals. This was the first time Lorena knew that her former teacher was actually her supervisor even though she was quite high above Lorena in the state hospital hierarchy. She wondered if Mrs. Slagle would be visiting the State Hospital in Kankakee soon and made a mental note to tell Mrs. Radicky when she got to the OT Shop on Monday morning.

Mrs. Slagle went on to discuss the formation of the Society for the Promotion of Occupational Therapy the previous March in Clifton Springs, New York. She gave a brief description of the few people who attended and the conflicting ideas they had expressed. Then, she described what had happened at the September 3, meeting in New York City where there were twenty-six people in attendance.

The occupational therapists listened without comment until Mrs. Slagle asked if there were any questions. Three women all spoke at once. Mrs. Slagle asked for order and that the women raise their hands. She called on each in turn. The first question was "Where will the classes be held to teach others to become occupational therapists?" Mrs. Slagle replied that the government had not yet completed their plans for these rehabilitation workers. She was not sure when the Army would be ready to enroll teachers and students for the program. But she would be organizing classes at the Henry B. Favill School of Occupations. The second question was "How many teachers would they need to teach these classes?" Again, Mrs. Slagle replied she did not know yet. The last questioner was Lorena. She asked "How much time will there be to tell our employers we are leaving if we decide to join the group needed by the Army?" This question stimulated a chorus of voices saying, "Yes, how much time?" "Should I warn my supervisor now of what I am considering?" "Do they just want teachers or do they also want some of us that are already therapists?"

To all the questions, the stately small woman's answers were the same. "At this time, I do not know. I just wanted you to be prepared. Your own good judgment will help you decide whom to tell. I will contact you or someone else will as soon as we have solid plans." She then passed around a clipboard with a pencil asking all the women who were interested to write down their names, post office addresses and if there was a telephone, to write that number as well. She suggested that the women look at the book *War Work for Women.* As soon as she adjourned the meeting, there was a rush to look at the book. Carolyn reached the book first and sat down in a chair in the front row of desks. Half a dozen of other women crowded around looking over her shoulders as she turned the pages. The earnest mood of the women was felt almost like thick air. There was such patriotic devotion to help heal the warriors after their return. The topics in the book were about canteen work for the YMCA, nursing, industrial work to support the troops, such as sewing uniforms, and entertainers such a musicians. There was nothing about occupational therapists. But Mrs. Slagle, who had stayed around to chat with some of her former students, explained that the idea was too new to have been put into the book.

Eventually, some of the occupational therapists decided to walk to the Blackstone Hotel and have tea together before saying goodbye. They knew they would not see each other again for months, or if the war lasted long, years. And now that almost all of them had jobs, they could afford tea at the Blackstone. It was even more elegant than the Palmer House.

The walk was cold and windy in the November weather. At least it was not raining. The wind carried their voices away so that talking ceased as they shouldered into the wind. As they got closer to Lake Michigan, the wind seemed even fiercer. At last they pushed through the glass doors into the warmth. The maitre'd found a table for all six and the women removed their heavy winter coats and left them with the coat check girl. They continued the discussion of what war work would be like for women. Each woman shared any tidbits they had heard or read.

The tables around them were occupied with couples and small groups of men and small groups of women. One of the tables had several men wearing uniforms. One of the women, who thought she knew the military because her brother had joined up, began to explain what the various insignia meant. For most of these women, it was their first time to begin to absorb what it meant to have a country where military garb was suddenly of prime importance.

Obviously, these women did not relish going back out into the wind which tore away their voices. But, at last, they paid for their tea and cookies, and arose to reclaim their coats. Lorena recognized how good it felt to be able to enjoy visiting the Blackstone without worrying about having enough money. She knew she carried enough to buy her ticket back to Kankakee and have more left over. The meal here at the Blackstone with Miss Ring was in her mind as she had these thoughts.

On the train that Lorena boarded to go back to Kankakee on Sunday afternoon, there were several cars full of new military recruits that were attached to the back of the train. There were fewer soldiers in the regular train cars than there had been on the trip into the city. Most of the passengers were civilians, farmers and their wives, small town residents, returning after a weekend in the city. Occasionally, one of the new recruits would wander through the car.

When she returned to the nurses' dormitory, Edna May informed her that she had been accepted into the Army Nurses Corp. and would be leaving next week for Walter Reed Hospital for a short training course. Edna May explained that the Army Nurses' Corp. had been established in 1901 so it wasn't even twenty years old yet. The two women stayed up late talking and beginning to say their good-byes. They knew it would take all week to say everything to each other that they wanted that was important. Edna May promised to write as soon as she was settled.

CHAPTER 20

THE CALL

Lorna thought about "war work" for several weeks before she decided that she would discuss the possibility of leaving Kankakee State Hospital and joining the Army rehabilitation workers. Finally, she felt as if she was betraying Mrs. Radicky, who had been her mentor and guide for these last two years, that is, she would be a betrayer if she didn't inform her soon. The opportunity came for her to tell Mrs. Radicky when they were walking uptown to shop for some new yarn for the patients to make mittens and other things for Christmas for the patients. As they crossed over the bridge, Lorena said, "Mrs. Radicky, the Army is looking for occupational therapists to work with our injured soldiers. I am thinking about whether I should join up." Then she gulped in a breath of frozen air.

Mrs. Radicky said, "I wondered when you would begin to think about that. I have seen the recruitment posters in the post office for a month or more. If I were your age, I would certainly be thinking about it. I know the nurses are enrolling. The matron has mentioned how hard it is to keep nurses now because many are leaving for the Army."

Lorena was so surprised by this response that she was speechless for a minute. She was afraid she was going to have to withstand Mrs. Radicky's attempt to dissuade her. Apparently Mrs. Radicky had not forgotten what it was like to be Lorena's age. In fact, Lorena wondered if she were a little envious of the possibility. Also, Mrs. Radicky did not have to deal with the conflicting ideas that Lorena's upbringing thrust upon her. She knew the Quakers would not approve of the country's entry into the war. Certainly Miss Addams disapproved of the US participation in the Great War. However, the overwhelming feeling from advertising posters and the nurses with whom she worked was so focused on helping our boys at the front.

Mrs. Radicky went on, "Please just tell me as soon as you make up your mind, so I can try to find someone who can help me. I am sure she will not have your training but I will need help. There are just too many patients for me to teach. I need to teach someone else how to teach them. Have you done anything official yet such as filling out an enrollment form?"

"I simply had thoughts. That's all I've done so far. With so many people around me joining up, seeing all the soldiers on the train, I can't help but think about whether or not my duty is to join up too.

And with that, the subject was dropped for the time being as they went into the dry goods store to make their choices. At this season, there was usually a great pile of red yarn. Today, the drabber colors for men's socks were in much better supply. They had to ask the clerk behind the counter to assist them to find the skimpy pile of red wool skeins. They bought all of them. Knitting needles were the next thing on the list of supplies needed. Gradually, they worked their way down the list and packed their purchases into the folded canvas bags they had each brought.

It was beginning to get dark as they retraced their route, trudging across the bridge, avoiding the slippery spots.

Christmas would have a different feeling this year now that the country was concentrating on the war effort. Fewer gifts for patients had been received from the churches in the community because they sent their gifts to the military camp instead. In the past years, it was not an uncommon experience for a merchant to drive up to the front of the hospital on the day before Christmas and bring bags of small gifts and candy for the patients. Several of these merchants had told Mrs. Radicky while she was in their establishment, that this year they would not be bringing the gifts to the hospital but rather to the army base. The staff was working hard to try to make up for the deficit in gifts. Mrs. Radicky had pleaded with her friend's husband, the owner of a bakery shop, to supply her with enough sugar to make molasses candy for the patients. An evening, a few days ago, after the cooks finished cleaning up after supper, in the big kitchen, Mrs. Radicky, Lorena and several cadet nurses had stirred taffy, then buttered their fingers and pulled the sticky loops until they began to harden. Then they buttered their scissors and snipped the loops into pieces that cooled on waxed paper on the tables in the big kitchen. After the candy cooled completely, they cut squares of waxed paper and twisted them around each piece. This candy, along with a few walnuts would have to suffice instead of the usual bag of chocolate creams, an orange, nuts and a popcorn ball for each patient. The war was making itself felt even in small things. However, no one complained about these small sacrifices. They seemed to feel it was their opportunity share in the war effort. They might not be able to go to France to fight, but at least they could make do with things at home so the soldiers could have what they needed. Even the patients expressed these thoughts.

Edna May's first letter arrived. It told of her posting to Fort Sam Houston in Texas for a short training course before being sent to France. She described the tent barracks where she slept and the work in surgery which she had not experienced since the short exposure in nurses' training. Her patriotic fervor seeped through every sentence in the letter. Lorena sat down immediately to answer her letter hoping Edna May would receive it before she embarked for France.

Lorena could feel herself being drawn into the "do it for the boys over there" frenzy like iron filings drawn to a magnet. She recognized it but seemed unable to restrain herself from joining in. It was during this time that she felt she must answer the call to war work. She wrote to Mrs. Slagle of her decision and then prepared to wait.

Chapter 21

Preparations for the Dance

Weeks passed and Lorena did not get a reply to her letter. In these winter months, inactivity seemed a good way to curl up and hide away from the biting cold of Mid-West. The war fever cooled a mite but still flowed beneath the surface of many conversations.

Wartime activities to entertain the troops accelerated. An invitation arrived from the Commandant of Fort Sheridan, the army officer-training base in Lake County north of Chicago. A spring dance was being organized to prepare the new officer recruits for their departure for France. All the nurses and other younger female workers at the Kankakee State Hospital were requested to please attend and do their duty to help our soldiers remember their homeland with pleasure. Such a hubbub followed the posting of this invitation in the main building. The young women jockeyed to see who would have to stay at the hospital to work and who could spend the weekend entertaining the troops. The letter from the commandant explained that all the women, who came to the dance and the weekend of festive activities, would be housed in the homes of families in nearby Highland Park.

Mrs. Radicky saw the letter posted on the door in the main building and encouraged Lorena to make arrangements to attend. Dancing and going to parties was something Lorena was not familiar with and it made her uncomfortable to think of what might be required, such as flirting and conversing with strange men who were on their way to be killed or maimed. How could a woman make easy conversation under those circumstances? She had not learned to dance at the Quaker schools she had attended since the religion frowned on this sort of intimacy between females and males. The only dancing she had done had been when one of the nurses brought her Victrola and records down to the parlor and the nurses danced with each other. Lorena had learned to waltz and schottische. She expressed some of these thoughts to Mrs. Radicky who responded by reminding her of her patriotic duty though Mrs. Radicky was probably also expressing her own repressed desire to join the dance group. If she could get Lorena to go and come back and tell of the experience, she would be able to experience it through Lorena.

Lorena thought about Colin and his letters from the Canadian front. Remembering Colin's discomfort convinced her she had a duty to the men leaving for the front. She would do it for Colin. She put her name on a list in the director's office of the women who would go to the spring farewell weekend for the officer candidates. During the next week, as often as she could, she got someone to play music on the piano in the parlor while she dragged one of the off-duty nurses into a waltz or schottische. If the off-duty nurse was also planning to join the group going to Ft. Sheridan, she did not require nagging, as all the women wanted to be good dancers. It was their patriotic duty.

Finally, the weekend for the dance was immediately ahead. Each woman attending from Kankakee was directed to be at the railroad station at least an hour before the train departure time. The Army had acquired one whole coach for this group. It was free and it would take them directly to the Highland Park train station where they would be met by a Mrs. Webster who would introduce them to the hosts where they would stay overnight the two nights they would be there.

A list of what to bring had been provided so that those women who seldom traveled would not neglect something important. Since Lorena had traveled a good deal of her years, she read the list and realized she had already packed most of the items. During the last month, after she had agreed to join this group of patriotic women, she had gotten some bluebird colored blue velvet and sewed herself a lovely frock. It had been a complete surprise when she saw the bolt of lovely cloth in the drygoods store. The round neck of the bodice was piped with royal blue satin. The waist front fell like an apron over the skirt. It also was piped with the darker blue satin and had decorative blue crystal buttons along the sides. It was a magnificent dress, Lorena thought. The cloth alone had cost her eight dollars. Over the last two years, she had used her sewing skills and ability to use craft techniques to gradually add to her wardrobe. Since her youth had been mostly one of poverty, she was surprised at how she enjoyed the luxury of very nice clothing. With the remainder of the blue velvet, she covered one of her small brimmed straw hats with shirred blue velvet and accents of the darker blue satin.

It was still quite cold in the upper Mid-West, despite the fact that official spring was in the offing. The previous fall she had discovered a bolt of navy blue Astrkhan cloth with mohair. This bolt of small closely curled wool cloth had the price marked down. Lorena had purchased all five yards on the bolt. She bought some serviceable mercerized sateen for the lining. She had sewed a loose fitting belted style coat with slash pockets. It was finished before Christmas of 1917. In this almost spring weather of March, she would need to wear it. Once when none of the nurse roommates was present, Lorena donned all her various garments that she planned to take in turn and went into the hallway to swish and model to herself in the long mirror. She realized as she looked at herself, that she had grown into an interesting looking woman. So seldom did she feel there was time to look into the mirror, that it was rather a surprise to realize that she liked how she looked.

Chapter 22

The Dance

The train car that got detached on a side-rail in Chicago and then hooked unto another engine for its trip north to Highland Park, had every seat full. It was indeed a coach load of valuable entertainment for the men on their way to fame, maiming or death. Lorena had enjoyed her window seat. It was almost dark as they left the station in Chicago. Occasionally they could see lights on Lake Michigan off on the right as they moved north of the city. At the Highland Park station, she could see a woman not too much older than she waiting on the platform holding a clipboard and watching the arriving train expectantly. It must be Mrs. Webster, Lorena thought. And she was correct.

As soon as the train stopped, Mrs. Webster stepped on board and asked those women already at the door, to please sit back down until she gave instructions about how they would find their hosts. She explained that there was a bus outside the train station waiting to drive each of them to the home where they would be staying. She explained the schedule and how the bus would pick them up tomorrow morning to take them out to the army base to watch the men in parade on the parade grounds. They would have the mid-day meal with the men in their dining room. Then they would be returned by bus to the homes of their hosts to rest and prepare for the evening dance. They would again be picked up in time to arrive for the evening of entertainment at 7 p.m. In Kankakee, each woman had been given a sheet of etiquette to observe with her hosts as well as with the officers. Mrs. Webster briefly reviewed these rules and suggestions. Her last duty, she said, was to read off the names of the hosts, so that when the bus stopped at that home, the women staying there would know it was the place for them to descend from the bus. Several women would be hosted in each home it seemed. As she read off each name, she hand a slip of paper to that woman with the name of her host. Lorena Longley was the last name she called out and Lorena realized she alone would be staying with Mrs. Webster as Mrs. Webster lived on the base.

After all the others had disembarked the train and gone carrying their valises to the bus, Lorena followed her hostess to a military car outside the station. The uniformed driver took her valise from her and put it into the front seat beside the driver's seat and then opened each rear door for the ladies. As they drove away from the station toward the army base, Mrs. Webster explained that her husband was a doctor in the Post Hospital. The couple occupied one of the two story homes for officers. The soldier driving the automobile pulled up in the circular gravel driveway before the elegant porch which had railings all around. Lorena took her cue from Mrs. Webster who waited for the soldier to open her door before getting out. There had been few automobile rides in Lorena's life. Mrs. Webster led her unto the porch and through the unlocked front door which held a large oval of beveled glass. There were fresh flowers in an oriental ceramic vase upon the table in the entry hallway. Mrs. Webster led the way up the oak stairway followed by Lorena followed by the soldier and valise. Mrs. Webster called her Miss Longley. She dismissed the soldier after he set the valise upon the bureau. Her hostess showed her where she could hang up her dresses, and how to find the bathroom in the hallway near the stairs. Then she excused herself and said she had many other things to do to prepare for tomorrow's events. If Lorena needed anything, she should pull the cord of the bell hanging by the door to her room. A servant would answer the ringing of the bell.

Lorena felt slightly flustered at being in such a home but she remembered how she had overcome her anxiety in many other unaccustomed situations. Her usual self-confidence buoyed her up as she prepared to get ready for supper. Mrs. Webster had told her it would be served in about half an hour. She realized she was quite hungry. She had packed a snack of bread and cheese in her valise but due to the excitement of the trip, it was still there. She hoped it had not made her clothes smell of stale food.

The evening meal in the dining room was a thick beef and vegetable stew with biscuits. There was no dunking of the biscuits into the stew as Lorena would have preferred. She closely watched her hostess in order to do what was proper. Captain Webster had returned from the hospital for the evening meal. He was a gracious gray haired, clean-shaven man. After asking about her train trip, he told the women at the supper table that there were a number of men from the Officer Corp who had come into the hospital this afternoon with fever, aches and pains and difficulty breathing. They were too sick to participate in the weekend festivities though they had been eager for this event. One of the men had been an instructor who had just transferred from Camp Funston in Kansas. He had reported a similar outbreak there just before he left on March 8. He thought he had missed catching it but here he was feeling the same way. Captain Webster looked worried and ate little supper. As soon as the meal was over, Lorena offered to help clean up but Mrs. Webster informed her that the servant would take care of everything, that Miss Longley had had a long train ride after working for six hours. Lorena was relieved to have some time alone before sleeping. Recently she had begun a journal so she sat down to write her impressions of the trip so far.

> I wonder if I should really be here. I do not feel like I fit in to this sort of rushed weekend. Since Edna May has gone, I have felt like I do not fit in much with the nurses anymore. I really miss her. I wonder if we will ever meet again. She was such a wonderful friend. I hope I have a letter from her when I return to Kankakee.

The pen fell out of her hand onto the bed-sheet and made a dark stain. Lorena got up and went into the bathroom and took her wash cloth off the hook and wet it at the bathroom sink. She was able to sponge out much of the ink but it waked her up so it took her another two hours of alternating reading with attempting to sleep, before she actually slept.

The next morning, she arose for breakfast at the time Mrs. Webster had told her. They walked to the parade ground. She was already sitting with Mrs. Webster in the viewing benches when the bus turned into the parade grounds to unload its burden of nurses. Mrs. Webster got up and went to meet the young women as they alighted. She led them to join Lorena on the newly constructed viewing benches. The event started with the marching band slowly going through its paces as it rounded the parade ground twice. The second time, a group of uniformed men bearing guns marched onto the field behind the band. Different groups of men in uniforms or men on horses followed and marched to the music of the band which had found its place across the field from the viewing benches. Some of the mounted troops had taught their steeds to march to the music also, it seemed. For Lorena, who had never seen such a thing before, it was very exciting. Mrs. Webster, on the other hand, seemed slightly bored as she made frequent side conversations during this demonstration of marching skill.

When the show was over, the women returned to the bus, which had remained on the side of the parade grounds. This time, Mrs. Webster and Lorena boarded the bus as well. They were driven to the mess hall for lunch. They went through the food serving line just like the soldiers who followed them. The women were seated at several isolated tables near the back wall. Finally it was time to return to their hosts for a rest. As soon as Lorena's head hit the pillow, she fell asleep, thus recovering some of her lost sleep from the night before.

The evening dinner was served to them after Mrs. Webster introduced each woman to her dinner partner. Captain and Mrs. Webster led the couples into a dining room in the officers' club. Lorena's partner was a young man from Western Indiana who had been receiving officer training here at Fort Sheridan for the past two months. He was an interesting dinner companion until he began to discuss his outstanding education at the University of Chicago. He had studied liberal arts and languages. His facility with the German language was why he had been selected to be part of a special corps to deal with prisoners of war in France. Then he became quite boring, as it seemed he wanted to impress Lorena and all the women with in earshot of his prowess with horses and guns. Finally, the five-course meal was finished and the officers led their partners through the chilly night air across the parade grounds from the officers' dining room to a gymnasium, which had been decorated with crepe paper streamers. A small platform had been assembled rising slightly above the dance floor for the ten-piece band and chairs lined the walls. A beverage table at the other end of the gymnasium floor held a punch bowl. It looked quite festive. Almost as soon as the couples began to enter the large space, the band struck up "Over There". Couples swung unto the floor and the dancers sang along with the band. It seemed that everyone knew this sentimental song. Lorena stood beside her dinner partner until he turned to her, bowed slightly over her hand and asked if she would like to join the dancers. She felt it was probably expected of her and was the polite thing to dance with her dinner partner. She nodded her head yes, as the music was almost too loud for voices to be heard. He put his hand on her waist and pulled her into the dancers in the middle of the gymnasium. Lorena felt proud of her newly acquired dance skills as he led her around the dance floor. Her partner knew almost nothing about her, as he had been too busy telling about himself. He did not really seem interested in her as a person, but only as a dance partner. She was pleased that her performance seemed satisfactory. However, after the obligatory first dance, Lorena felt free to dance with whomever asked her. Because she had come here as a patriotic duty, not to find a husband, she cared not whether she danced with a certain appealing officer, or not. She just enjoyed the dancing, so in her mind, she accepted each dance partner on a first come, first serve basis. There were hundreds of officers in the gymnasium and perhaps only sixty women. She realized that some women whom she did not recognize must be from the area near the fort. She danced dance after dance after dance. Even if it was a rhythm with which she was not familiar, she willed herself to allow the man to lead and she would do her best to follow the slight pressure from his hand on her waist or on her right hand.

Because there were few breaks between dance songs, she had little opportunity to speak to any of the other women. Besides, she knew that she and the others from Kankakee had been brought on this trip to talk to the men, not to the women. When the band did take a short break about each hour, Lorena, like all the other women, flocked to the punch table to quench their thirst or to the restrooms in the hallway. Even in March, they were all perspiring, as they were never able to sit out a dance. The moment a woman sat down, some officer was beside her chair, asking her to dance.

Lorena was aware that some of the officers were drinking alcohol because she had smelled it on several partners' breath. However, she did not know where they were getting the alcohol because the punch tasted non-alcoholic. She did not see them pouring alcohol into the punch. That would remain a mystery but she was aware of the change in their behavior as the evening wore on and the men had had more alcohol. For some, their dancing became smoother. For some, they began to be quite clumsy, grasping her waist and hand for balance. The whole experience did not lend itself to making lasting friendships with these men that they had come simply to entertain and make their last days in the USA memorable.

At mid-night, the band again played "Over There" and all the dancers, as well as the extra men without partners sitting against the walls joined boisterously in the song. Then the band fell silent and began to put away their instruments. Mrs. Webster and several other chaperons herded the group of women unto the bus. Several of the Kankakee women were also stumbling and had to be assisted to their seats. The other Kankakee women seemed embarrassed by this lapse in their coworkers' behavior. Mrs. Webster did not appear to be surprised.

After the bus drove away to deliver the women to their pre-arranged places of rest, Captain & Mrs. Webster and Lorena walked across the frosty parade ground and to their home in the row of officers dwellings. After making sure Lorena and his wife were safe inside, Captain Webster walked toward the hospital to check on his newly admitted patients.

Chapter 23

In Flew Ensah

Captain Webster straggled in to his home during breakfast which was being served to Mrs. Webster and Lorena by the male servant. He had spent the night in the hospital directing the care of the increasing number of men with fever, chills, vomiting, aches and pains. A number of the officers who had attended the dance had come into the hospital too, due to drinking too much liquor. However, Captain Webster reported relegating their care to an isolated ward with few nurses on duty. He showed little sympathy for people who drank too much. However, he could not seem to stop talking about the flood of men with some sort of contagious infection. He said it reminded him of what his father, also a doctor, had said about an influenza outbreak in 1890.

After breakfast, the bus with the women from Kankakee State Hospital pulled up and Lorena in her navy blue Astrkhan coat, said goodbye to her hosts as she handed her valise to the driver. Soon, all the women were back on the train coach. Those who had drunk liquor at the dance were asleep in their seats. The other women discussed the experience between themselves.

It felt comfortable to get back to the routine of the big hospital after the excitement of the army camp. However, the women who had gone lived on the excitement of that event for almost a month. Several of the nurses who had gone on the Fort Sheridan outing decided to join the Army Medical Corp. The complement of nurses at Kankakee State Hospital was getting ever thinner each week.

On Wednesday morning when Lorena awoke, her throat felt tight and dry and she shivered even under the covers. When she raised up to find her slippers beside the bed in order to go to the bathroom in the hallway, she almost fell from dizziness. She grasped the bedpost for support. Something was very wrong with her. She asked the new nurse who had taken Edna May's place in their dormitory room if she would please tell the housemother to send a note to Mrs. Radicky that Lorena was too sick to come to the OT Shop today. This was the first time that Lorena had been sick since she had come to work at Kankakee State Hospital. Even when she had cramps during her menstrual period, she did not take time to be sick. She realized she was much better able to ignore the pain if she had to walk around and help patients work on their crafts than if she sat still.

Lorena did not even go down to breakfast. In a short while, Lena appeared beside her bed with a cup of hot milk. Lorena could not tell how long she had laid in bed as her head was quite thick feeling and time did not seem to matter. With Lena's help, she sat up in bed and began to sip the hot milk into which Lena had sprinkled some nutmeg. She had drunk almost the whole cup full before she began to cough it back into the napkin Lena held for her. Lena then said in accented speech "Miss Lorena, I think I need to call the doctor". Lorena was so sick she simply nodded her head.

About an hour later, the infirmary doctor awoke her as she lay in sweat drenched sheets in the cold room. He felt her pulse and listened to her chest. He asked her how long she had been feeling like this. Then he told her "Miss Longley, I am going to have you moved to the infirmary so I can care for you there." Again Lorena simply nodded her head in assent.

Two strong young men came with a rolling table with a thin mattress on top, which they left on the walkway outside the dormitory. They came up to the dormitory room and each got on either side of Lorena, wrapped her in her blanket and walked her slowly down the steps. They assisted her in getting onto the rolling table and covered her tightly with her blanket. The March wind was still strong.

When they got to the infirmary building, they lifted her off the rolling table and carried her inside to a bed. She had drifted in and out of consciousness on this short trip. As she lay back in the bed, she realized that there were several other women in the same dormitory ward with her. She was aware that two of them had been on the train trip to Fort Sheridan. Then despite her chills, she drifted off again. She was not even aware of the nurse who stripped off her wet clothing and bathed her with a cool cloth, then put a clean dry nightgown back over her before re-covering her with her own blanket and another blanket on top of that.

For several days, she drifted in and out of reality before she began to rally. While she was in this intermittent unconsciousness, one of the nurses who had been in the infirmary when they carried Lorena in, had died. The other was in a similar state of recovery as Lorena. With in a few hours of their beginning to feel better, the two women began to discuss their experience and how they might have contracted the disease. Their heads were approximately six feet apart as they lay in their steel-framed hospital beds. Lorena was able to remember to tell the nurse about Captain Webster's account of all the men who had been admitted to the hospital in the army camp. Lorena wondered aloud if she could have caught it from Dr. Webster. The recovering nurse in the other bed said she had been dancing with a man who began to complain of weakness and had led her outside where he vomited. She had thought he just drank too much.

They finally realized during their conversation, as they lay in the two beds, that the third woman they both remembered in the other bed nearby was no longer there. However her bed contained another woman, as did all the beds this infirmary ward. Lorena asked the infirmary nurse, Anita, where the sick nurse was who had been there when Lorena came in and if she had gotten well enough to go back to work.

Anita paused for several moments before answering. Then she replied, "The two of you are the lucky ones. She passed on yesterday. We feared for all of you but thankfully, the two of you are getting better. Some others have also come to the infirmary with a similar illness. Now some of the patients are even getting it. The patients with the sickness are in another room here in the infirmary."

This new information was too much to absorb for a mind just returning to normal function. Both Lorena and the other sick nurse just lay back silently as they absorbed this grave news.

A few days later, Lorena and the other nurse were well enough to be taken by wheelchair back to their nursing dormitory. Lorna tried to go back to work a few days later but could tolerate only an hour in the OT Shop before she became weak and fatigued. Gradually over a week, she built up her tolerance for longer times in the OT Shop.

By the middle of April, this sickness had seemed to be gone. The infirmary became almost empty again. Rumors around the hospital reported that two of the nurses who had taken the train to Fort Sheridan for the weekend, had died following their return. Lorena felt especially fortunate to still be alive and recovering.

Chapter 24

The Interview

Finally after the first of May, Lorena received a letter from a Medical Corp colonel, telling her that an appointment had been made for him to meet with her and discuss her desire to work as a reconstruction aide in the army. He gave an address in Chicago on La Salle Street. She showed the letter to Mrs. Radicky who told her to take whatever time that she needed for her interview.

The appointment was at ten o'clock on a Tuesday morning. It was difficult for her to miss only one day of work at the OT Shop in the state mental hospital. Again, she wrote a quick note to her friend and colleague Carolyn and asked if it would be possible to stay overnight on Monday night before her appointment on Tuesday morning. Her reply came by telegram, as Carolyn apparently feared she would not receive a letter in time. The telegram said "You are always welcome STOP Look for you Monday evening. STOP Carolyn Spence-Warren."

Immediately, Lorena began to look around the nurse's dormitory where she had spent the last two very happy years, as if she were saying good-bye to it like a person. Then she stopped and reminded herself that she might not have a successful interview and might be rejected for the reconstruction aide group. None-the-less, she began a mental inventory of her possessions and what she would do with them if she were asked to join the reconstruction aides.

On Monday she took the train as soon as she could get to the station after the OT Shop closed. She arrived in the Chicago railroad station after supper. She had eaten a sandwich packed by Lena during the train ride. By now, she knew the route so well she did not even have to think about her ride to Calumet Street and the short walk to Carolyn's home. The reunion of the two occupational therapists was always a joyful one.

Next morning, she took her valise with her when she left Carolyn's house, as she would go from the interview to board the train back to Kankakee.

The place where the colonel interviewed her was in a hotel room on Michigan Street. He was a silver haired man in a green uniform. His desk faced away from the window on the lake and toward the door. She basked in the view of Lake Michigan as she sat facing the colonel. While he flipped through the description of her work at Kankakee written by Mrs. Radicky and the copy of the curriculum she had studied at Hull House, the colonel described the six weeks preparation course that the reconstruction aides would be required to take. They then discussed the five-month course that Lorena had already completed before she began her work in Kankakee. She handed him the certificate from her coursework at Hull House. The colonel asked her if she would consider teaching other artists and craftswomen how to work with patients. Lorena turned this suggestion over in her mind for a moment before replying "Colonel, I would really prefer working with the injured men, rather than teaching others how to do it. Even if I have to take the six week course, which will probably teach me things I have not already learned, I'd rather work with the injured soldiers."

The colonel was quiet a moment and then excused himself and stepped out of the room. After a few minutes he returned and said "Dr. Fliss thinks it will not be necessary for you to take the six week preparatory course since you have already been working in this job for two years. You will need to go to Washington DC to meet with someone in the Surgeon General's Office. When can you be ready?" He secretly hoped that when she got there, they would be able to persuade her to become a teacher for other reconstruction aides.

Lorena gave her agreement and told him that she needed to have two weeks to prepare for her trip. This was agreeable to him. The colonel gave her a train ticket to Washington and instructions about how to get to the Surgeon General's Office. Then he said "Young lady, you will not be in the Army. You will be considered a civilian worker. You will be paid $50 per month. Here is a voucher for $20 to pay for your travel to this interview and for your meals on the train. You can cash the government voucher at any bank."

The trip back to Kankakee by rail, Lorena suddenly took on a new awareness of military personnel riding the train, the beautiful spring farmland through which the train was passing and the recruitment posters everywhere. She realized she had made a grand decision to join a war effort. This would not please the

Quakers who had provided so much of her schooling. But she would just have to forget those ideas for the time being. Besides, she reminded herself, she would not be killing anyone; rather, she would be helping the injured.

Chapter 25

Washington DC

On May 25, Lorena dropped letters in the Chicago railway station postbox for her sister, Edna May, and Colin to let each of them know of her mailing address. Then she boarded a coach for the train ride to Washington DC. Having never been further east than Chicago's South East Side, she found the whole adventure of watching the countryside to be refreshing. Late May in the Midwest is a beautiful time with new leaves, flowering trees and bushes. Occasionally, thoughts of what a French battlefield might look like in comparison crept into her mind. But she refused to let these anxious thoughts destroy her time of tranquility.

After twenty hours on the train, sitting up in the coach, she felt absolutely flailed by the time she stepped off the coach in Union Station. She collected her luggage from the rack. She had her valise and her case of tools from her time in classes at Hull House. She had not needed them while working at Kankakee State Hospital because the OT Shop had all the tools and more. The instruction sheet telling her what to bring had said to supply her own tools. As the train entered the environs of the capitol, she had taken out the second instruction sheet given to her by the colonel about how to get to the YWCA where she would sleep during her short time here in Washington D.C.

She shared a room with another woman at the YWCA at 624 Ninth Street NW. There was a brand new swimming pool so she had to rent a swimming suit. The novelty of this experience would remain with her for a long while, as it was her first experience with public swimming. Each day, she took the streetcar to

Walter Reed Hospital where she met with Miss Elizabeth Green Upham from the Federal Board for Vocational Education who was in charge of gathering together the reconstruction aides. Miss Upham was a busy woman who often went to the Capitol to talk to legislators about her project to get a law for rehabilitation of soldiers. Miss Upham conducted orientation classes for ten women from different parts of the States. Lorena was the only one who had had formal occupational therapy training.

The first order of business was to get fitted for uniforms. Each aide was issued three white aprons and three blue chambray long sleeved dresses with a dozen wide white buckram stiffened collars and wide white cuffs. The dresses and aprons reached to twelve inches from the floor. The three caps that went with the uniform were made of the blue organdy gathered into the white band. She was also issued a gray sweater, two pairs of cuff links, an O.T. collar pin, two pairs of woolen tights, three pairs of flannel pajamas, four suits of woolen underwear, six pairs of merino wool stockings, six pairs of cotton stockings, three pairs of sturdy shoes, a pair of gloves, a raincoat, rubber boots and a waterproof sou'wester. She knew she would have to mail her clothing she brought with her home to Kentucky to await her return. She would be required to buy a street uniform when she was not working in the hospital. It was a blue serge suit and a black velour hat for winter and a straw hat for summer. An Ulster cape was also required. By the time she bought all these extra garments for her street dress, it would cost her $100 or almost all she had saved at Kankakee. It did not seem quite fair but since she was only a civilian worker rather than in the military, they would not supply everything.

There was a similar class of reconstruction aides who were training in physiotherapy in Walter Reed Hospital. The only difference in their uniforms was that they had blue dresses with short sleeves. The two classes of women seldom saw each other since their training kept them busy from dawn to dusk.

The class learned about working with occupations and purely medical functions. Miss Upham taught the class of reconstruction aides about how to occupy a man during the early stages of convalescence. She talked about motivation. "Stay out of the doctors' and nurses' way," she said bluntly. It did not take long before she recognized that Lorena had greater experience than her other students. Soon she had persuaded Lorena to teach the other aides how to do chair caning and rug making. Lorena was teaching the others before she realized this was what she had told the colonel she did not want to do. She kept a good spirit and attitude about being subtly tricked into teaching but she still knew that her first call was to work with the men. She also had felt sure she would go to France but now she realized that many reconstruction aides would be staying in the USA working with the invalids who returned from France.

Part of the training to be a reconstruction aide involved working with the one ward of injured soldiers who for the most part, had been injured during their basic training in camps in the United States. On the fourth day at Walter Reed Hospital, the group of aspiring reconstruction aides was shepherded to the ward with these men. The smell of disinfectant over healing and putrefying flesh was overpowering. Miss Upham assigned each trainee a man to talk to and discover what craft would be most appropriate to teach him.

Lorena's patient was a 20-year-old from a ranch near a small town in Texas. While standing on the dock waiting for his turn to mount the gangplank to board the boat, he had been roughhousing with some of his fellow soldiers. He stepped into a coil of rope just as it was pulled to use. It suddenly wrapped tight around his leg pulled him off balance and into the murky waters of the harbor. The ship bumped against the piling and his foot was caught between and traumatically amputated. Reconstruction aide trainees had had the opportunity to read a small description of their patients before they met them in the ward. This young man had already been working with the physio-reconstruction aide trainees to use crutches properly while awaiting his prosthesis and for his wound to heal. His main complaint to Lorena was that he didn't even get his wound on the front. He felt ashamed to how he got the injury and felt he would never be able to return to his Texas ranch, as a one-footed man would have difficulty mounting a horse. Lorena met the physio-reconstruction aide with whom he had been working and discovered that despite his complaints, he seemed able to master everything the physio had tried with him. Between them, they decided that braiding a lariat should be his first project. Then he should learn how to tan and shape leather so he could replace by himself the leather pads that would be need for his prosthesis. Working with this bitter young man was not easy but gradually over the few days she worked with him, he began to show more focus on his work and less on feeling sorry for himself. Each day, Lorena received the story of another patient and gradually she had four patients that were hers to work with.

Shortly after Lorena's arrival, the War Department decided that reconstruction aides should be included a new department called the Division of Physical Reconstruction. By listening whenever she could she discovered that the transfer of the reconstruction aides out from under the supervision of the Orthopedic Department had been a sort of punishment. The Orthopedic Department had been somewhat autocratic recently about in their approach to personnel. However these orthopedic doctors still had complete power to prescribe activities for the injured men.

It seemed almost unpatriotic for the different groups of healthcare workers in the War Department to be fighting among themselves. It was a new experience for Lorena to see powerful men trying to outdo one another. Each evening as she rode the trolley back to the YWCA, she ruminated over the interpersonal contests she had witnessed during the day.

When nothing had been said to her about her date to leave for France and two other classes of reconstruction aides had left already with Lorena not among them, she approached the Director of the Division of Physical Reconstruction and asked him directly when she would be allowed to sail to France. This craggy old man with tufts of eyebrows almost obliterating his icy blue eyes harrumphed and pulled back from his desk. He looked her up and down before replying that in the military, people took orders from superiors and did not give them. Lorena made her best attempt to look subservient though it was not her usual mode. She spoke in her softest most persuasive voice when she said "Col. Rider, I do not mean to be troublesome, but I most earnestly wish to help the injured men in France. I feel I could be more useful there than I am here teaching crafts to other women. I am not afraid of the kind of injured men that I see coming back here to Walter Reed Hospital. I feel I would be most helpful at the hospitals near the front."

The old doctor gave her a long look before replying, "Miss Longley, I believe you could adequately work with the men at the front. The other reconstruction aides who have been trained here have been sent to hospitals in the USA. Only our most mature aides will be sent to France. Miss Upham has kept me informed about your assistance in teaching the other aides. I believe you have the inner strength to manage in the base hospitals near the front. I will speak to her about your request." He picked up his pen and tacitly dismissed her. Lorena could hardly believe his response. She quickly stood, gave an almost imperceptible curtsey before fleeing out the door before he could change his mind.

For several days, she feared her visit had done nothing to speed the time of her departure for France. Nothing was said to her by Miss Upham so finally, Lorena decided to speak to her about her desire to leave. This led to Miss Upham's confession that Dr. Rider had indeed spoken to her about Lorena's desire to ship over. But Miss Upham had not thought she would be able to get another person to replace her in teaching the chair caning and rug making. However, now she knew that a new batch of girls was arriving to learn how to be reconstruction aides. She would look for someone that Lorena could train to teach chair caning and rug making. Lorena would just need to have patience. She reminded Lorena that this war had been going on for four years already. It would not be over before Lorena got to the front.

Lorena had to be satisfied with that. She realized that volunteering to work as a civilian for the Army meant that a person really gave up their freedom of decision making. This was a hard realization to accept.

CHAPTER 26

EMBARKING

In the next group of women arriving to be trained as occupational therapy reconstruction aides, there was a school teacher from Montana that seemed a likely prospect to become Lorena's replacement.

While the woman was not an occupational therapist yet, she had taught many crafts in a high school art class in an Indian School. She seemed to fit right into the class of women and be a friend to everybody. All her classmates went to her when a problem arose. Lorena observed this behavior and brought it up with Miss Upham. She said "Miss Upham, I believe that Flora Baer from Montana could take my place teaching the chair caning and rug making. I've been watching her and she is a good teacher as well as getting along with everybody."

After a slight pause, Miss Upham met Lorena's gaze and said "Yes, Lorena, you are correct. I've become aware of her attitude which is a proper one for teaching women, as has yours been as well. I think she could take over your teaching tasks. I realize how much you have wanted to sail with the other women for the front. I'll recommend her to Dr. Rider."

Lorena was so excited to finally be able to pack her bag and again organize her own tool case. She had enjoyed being here in the nation's capitol for a month, but now, she was ready to go.

A day later, she, along with nine of the other women she had been teaching, received an envelope with the Army orders, even though they were civilian workers. Her final destination was the hospital at Base 117 at La Fauche near Chaumont, which was the headquarters of General Pershing. She was to be at the Ellis Island, New York Harbor at 6 a.m. on Monday morning. Since she had kept her clothing clean, ironed and ready to pack in a moment, she had nothing pressing to prepare before leaving. Each evening after returning to the YWCA, she had washed out her apron and dress and hung them on the clothesline, which hung lengthwise of the basement. Then she took down the ones she had hung up the night before and ironed them. She rotated her aprons and dresses and undergarments so that all got equal wear. They would have to last through several months before they would be allowed more, even for Europe.

Because she had not had a chance to visit the Capitol and the White House, she decided to do so this last Saturday before she left. Then she could take the Sunday morning train with this last class of reconstruction aides to New York. She would take the Ferry to Ellis Island, which had recently been reorganized for troop dispatching. There she could stay in the Army quarters near the dock on Sunday night. They would be able to easily get to the dock for the 6 o'clock embarkation.

She found Flora Baer before she left the hospital this last time and asked her if she had any questions since she would be taking over the job of teaching the chair caning and rug making. It was then that she discovered that Flora had not been informed that she was to stay behind and teach rather than go to the front. She had not realized that all the other reconstruction aides in her group had received their orders. Her crestfallen face was expression enough of how she felt about this situation. Lorena was torn between feeling sorry for her and just saying goodbye without providing a shoulder to cry on. But her better nature took over and she laid her hand on Flora's blue percale covered arm and said "I'm sorry. I know you wanted to go with your classmates. But Dr. Rider and Miss Upham think you can teach the aides better than I can. They want you to stay because of your skill in teaching." Lorena heard herself and wondered if anyone could believe this contrived message.

However, Flora did appear to become less sad looking as she heard this compliment.

"She'll do just what I did. In a few weeks, she'll ask them to find somebody else, just like I did." Lorena told herself to relieve her guilty pleasure in leaving Walter Reed Hospital and heading for the Front.

The visits to the major public buildings for the US government reinforced Lorena's surge of patriotism as she prepared to leave her native soil. Lorena knew she probably would be miles from the Front, but she realized that accidents happen. Just look at her first patient here at Walter Reed Hospital. He surely never expected to be injured before he even got on French soil. An accident could happen to her before she got to her Army Hospital at La Fauche. After she got to La Fauche, misfired weapons or a fast moving troop retreat could cause injury to her. Life during war was an uncertain proposition even if you were not a soldier.

She had rented a locker in the train station for her tool case and her valise during her White House-Capitol tour. After retrieving them, she boarded the train to New York and began to walk the aisle looking for her reconstruction aide compatriots. In the third car, she found four of them sitting together on plank benches around a small square table fixed to the floor. A middle aged woman stranger wearing one of the reconstruction aide uniforms motioned her to the vacant table next to them informing her that the others from their group would soon be joining them as well. The middle-aged woman was named Miss Marguerite Henderson. She would accompany them and be in charge of the group. After these introductions, two of the women at the table moved over to sit with Lorena. After stowing her luggage in the receptacle at the end of the passenger car, Lorena relaxed and took a seat on one of the benches near the small table by the window.

The other reconstruction aides had all assembled by the time the train started. The two women who had moved began to whisper descriptions of their party the previous evening. It gave Lorena a preview of the kind of women she would be working with. Even their parties were rather sedate. They had gathered in the YWCA room of two of the aides and made non-alcoholic punch from some apricot juice and ginger ale sent by the mother of one of the women from nearby rural Maryland. One of the women, Helen Vander Gaast, another re-aide from Chicago, had sneaked a flask of whiskey into the YWCA. The other women were surprised by her daring and challenge to the rules of the YWCA. No one but the bearer of the whiskey was willing to try it and in fact, they ask her to leave the party lest she get them all in trouble. Finally, after fifteen minutes discussion, they were able to persuade her to pour the whisky down the drain in the sink in the hall bathroom. One of the girls stood outside and guarded the door while two others poured the whiskey out and rinsed the bottle and sink so there would be no tell-tale odor. They had looked for Lorena to invite her to the party, but her roommate said she was out touring. They quickly forgot her with the adventure of emptying the whiskey. None of the women wanted to be left behind in the USA just because they were foolishly sharing punch with alcohol in it. Lorena felt relieved that these women were so sensible. They would need to be able to trust each other when they got to Base 117. It would not do to have anyone with poor judgment among them. She would have to observe Helen Vander Gaast from New York, and see if she had other lapses in judgement.

The trip took them through the verdant countryside of the middle of summer. Fields of beans, potatoes, cabbages and onions lay next to groves of trees still mid-summer green. A few houses visible from the train had flowerbeds or flower boxes. The train tracks did not go through the best part of towns. Often the view was into someone's back yard and privy. Most of the men who filled the other tables and benches in this car soon slept. They did not try engage the reconstruction aides in conversation. Perhaps Miss Henderson's presence warned them off.

The trip had taken approximately 12 hours, so it was dark when they reached New York Penn Station. Several of the women at the two tables and benches had fallen asleep despite the hardness of the seats. They had laid their heads right down on the table or against the window. Lorena had remained awake during the entire trip. There was a small bus there to transfer the women and their luggage to the ferry to Ellis Island.

Their assigned barracks area was filthy. At this hour of night, they did not want to sweep and scrub, but that is what was necessary before any were willing to lay down their heads. Miss Henderson found an official and requisitioned a broom, mop, bucket and rags. The women set about making their sleeping section tolerably clean before sleeping.

Similar rooms full of men surrounded their long dormitory room in the barracks. The men had agreed to allow the women to use the bathroom for fifteen minutes. There was no bathroom or toilet assigned to the women. The women took turns going to the toilets, during the time they were cleaning their space. These men were also on their way to the Front tomorrow on the ship *USS Tiger*, a merchantman that had been reconfigured to transport troops. The ship's massive bulk was visible through the small panes of the east windows. Miss Henderson gave each woman an influenza mask to wear since they had to sleep in such close quarters here and on the ship. She talked to her group of women about the epidemic, which was appearing almost anywhere these days.

Lorena found it difficult to sleep in this dormitory room with nine other women. The metal bedsprings covered by a thin mattress, squeaked unmercifully each time its occupant moved. Despite being tired from the late arrival of the train, and the cleaning, Lorena was still unable to sleep. The influenza mask was uncomfortable. She was too tired to even inquire about their accommodations on board the *USS Tiger*. Lorena knew she must have finally slept, because she awoke to the blast of the ship's horn. All the women in this dormitory room awoke at their varying rates and dressed, repacked anything they had taken out. There had been no bargain with the men about using the toilet this morning, so Lorena stood in the hallway outside the toilet and asked each man exiting if he were the last. Finally, one man went in and asked the men in this toilet to please use the one at the other end of the building so that the women could use this one. This nice soldier also told the women that they had one hour from the time of the ship's horn until the ship would cast off. Lorena relayed this information and the availability of the toilet to her compatriots. They rushed into the toilet, did whatever was necessary and rushed out. They stayed close to each other as they hurried, carrying their luggage to the dockside. There they saw another group of women in occupational therapy reconstruction aide uniforms. These women had come from Boston with the same destination, Base Hospital 117 at La Fauche. Miss Henderson greeted them and informed them that she was in charge. Her title would be head aide.

Masses of young men were standing at attention on the dock. An officer went from group to group handing out cards upon which to write the name and address of the nearest relative in case of death. Lieutenants were leading groups of men in platoons up the gangplank. The dockside was almost empty when a colonel came to the two groups of women and told them to board. They knew he was a colonel because he told them he was Col. Wilson. They followed him and Miss Sanderson aboard. A sailor met them and conducted them below to a 24 by 12 foot room with twelve bunks. There were two small covered portholes so the women knew they were on the outside of the enormous ship. Otherwise, the trail through stairs and hallways had quite confused their sense of direction. The two groups of women now joined as one, had just gotten into the large cabin when the ship lurched and they knew they were underway. Lorena threw her valise and tool kit into the large bin on top of other luggage near the door and climbed up on the top bunk also near the door. Miss Henderson motioned a seaman inside to demonstrate the life jackets. Then the women were drilled about what to do in case of enemy attack. The seaman called it a "drowning drill."

CHAPTER 27

THE CROSSING

The women had been prepared for many eventualities, but not seasickness. Lorena did not remember such an extended time of miserable nausea. It had started so suddenly that they had not even had a chance to build any camaraderie before the ship was rolling. The closed space with the odors of vomit and shit from so many women was quite overwhelming. It was not quite so bad on the top bunk as she imagined it was for the women on the bottom. The nausea was debilitating enough that she could not drag her body out of the bunk except to squat over the enamel chamber pot under the bottom bunk, then clip the cover back on so it would not overturn and spill when the ship rolled. Each time she did that, she had to remove her influenza mask. Eventually, she just tucked it under the pillow she had made of her cape. She said to herself, "I've already had the flu anyway."

By the second morning, Lorena forced herself to seek the open air. When she opened the cabin door, she discovered a guard was stationed outside the cabin for the reconstruction aides. She asked him why he was there and he simply replied, "To protect you from the men." He then went on to tell her of the area on deck which had been assigned for the women and restricted from the men. He showed her a small pencil drawn map of the deck and where the women were to stay in order to be safe.

With the map in her mind she climbed the narrow stairway holding fast to the handrail mounted on the wall. The ship rolled only slightly but Lorena had heard about "sea legs" and she knew she had not gotten hers yet. On deck, she met another woman who was also getting some fresh air. Both women had put on their long blue gabardine coats despite it being nearly July 1. The wind off the Atlantic Ocean was cold. It whipped both her Ulster cape and her skirt around her legs. She had to put one hand upon her uniform cap to secure it. Through the camouflage netting over parts of the deck, the two women could see that they were part of a huge convoy of ships.

Lorena took the initiative to introduce herself to the other occupational therapy reconstruction aide. "I am Lorena Longley, originally from Kentucky but most recently from Kankakee, Illinois. And how about you?"

The only other occupant of the "women's section of the deck" replied in a New England accent that Lorena always associated with snobbery. "My name is Martha Garrison and I hail from Lexington, Massachusetts. I taught art in a private school for girls in Western Massachusetts until the war call for aides came out."

Lorena went on to explain "I've been working in the Eastern Illinois State Hospital for the Insane." She described her life's career in a few brief sentences.

Martha said, "Please tell me more about your training at Hull House. I thought about trying to work in a settlement house myself but my father wouldn't hear of it."

Lorena told of her trip to Chicago from Oskaloosa then reciprocated with "And how did you decide on art training and how did you hear about the opportunity to join the reconstruction aides?"

"Well, my parents encouraged me to choose a course of study that would help me find a good husband. Since we were close to Radcliff, I decided to go there. One of my first courses was a painting class. The teacher was just wonderful! She encouraged me to take other art classes and before I knew it, I found feeling fulfilled myself only when I was doing art," Martha recounted.

In her usual way, Lorena used her skills in leading other people to talk about themselves. "Did anybody try to discourage you?" she questioned.

"Oh, yes, some of the faculty thought I should do something else, but my parents thought art was a good thing for a wife to know. They encouraged me to go to the parties at Harvard, but I found most of the men much too intellectual to be much fun."

Lorena asked, "Did you ever think of doing anything else?"

"Oh yes, I met a student from the Cooper Union art school in New York, and I wanted to go down there to study more, but my parents refused to allow me to go on to study in New York City, so I took the teaching job in Springfield. That was easiest." Martha she went on to described the small campus in which she taught art. When the opportunity to study reconstruction aide work, it was like being let out of jail. Her father was a prominent lawyer in Lexington and could not refuse her when she appealed to his patriotism.

As the two women talked, the clouds appeared to break and the sun shown through, bathing the deck in sparkling lights from the wetness. Despite feeling rather peaked from lack of food and lost fluids through throwing up, Lorena began to feel a little cheered. Talking to another person invariably lifted her spirits. Neither woman felt like eating breakfast. The guard outside their dormitory cabin had explained that breakfast would be served to them in the dining room on the first deck. The two women decided to try just having something to drink. They made their way to the mess hall aware that the eyes of men were watching them wordlessly. Apparently their uniforms made them immune to wolf whistles and cat calls. Not many men were on deck or in the mess hall either. Obviously the women were not the only ones suffering from seasickness.

The mess hall was sparsely furnished with long benches screwed to the floor on either side of long tables also screwed to the floor. The women saw a short line of men approaching a table with large cooking pots. Red faced cook's helpers were ladling out some sort of gray porridge into metal bowls. The women stood in line behind the men. As soon as the men in line realized that there were women there, they stepped aside and magnanimously gestured the women to the front of the line. Lorena protested that she did not want to eat, only drink some of the tea, which was being poured from a gallon sized gray speckled enamel teakettle into metal cups. Each woman took a cup, poured some milk from a gallon sized ceramic pitcher into the cup and stirred in a spoonful of tan sugar crystals. They looked around the mess hall for a seat. At the far end of the hall, there was a table with a piece of folded cardboard on it labeled Reconstruction Aides. The hurried toward it trying not to slop their tea as the ship gave slight rolls.

Now, they were very aware of the eyes upon them. Lorena went around the table and swung her legs over the bench and under the table without spilling a drop. Martha sedately slid between the table and the backless bench and sat facing Lorena with her back to the room of men. They sat rather subdued, knowing they were the center of attention. Neither woman removed her coat, feeling that the coat itself was a barrier between her and the many men in the room. Eventually, Lorena remembered that her tea was cooling rapidly so she lifted it to her lips. It was neither bad nor good, just wet and sweet. She sipped it slowly remembering that it could easily come back up. She slipped her white linen handkerchief from her uniform pocket just in case. But the tea seemed to actually settle her stomach. She peered across the table to see how Martha was reacting to the tea. Martha had seen Lorena slip her handkerchief out and had followed suit. But she seemed to be relishing her tea. The two women self-consciously began to discuss the tea they were drinking. Suddenly, Lorena wondered if they might be allowed to take a kettle of tea down to their compatriots in the reconstruction aide cabin. She voiced this thought to Martha who responded positively but said she didn't know if they should ask about it or not. After due consideration and bolstering one another's courage, the two women picked up their empty cups and carried them to the large washtubs set at the side of the hall. They had observed the men depositing their dirty dishes there. Then side by side, they approached the serving line again. The man immediately in front of them in line turned slightly to see if they were coming for a serving of porridge, so Lorena asked him who she needed to talk to get some tea for her compatriots. His rather ungrammatical response "Mam, them cooks is about to wind er up. Jist ast em." He stepped aside to let them pass toward the galley door, which was held open by a large hook.

Lorena stepped over the raised metal ship compartment threshold into the cavernous galley. One of the cooks turned and recognized through the steam from the stove that there were strangers in the galley. He began walking toward them in a rather threatening way until he realized they were female. Suddenly he appeared shy despite his burly bare arms and trunk like torso. His deep voice sounded like it came from deep in the trunk of a tree when he said "What kin I do for yuh ladies?"

Lorena voiced their request for a kettle of tea for the seasick women in their cabin. He nodded his assent and rumbled back to the water tank by the stove to fill an empty teakettle. Then he found a metal tray onto which he put several stacks of cups, a bowl of sugar, teaspoons and a small metal pitcher of cream. When he lifted it and realized how heavy it was, he called another of his galley workers to carry the tray and follow him as he lifted the steaming teakettle. Lorena and Martha fell gratefully into line behind the two male kitchen workers. It would have been a physical struggle to carry the heavy teakettle full of hot liquid as well as the heavy tray of cups and other necessaries through the narrow hallways, down the narrow steps and over the high threshold into the cabin.

In the narrow hallway approaching the door to the cabin, the two women wiggled past the men carrying the tea implements and asked the guard to please open the door for them. Each woman stepped over the high threshold and felt the blast of the bad smells of seasickness. None-the-less, Lorena cheerfully said, "Ladies, we have brought you tea." Then she turned to the bearers of the tea things and instructed them to set the tray and kettle down inside between two sets of bunks. The men did as instructed and gave slight salutes as they looked around the dormitory cabin before leaving. These men were used to the smells of seasick passengers and did not flinch. Lorena's impulse was to grab the metal door and fan fresh air into the room, but she felt her first duty was to serve the tea. She asked each woman in turn if she would like tea, with or without sugar and milk, then she poured the liquid while Martha carried the tea through the narrow spaces between the bunks to their compatriots.

By the third day, most of the women were able to at least rise from their beds long enough to go to the bathroom and the one toilet reserved for women passengers. It was still necessary to use the slop jars sometimes as there were only two toilets in the designated bathroom.

The remainder of the crossing was uneventful, if one considers being separated from the men on the ship but knowing they are watching you every minute you are outside the dormitory cabin can be considered uneventful. Eventually, before the ten-day crossing was finished, all the reconstruction aides had recovered from their seasickness enough to be able to join the other women in the line in the mess hall and at the table labeled for the reconstruction aides. There were no escapades of the aides crossing the visible and invisible barriers between them and the men. Helen Vander Gaast seemed quite mature and unlike the report of her behavior at the leave-taking party. When Miss Henderson was not around, there were a few playful conversations about trying to meet individual handsome men they had seen on deck or in the mess hall, but no one was foolhardy enough to attempt such a peccadillo.

Chapter 28

The Arrival

June 26, 1918, the *USS Tiger* and the rest of the convoy reached Portsmouth, England. The harbor was so full of ships; it was difficult to see the waterfront. None of the passengers of the convoy were allowed off their ships. Gradually, one by one, the big troop ships were relieved of their passengers, in groups of approximately 200, to be deposited on another ship. The women were instructed to wear their woolen tights and sweaters under their cape to keep them warm on the small craft. It seemed to take an interminable length of time to offload the smaller groups of passengers into row boats and take them to their smaller ship for reboarding. It was nearly dusk when the 24 reconstruction aides who were the last ones to disembark made the short trip to their craft for crossing the English Channel. This smaller ship had no bunks. They had to sit on benches along the deck for the entire crossing. On deck, they did not have to wear the uncomfortable influenza masks. Because she had already had the flu, Lorena was not required to wear one. Already, the Army doctors knew that the people who had had the flu would not catch it again. The smaller ship got underway as soon as the passengers were all aboard.

Their last meal on the *USS Tiger* had been at noon so all the reconstruction aides and the infantrymen were hungry. For the first time, the women had the experience of eating the K-rations. Each passenger was handed a small paper bag, which contained a flat paper cup, paper wrapped water crackers and some dried prunes. They removed their masks. They spit the prune seeds back into the bag. Cool water was carried in a large metal teakettle and poured into the paper cups.

The women had clustered together on the benches. They could hear the engines start as the craft was small enough that the engines were not far from the passengers. Again, some of the passengers experienced seasickness from which they had recovered only a few days before. In this situation, it was just best to hang over the side of the boat to give up the crackers and dried prunes. The ocean was not too rough so Lorena did not throw up her meal.

The toilet for the women on this boat was much more of a challenge. Two army blankets had been attached by clothespins to a length of rope, which was strung between hooks on poles near the corner of the pilot's house on deck. Every time a reconstruction aide had to use the toilet, everyone on the other side of the blanket could hear every splash and swish. The toilet was a large ceramic crock secured in a wooden frame with a rough wooden seat and hinged cover to prevent splashing while at sea. There was no washing basin. The women knew they were gradually learning to disregard their inhibitions about privacy requirements for the gentler sex.

They were not allowed to go below decks in case the ship would be sunk. They were forbidden to even whisper. The men could not smoke lest the enemy see their cigarettes. The tension was so high, that hardly anyone slept. The wind off the English Channel blew away all the bad smells of humans crowded together. A few of the most seasick spent most of the voyage clinging to the rail.

Morning light illuminated the French Coast ahead of them. They realized they were part of a flotilla of boats like their own. As they gently rocked, they could see boats taking turns to pull up to the quay and empty their decks of the Army men on board. Soon it was their turn. By now, after a night on the ocean with no place to put their heads, the reconstruction aides were a rumpled pale looking group of women. None-the-less, men seemed to cheer up just seeing them there. As the men disembarked, they formed up into marching units and were led off by their officers to waiting trains. Miss Henderson left the women with Lorena in charge and went off to find an officer who could give her more information about the travel accommodations for the "Re-Aides" as they had begun to call themselves. The women tried to look inconspicuous clustered together in their dark capes. They could occasionally see a wayward glance as the platoons of men marched past. Lorena's feet began to ache, as these new shoes were not yet broken in comfortably. Eventually, they could see Miss Henderson and an officer approaching them down the length of the dock. The officer seemed to be looking them over carefully as he approached. Miss Henderson matched him stride for stride. Her skirts flowed out around her somewhat controlled by the weight of the cape.

Miss Henderson introduced him as Major Johnson. The major then puffed up slightly as he said "Ladies, I know you were sent with good intentions but in the midst of war, we do not need the responsibility of taking care of you. So do your best to not get in the way of the Army. Miss Henderson has some orders for you. We were not expecting you and so it will be a few hours before we find a place for you to sleep tonight. The trains are too full of soldiers to find room for you. So stay here until someone comes for you to show you where to go until we can find a train with space for you. If you need to respond to the call of nature, please go to that outhouse just at the end of the dock. One of you will need to stand guard outside." With that, he stalked off without so much as a goodbye or a salute.

Miss Henderson was a good leader and good example for the tired women. She encouraged them, now that the sun was warming the ocean air, to remove their capes, fold them and then sit upon them on the dock a few feet from the dirty waters of the harbor.

It seemed an inglorious end to their voyage to be sitting on a dirty dock in a shipyard, especially when there was no food in sight. Eventually, Miss Henderson wrote a note to Major Johnson and sent Lorena off to find him. After a walk the length of the dockside, Lorena saw a group of officers in a small building. She approached, entered and asked them of the whereabouts of Major Johnson. One of the officers straightened up and said, "Follow me." He led Lorena into another small room. He stopped, saluted and said to Major Johnson who was bent over his desk "A lady to see you sir." Then he turned on his heels and exited.

Major Johnson looked irritated as he raised his face from a ledger. Lorena gave her half curtsey and handed him the note from Miss Henderson. He took it, opened it and read it without speaking. After a few moments, he barked out "Captain Edwards, come in here."

A nice looking young man with an open face quickly entered the door and looked expectantly at his superior officer as he said "Yes, sir."

"Go with this young lady to where the other women are and lead them to the mess hall. They have not eaten. Stay with them until they are finished. Then show them the hotel where they will be sleeping tonight." Lorena's heart soared as she realized they might be able to be comfortable for one night. The major went on "Captain Edwards, you are to be in charge of these reconstruction aides until they leave on the train. Take this paper to the hotel keeper at the Hotel Canard Blanc in Poisson Street." He handed the young officer a folded paper. Captain Edwards saluted toward the top of Major Johnson's head as he returned to his ledger. He then backed out of the room and indicated for Lorena to follow him. When they were outside the building, Lorena hastened her step until she was abreast of him. They walked side-by-side down the dock, neither speaking.

Chapter 29

Le Havre

The Hotel Canard Blanc was on a back street near the harbor. It was clean though the Re-aide women were crowded three to a bed. There was a bathroom on the first floor. The women took turns enjoying the luxury of a bath knowing that it might be the last one for months. The concierge of the small hotel told them in sign language that they must conserve water as it took too much time to reheat the water in the storage tank. She led them into the bathroom and put her hand near the bottom of the tub. Then she showed them the tank over the stove in the small room next door where the water was heated. Then she pointed to the clock and showed one hour. In conversation between themselves, the re-aides understood that they must conserve the hot water. Consequently, their baths consisted of approximately two inches of water in the bottom of a galvanized tub. Each woman helped the bathroom attendant lift the tub of dirty water and pour it through a hole in the tiled floor. The attendant then prepared the bath for the next bather. The toilet was in a closet in the hallway near their sleeping rooms. Lorena was the last one through the bath. By this time, the warm water had all been used and the attendant was tired and crabby. Lorena gestured that she could leave, as she Lorena would empty her own water. Lorena just wanted this last bit of bathroom privacy before leaving for the hospital in La Fauche. After the attendant exited, Lorena bent her naked body over the tub and washed her hair. Her scalp had been itching for several days. She had asked one of the other re-aides to examine her head to make sure she did not have lice. There had been no lice on her scalp, just a dirt and scales of skin from over two weeks since the last hair washing. Even though she brushed it whenever she had an opportunity, it still was not as good as washing it. She was grateful though, that it was only dirty hair. People who slept in bunks often caught whatever creatures the previous occupant had left.

The cold water and the bar of soap did not make her hair feel clean but she knew that she had done the best she could to make herself clean. Besides, they wore their uniform hats whenever they went out now.

By the time she got back to the hotel bedroom and donned her flannel pajamas, both her bedmates had fallen asleep on the opposite edges of the bed. The only choice left for her was to climb into the space in the middle between them. The bed sagged slightly so as she pulled the cover up both the sleeping women rolled slightly over toward her. She wondered if she would be able to sleep. But when she awoke the next morning, she realized her fatigue from the sleepless night on the small ship had allowed her to sleep soundlessly with a body cuddled up to her on either side. She realized that their sense of privacy had receded another degree. She was glad that she liked and respected these women. Otherwise it would be extremely difficult to live in such close quarters with them. How many of the men liked and respected their comrades in the trenches, she wondered.

The morning ritual of taking turns for the toilet, brushing teeth in the basin provided on a bureau in the room, and then dressing took nearly an hour before all the women were ready to descend to the dining room for breakfast. There were two women waitresses for the breakfast meal. Neither spoke English. Lorena wished she had studied French rather than German at Penn College. She wondered if she could purchase a French dictionary here. When she left the dining room, she stopped at the concierge's table and said in a questioning voice "Dictionary, dictionary?"

The concierge looked at her with an uncomprehending look at first but suddenly her face beamed and she took Lorena's hand and dragged her behind the table and into the concierge room. Lorena knew this because a small wooden sign nailed to the door read "concierge." There, the middle-aged woman went to a shelf and took off a French dictionary. She handed it triumphantly to Lorena. Lorena took it in her hands and opened it to realize that this dictionary would help a French reader but what she wanted was a French-English dictionary. None-the-less, she smiled at the concierge to reward her for her effort. Then she said, "English-French Dictionary. French-English dictionary?"

She looked expectantly at the woman who looked blank again, and then suddenly she smiled and said, "Biblioteque? Librarie?"

Lorena shook her head sadly, as she had no idea what the woman was saying. She again wished she had studied French instead of German. What should she do, she wondered? She remembered she had some paper and a pencil in her pocket. Out they came and Lorena drew a book and a hand with some coins in it reaching out.

The concierge smiled widely and replied "Je comprend". She took Lorena by the hand and led her out through the small lobby and down the street, around the corner and into a small newspaper, candy, tobacco and bookshop. She spoke to the sales lady in rapid fire French. The woman reached behind her on the bookshelf and brought out a tiny compact French-English/English-French dictionary. "Cinq francs." She said holding up five fingers. Lorena realized she had only American money in her pocket. She held it out to the woman who studied it before taking one quarter. Lorena wondered if this was the correct amount but it did not seem unreasonable. She had heard stories of American soldiers being exploited and charged too much so she was realistically suspicious.

Lorena thanked the woman in English, knowing she would not understand. However, the storekeeper seemed to comprehend her English slightly better than the concierge. Lorena tucked the small book and extra coins into her ample pocket while the concierge and the storekeeper had a brief conversation in French. Then Lorena and the concierge went back to the hotel. Lorena tried to give the concierge a dime for her help but the woman refused it waving her hand "No, no, no." This word Lorena could understand.

She took the dictionary up to her room hoping to find a quiet place to try to learn a few French words but her roommates were busy repacking their luggage to travel. They were relieved to see Lorena as they were leaving for the train station in a few minutes. Lorena quickly repacked her valise to join they others going down the stairs. Miss Henderson had to sign some vouchers at the concierge's table so she could be paid for their food and lodging. Then the women walked in an orderly fashion two abreast to the train station each carrying her own luggage.

CHAPTER 30

TO CHAUMONT

The train car into which the women filed had been adapted from a livestock transportation container into a place for passengers by cutting some windows into the here-to-fore solid wooden walls. The doors still opened in the middle of the car. Backless benches had been crowded crosswise into the car and nailed to the floor with brackets. The women automatically dropped their luggage in an orderly row between two benches. Because they were to be the only occupants of this car, they were not crowded. Again, they found themselves segregated from the men. Was it going to be that way when they got to La Fauche also they wondered to each other? Fortunately, these women were a hardy lot; resigned to whatever challenges they met.

The train trip along the Seine River took them through the ancient city of Rouen. Occasionally they caught sight of the river in the distance. Lorena took this opportunity to look up in the dictionary some of the words she saw on the signposts. Many of these words were not in her small dictionary. She realized it was quite an abbreviated introduction to the French language. She did see a line of people waiting below a sign that said, "rations de vivre" and was able to find it in the dictionary. It meant food rations. As they approached Paris, the towns seemed closer together; Herblay, Sannois, Epinay, St. Denis, Aubervillers. There was little war damage to the countryside visible from the train. Lorena had heard so much about the devastation to the French countryside that she was surprised not to see evidence of it. Stops at some of the villages had slowed their progress.

They arrived in the Paris railway station at nearly eight in the evening. Miss Henderson went to find the officer who could give her the vouchers for the next length of the journey. The women stood together on the covered platform with the luggage nearby. They did not want to move about lest they lose each other in this crowded place and also perhaps fail to see Miss Henderson's return. They had not eaten since morning. A woman with a cart of small loaves of bread passed by. Lorena consulted with the other re-aides. They decided to pool their money and buy six loaves. Lorena ran after the women and held up six fingers. Apparently some of the other re-aides had gotten French money in Le Havre because when she opened her clutched hand to pay for the loaves, she saw some coins she had never seen before. She held out her hand to the woman who picked a few coins out of her hands and said "Merci Mademoiselle."

At Lorena's elbow was another re-aide that helped her carry the six loaves back to the group. Lorena then opened her tool kit and took out a craft knife. She wiped it on the underside of her apron and then began to cut the loaves of bread into four sections apiece. Each woman had a quarter of a loaf of bread. But they had nothing to drink. They had been warned not to drink the water. Eventually, a man with a steaming kettle appeared. They saw him pour some steaming liquid into a man's cup and take a coin from him. Lorena knew that her refolded paper cup would not withstand hot tea or coffee. Then she remembered the glass jar of nails she had in her tool kit. She opened up the kit and unpacked those things lying on and wrapped around the glass to keep it safe from breaking. She emptied the nails into her handkerchief and tied it up and laid it back in the bottom of the tool kit. Then she called out "Sir, sir!" The man did not turn around. The other women were watching her. She put the glass jar into her pocket. Out of her other pocket she took the little dictionary and looked for the word sir. "Monsieur, monsieur!" she called out. She knew her pronunciation was bad but the man stopped and acknowledged her. As he approached, several of the other women found things in their luggage that could substitute for a drinking glass.

Shortly thereafter, Miss Henderson returned with an officer, who looked them over and remarked to no one in particular, "I wonder what they will do with them when they get there." There was an edge of derision in his voice. The re-aides were becoming used to the skepticism that the Army officers seemed to have about them and their mission to help heal the injured soldiers.

After some time, after all the bread was eaten except the one quarter loaf that Lorena saved for Miss Henderson, the head of their little group of women appeared from within the main hall of the railway station. Behind her walked another officer in a summer dress uniform. Miss Henderson introduced him as

Major Hayes, the officer in charge of troop shipments. She reported that he had agreed to find them a place on the earliest train leaving tomorrow morning. However, they would have to wait here on the platform for another 10 hours.

Lorena gave Miss Henderson the quarter loaf of bread as she suggested that some of the women could spread their capes on the platform and sleep while some others kept watch over them. They could sleep in shifts. Lorena volunteered to take the first shift and asked for a volunteer to join her. Every re-aide raised her hand to volunteer so Lorena chose the redhead from Ohio named Miriam Wentworth. Martha Garrison, her shipboard friend made a face at her when she was not chosen. Lorena gave her an apologetic look and vowed to make it up to her.

Lorena saw a straw broom propped in a corner of the platform between a brick buttress and the wall. She gripped the broom and swept and area clean near a bench. The other twenty-two aides including Miss Henderson laid their capes on the platform near a bench with their valises at one end. The women then lay down and rested their heads on their valises. It was a balmy evening so they were as comfortable as was possible under the circumstances. Miriam and Lorena seated themselves upon the bench. They vowed to each other to keep themselves awake.

During this nighttime watch, the two women came to know each other in a way that would increase their trust during the time they worked together. They took turns questioning each other about their background.

Lorena asked, "Miriam where do you hail from? I'm originally from Kentucky."

"I was born and raised in Toledo, Ohio. I have five younger brothers and sisters. Mom worked as an elementary school teacher after Dad was killed. He worked in a rubber tire factory. There was a terrible fire and Dad got burned badly. He died a few days later. So that was when Mom had to go back to work."

Lorena continued her quest to know Miriam better by saying, "It must have been very difficult for your mother to raise six children, especially if she sent you to college."

"After Dad died, the factory owner gave Mom $300. That didn't last very long so she went back to teaching. She had done that before she married Dad." Miriam sighed and continued, "I was such a good student that my teachers helped me to find money to pay for school at the university. I had to work to earn part of the money for my expenses. I took several extra years to finish. I did seamstress, millinery work, and sometimes took care of sick people. At the university, I majored in art, expecting to follow Mom into teaching, maybe even college teaching. However, I saw the recruitment posters for war work for women and that changed my plans."

At midnight, Miriam and Lorena gave over their job as guards of the women to Martha Garrison and another woman named Alice Simpson. The two sleepy re-aides clutched their capes about them and fell asleep.

The train whistle awoke them at 5:30 a.m. The women rushed for the regular passenger cars that were to carry them to Chaumont. They would have to use the toilets at the end of the train cars, as there was no time to use the restroom now. After the cattle cars, this was indeed luxury to ride on regular passenger benches, even though they were bare wood, not upholstered. All the re-aides were able to get into one train car leaving only a few empty seats, which were soon filled with uniformed doughboys and their packs.

Seeing Paris from the train window was all they were allowed of the famous capitol. The night on the platform had so fatigued most of the re-aides, that as soon as they left the city, they slept on each other's shoulders. Consequently, they missed most of the view of the French countryside, which while not destroyed by war, was not verdant with crops because of the poverty of the farms lacking men to work the fields. Additionally, each group of infantry, no matter of which country had marched through the area, had stripped the land of whatever vegetables and fruits there were. For mid-summer, the land definitely had a barren look when those sleepy re-aides momentarily opened their eyes.

The train followed the valley of the Seine River. There were frequent stops on sidings while other trains went past going the other way. It seemed as though they stopped at each village as well. Twice, the train tracks crossed the Seine. It was dark when they reached the rail platform at Chaumont on June 29th.

It was apparent that Chaumont was a place of importance as there were so many officers and soldiers rushing around. General Pershing's headquarters was here. Miss Henderson already had the name of the officer she must see here for transportation to La Fauche. The women were shown to a large tent that had just been vacated by some doughboys who marched off to the front. Miss Henderson asked the women to wear their influenza masks and to check the slender cots for lice or other vermin before they lay down. The women had discussed this possibility while on the transport ship since they had not known who slept in the berths before them, but they had been too sick to worry about checking. Fortunately, none of the women caught any lice on shipboard.

Chapter 31

La Fauche

The women were transported next evening from Chaumont to La Fauche in the back of a small covered supply truck. The canvas over the back of the truck was painted brown. There were benches along both sides and across the back of the driver's area. There were several men who were destined to be orderlies who accompanied them in the truck. They volunteered to sit on the floor and allow the re-aides to sit on the benches. The luggage was crammed under the benches. The few pieces that would not fit were used as seats by some of the men. Several of the men seated on the floor had their backs propped against the knees of the seated re-aides. Lorena's legs went to sleep during the ride.

The truck had to drive without lights, as the driver did not want to become a target for airplanes trying to attack General Pershing's headquarter. The truck moved slowly over the ruts left by the artillery and supply wagons. Fifteen miles took nearly five hours, as there were so many detours around mud holes, and attempts at corduroy roads to remedy the mud. There was other uneven earth where roads should be. Miss Henderson reported that the officer who had arranged for this transport told her that once they arrived at Base 117, they would be assigned to a sleeping tent. One barracks had been assigned for the curative workshop. When they arrived, Miss Henderson was to seek out Major Fenworth who would show them where to sleep and where to start their work.

It was after midnight when they arrived. Despite the late hour, Base 117 at La Fauche was not asleep. It appeared as if most activity must take place after dark despite the mandate of "lights out". The truck bumped into the main road of Base 117 and stopped before a large brown tent. Miss Henderson went inside the tent as the tossed and bruised re-aides descended from the benches in the back of the truck. There were wooden duck-board tracks upon which to walk. They were narrower than the boardwalks Lorena was familiar with. The re-aides each gathered their valises and tool cases to the side of the duck-board walk that led into the brown tent. Soon Miss Henderson reemerged with Major Fenworth and an aide carrying an unlit lantern. The major looked the group of rumpled women over before turning away from them and striding off down a row of tents with his aide trying to keep up. He stopped at the flaps of a tent and motioned the women in side. "Put your grips in there and come with me to the building where you will have the space for curative work." He waited outside with some impatience while the women quickly chose their cots and put their valises and kits underneath.

The aide stuck his head through the flaps and said, "You need to leave someone here to guard your grips." Letitia Johnson and Mable Perkins volunteered to stand guard over the re-aides's possessions while the others followed the soldier to discover where they would work. Major Fenworth had disappeared by the time they came out unto the dark duck-boards between the tents. As they followed along, Lorena saw men's faces in other tent openings or raised tent sides, gaping at this procession of females. Soon, the tents gave way to wooden barracks. The Major's aide stopped before one with the door handing ajar and stepped inside. He took a match out of his pocket and flicked it with his thumbnail and stepped inside. He set the kerosene lamp inside the door of the barracks. He lifted the chimney and lit the wick. Then he picked up the lantern and took it to the center of the barracks and set it up on an upturned wooden barrel. There was an audible intake of breath as the women saw the mess they had to clean up before they could start their work. The lantern only illuminated a small area of the barrack. Lorena asked the soldier to walk in front of them as so they could see the whole space. He carried the lantern as he walked down the middle so the light would not leak through the cracks between the boards in the walls. The wood was still new looking, Lorena could see in the occasional flash of the lantern. The young man stepped around the remnants of the previous occupants—a broken cot, some empty ammunition boxes and several burlap bags. The dust erupted in small clouds with each step, though the dust was barely visible in the lantern light. Lorena could smell the dust. She heard several of the aides begin to sneeze. By the time they reached the far end of this empty barrack, Lorena judged it to be approximately 100 feet long and about twenty feet wide. A section at the end was partitioned off with a three-quarter wall. There were carpenter tools hanging on the other side of the partition and a workbench made of ammunition boxes was set up in the middle of this space. Lorena began to picture how the rest of the building could be broken up into different areas for different crafts. She assumed the other re-aides were also thinking about this problem.

Miss Henderson said quietly but so all the women heard her, "Let us go back to our tent and get some sleep. We can begin this work tomorrow." Obviously, she recognized their tired state and how discouraging the barracks was.

The soldier put out the lantern before they exited the dirty barracks in order to comply with the orders for "black out" he said. He guided the women back to their tent.

Lorena heard muffled sobs as the group neared the tent. She was so tired she felt like crying herself. When they got to their tent, the soldier set the lantern inside the door and relit it. There were Letitia and Mable asleep on their cots in the dark at the far end of the tent.

Lorena realized it was Martha Garrison who had been sobbing. Miriam Wentworth had put her arm around the weeping re-aide. She consoled Martha like a sister, with her arm around her as she led her to her cot. Several of the other re-aides clustered around. Lorena realized that Martha was shedding the tears that all of them needed to shed. They were a tired group who had seen the work they had to do before their real work could begin. The dirt and lack of furniture in the barracks assigned to them would discourage almost anyone.

Lorena addressed Miss Henderson, "I would like to go out and find some tea for the group to drink."

Miss Henderson looked at her gratefully as she began to examine the sleeping quarters to see if there were any amenities here. There weren't, just cots and a stack of blankets on the first cot by the door. She motioned Lorena outside and said, "I suggest that you take another re-aide with you as women alone are always vulnerable in a camp with so many men."

Lorena stepped back inside and tapped Alice Simpson on the shoulder. "Alice, will you come with me to find some tea or something else to drink? I know everybody would feel better with something in their stomachs." Alice followed her out of the tent and back toward the tent where they had descended from the truck. At the door of this tent, Lorena called out "Hello" since there was no way to knock. The young soldier who had showed them the curative workshop barracks stuck his head around the corner of a large wardrobe shaped cabinet. When he saw who was there in the dark, he stepped outside to ask what she wanted. She explained that the women had not had anything to drink since they left Chaumont, except the water that they carried in canteens.

"Follow me" he flung back over his shoulder as he trudged off in the opposite direction leading them further from their own tent. Lorena hoped she would be able to retrace her steps when it was time to return. All these tents seemed to look alike though they had small stakes with numbers sticking in the ground near them. She was too tired to memorize the numbers.

Soon they came to an area where three men were tending several cook stoves under a black canvass tarp on poles. The soldier asked one of the cooks for a teakettle of hot water and some tea for the reconstruction aides. One of the cooks asked "What are reconstruction aides?"

Despite her tiredness, Lorena attempted to explain their purpose. "Reconstruction aides are here to help the shell-shocked soldiers get well. We expect to help them learn some new habits and some new crafts to occupy them."

The man who had asked the question laughed and turned away muttering under his breath as he filled a teakettle from an enormous cylindrical shaped water tank that sat on some metal stands. He set it upon a cook stove. Lorena hardened herself inside to mentally fend off the subtle ridicule of his turning away. She felt Alice grip her hand hanging at her side. The gesture was a commiserating grip so Lorena squeezed back. In the dark outside the shelter of the black tarp, the soldier cooks could not see them comforting each other by holding hands. Both women knew that this would be taken as a sign of women's weakness. None-the-less, they relished the momentary comfort. The two women stood quietly in the shadows and waited for the water to heat. While they waited, Lorena asked the man for some cups, remembering that the women only had a few glass storage jars. The man seemed to consider this request as burdensome though he complied by grabbing a huge metal tray from a rack of trays and carrying it to a cupboard with rough open shelves. From the shelf, he filled the tray with tin cups. Into one of the cups he poured some sugar. He did not even ask how many were needed but Lorena counted them as he put them on the tray. There were enough. He reached into an enormous "ice box" and removed a jar of cream which he added to the tray. He put the loaded tray on a nearby table of rough wood.

Eventually, the cook handed Lorena the two gallon sized teakettle of hot water. Alice picked up the tray and the two women stepped slowly and tentatively through the night, seeking their way back first to the officer's tent, then back to their own tent. This adventure made them into heroes to their compatriots. While they were away, the other re-aides had taken the pile of woolen army blankets and distributed them to each cot. Lorena wondered if she would be comfortable sleeping on a wool blanket in such warm weather. But by the time the women had all had some tea and stacked up the cups on the tray again, Lorena was too sleepy to feel anything, let alone a scratchy woolen blanket. She pulled her Ulster cape over her and fell asleep to the sounds of other women already snoring.

Chapter 32

Preparing For the Patients

Not even the sun awakened the re-aides but the 5 a.m. reveille did. The bugle was close by the volume of it. A latrine was about two hundred feet from their tent. While Lorena and Alice had been getting the tea last night, Miss Henderson had sought out this necessary place and showed the re-aides how to find it in the dark. Now that it was light, the women felt slightly conspicuous walking on the duck-boards through the tents toward the small separate latrine building. It was built over a trench and had a seat with five holes like an outhouse. The smell was horrific. No privacy here thought Lorena as she sat down with her undergarment pulled down around her knees. She had not even thought to use it last night because she hadn't had enough to drink to even need it. But the tea before bedtime had made it necessary this morning. Five-inch squares of cut up newspaper sat in a pile on each of the small shelves behind each hole. Lorena reached back for one as she finished up and looked over at Miriam sitting on another hole. When Lorena went out, she saw that someone had stenciled in black paint WOMEN in large letters on both ends of this latrine. At least this time, they would have their own place. None of the women would have to stand guard at the door to make sure no man accidentally entered. She wondered about bathing facilities but right now, cleaning up the curative workshop barracks seemed the most important thing. A bath would feel good after they were finished, she decided.

As she approached the re-aide tent, she met some nurses exiting their own nearby tent. It was a sudden realization for her that there were more women here than just the re-aides. This was a reassuring thought.

Inside the tent it was pandemonium with twenty-four women all dressing at the same time, each trying in some small way to maintain her modesty.

Before starting their cleaning task, Miss Henderson told them to follow the nurses who were housed in the nearby tent. The nurses would lead them to the mess tent that was quite a distance away. Lorena joined Mable and Alice who were ready when she was. They saw some nurses emerge from a nearby tent. She hailed them with a "Hello". The nurses responded and asked the three re-aides to join them on their walk to the mess tent. She looked at each tent stake number in an attempt to remember the route for the future. All the tents looked almost alike. As they emerged onto the road dividing the tents from the buildings, Lorena saw a big gray Ford ambulance, several small wagons with no horses in harness, their tongues resting on the ground parked next to a barracks building with a sign reading US Army Medical Corp. There was a large Red Cross on a white background painted on either side of each ambulance. The nurses led them down the road, which was dry now but had deep ruts from previous rains. The mess tent was so marked and the nurse's led the re-aides inside and showed them the women's tables. A private was ladling out bowls of oatmeal into metal bowls. Another soldier dropped a spoon full of sugar on top of the oatmeal. Yet another private poured cream on the sugar. The women carried their bowls that were hot, by the rim and set them upon the women's table. In a corner, coffee was being poured into tin cups from a barrel with a spigot, lying on its side on a metal stand. Another soldier was pouring cream into the coffee cups of those who wished while another spooned sugar into the coffee. As the three re-aides watched, many of the men went back for more oatmeal and more coffee. After some consideration, Lorna and Mable decided to have another cup of coffee. They had slept such a short time and had much work ahead. Hopefully, the coffee would help them keep up their energy.

After returning to their sleeping tent, the three re-aides spent some time stringing clothes line across the tent and then unpacked a few clothes and hung them to air on the line near their cots. Perhaps tomorrow, they would discover how to get their laundry done.

Soon all the re-aides returned from breakfast and the latrine. Miss Henderson stood and asked, "Will you please all find a seat on the cots. We need to plan our work. I have some assignments to give you so we can start." She paused and looked for their agreement before she went on. "Lorena and Letitia, I want you to make a list of supplies we will need to clean the curative workshop. After you finish, please take the list to Major Fenwick. Miriam and Alice, I am giving you the task of making a list of the crafts that each re-aide knows how to do. Mable and Martha, I want you to make a list of craft supplies necessary for beginning work." She methodically went down her list. Other women were given the charge to find soldiers to bring barrels and boxes to the curative workshop to be used as tables and work benches.

When all the work had been assigned, the women dispersed to their various assignments. Lorena and Letitia sat on Lorena's cot and listed brooms, dust pans, rags, metal wash basins and buckets, a rubbish barrel, strong soap and a large barrel of clean water. They decided no mops, as they would only catch on the rough wood of the barracks floor. After they finished their list, Miss Henderson sent them off to Major Fenwick to request the supplies and help for transporting them to the curative barracks.

It was obvious from the response of Major Fenwick that he did not like dealing with anyone but Miss Henderson. He treated Lorena and Letitia as if they were children, questioning them about each item on their list. "Why do you need dust-pans? You can sweep the dirt out the door."

"Sir, we need to carry the dirt away from the door, as some of the men will be working on their projects near the door. We must avoid having them track dirt into the barracks again," Lorena explained.

Eventually, he assigned the same young soldier who had been their guide the evening before, to again accompany them to the big supply tent on the edge of the base. The brown supply tent covered stacks of wooden storage crates with the name of their contents printed on the sides. Outside of the supply tent, there was a wheelbarrow upside down on the ground. Lorena commandeered it and wheeled it along as the supply soldier led them through the enormous tent and into another just like it.

Eventually they had everything except the water barrel, which the soldier assured them would be delivered by caisson as soon as possible. They stacked the wash basins and bars of soap and rags into the wheelbarrow. Finally they got everything packed with four brooms balanced on the top. The two women set off toward the barracks knowing they would have made several wrong turns before recognizing the curative workshop barracks if it weren't for the soldier, whom by now they knew as Private Pollard. With his help, they began to unload their supplies. He then excused himself, expressing regret that he could not stay to help because he knew Major Fenwick would be expecting him back soon.

Four of the other re-aides had arrived at the curative workshop by the time Letitia and Lorena rolled the wheelbarrow to the door. These women did not need instructions. They grabbed those brooms and began to raise a dust. Lorena asked Letitia to await the water caisson outside the barracks while she grabbed the dustpan and rushed to rotate between the four sweepers. When the dustpan was full, she carried it outside and poured the piles of dust as far away from the door as she could. By the time the four sweepers had completed the length of the entire barracks, Lorena heard the water caisson drawn by a mule, pull up outside. Two soldiers unhitched the caisson and pulled it to the side of the door. Then they turned around and led the mule away. The women could hear them having a sotto voce conversation about why these women were so near the Front.

By noon, the cleaning group had the barracks immaculate. Barrels and boxes for worktables began to arrive. Late in the afternoon, the women sat down on their makeshift tables to plan for the next step. Mable, whose father had been a carpenter and who had passed his skill on to his daughter, volunteered to make one of the larger crates into a cupboard which could be locked so they could keep their tool kits in it. Miss Henderson would requisition a padlock for this cupboard. Each woman would be able to store her kit inside rather than under her bed. Several of the women, including Lorena decided they would rather carry their tool kit back and forth than be separated from it at night. The tools inside were her most valuable possessions, she decided.

Other such decisions were made before the women trooped off to use the latrine, to wash their hands in a basin set up on a box outside the tent and to find their way again to the mess tent. The sleeping tent was quiet by eight o'clock except for regular sleepers breathing.

CHAPTER 33

PATIENTS

By the second morning of their presence in Base 117, the curative worship was somewhat ready for the patients. Miriam and Alice's list of crafts and arts that the re-aides were ready to teach included chair caning, Turkish knotting, leather tooling, metal chasing, metal piercing, metal hammering, ceramics, macramé, chip carving, wood carving, furniture making, papier-mâché, painting and drawing. The re-aides had discussed Mable and Martha's list of craft supplies to discover if they could get materials. Each of them knew other crafts not on the list but they feared they would be unable to get the supplies. Martha and Mable had presented their list to Major Fenwick, who had responded that he had more important things to do than get these kinds of supplies. After he allowed this insult to lie between them, he turned to his ever-present aide Private Pollard and sent him with Martha and Mable to the supply tents. They had only been able to get a few of the supplies, leather, wooden 4 by 4s, paper and cord. They returned to the curative workshop with their load of materials on a small wooden wagon. Private Pollard was becoming quite fond of this new group of women.

Together, the re-aides apportioned the space left to them in the building into sections; a wood working section so that all the dust and chips would be in the same area to avoid irritating the lungs of men who had been exposed to mustard gas; a leather section near the door and the water caisson, an art section near the north windows; and a weaving section. They drew straws to decide which re-aides would have the morning shift from 6 a.m. until 2:30 p.m. or the afternoon shift from 2:30 p.m. till 10 p.m. for this season. They knew that as the days shortened, they would have to shorten their shifts, as they could not use lights after dark. When they were not in the curative workshop, they might visit patients who could not leave their beds if they had energy to do so.

On the third morning in Base 117, Lorena arrived at her first shift in the curative workshop along with the other ten who had drawn the first shift. There were no patients. The re-aides spent the time moving barrels and boxes, putting lumber on saw horses to make temporary tables, disassembling boxes to use the wood for other purposes such as carving. Lorena made a giant spindle upon which to mount the spool of cord for macramé and weaving. The few who had brought craft samples set them on windowsills.

While the re-aides were continuing their attempts to make the barracks into a proper workshop, Miss Henderson took Miriam Wentworth with her to meet the doctors and persuade them to send their patients to the curative workshop. She returned to the workshop before the second shift was to replace the first. She reported that she and Miriam had received short shrift from the doctors; however one of the doctors had told her that he had some shell shocked patients in a hospital barracks. He would be pleased if she and her re-aides would go to the barracks and meet some of these men. The doctor had said he would make recommendation about what crafts the men should do. The re-aides glanced at each other wondering what the doctor knew of the craft materials they had available here.

Miss Henderson dismissed the morning shift re-aides to go to lunch. The afternoon shift re-aides had all arrived early after their own lunch, as they were so eager to get to their work. They were disappointed that there were no patients with whom to work. Miss Henderson chose three from this shift to accompany her to the "shell shocked" barracks. Lorena was sorry she could not be one of these; however, she was glad to have a short respite from dirt and sawdust.

After having lunch in the mess tent with her shift-mates and some nurses, she decided to join two nurses who planned to walk the five miles to the town of Neufchateau. Her classes at William Penn College had taught her European history. She was eager for this small window of time in which she could actually see something of old Europe. She slipped her small French/English dictionary into her pocket.

The day was a warm one. By the time they got within view of Neufchateau, Lorena's blue chambray uniform had large circles of wet under her arms. Her companions were obviously more accustomed to this pace of walking, as they did not complain, though their uniforms showed wet spots too.

In the town center, in the afternoon, there were few people about. One of the nurses explained that the French took a nap after their midday meal if possible. The remnants of a morning market remained under some blankets hung from poles and stretched across to shade the tables. A basket of over-ripe vegetable sat on the ground between some benches. An unattended stall containing firewood ended the empty market stalls.

Across the road was the chemist shop that was their goal. One of the nurses needed to buy a chemical for cleaning the surgical tools, as the shipment from home had not arrived. In the window, Lorena saw several lovely vases with a chased design made from artillery shells. She took out her dictionary to look for the word "vase" and saw that it was the same as in English. The nurse bought the chemical by writing the name on a paper rather than trying to say it in French. Lorena tried saying "Vase, vase," and pointed toward the window. Finally, she too resorted to writing the word on a slip of paper and again pointed to the window. The man smiled in recognition of her efforts and lifted one of the shell casing vases and held it out to her. Lorena turned it over and examined it carefully. The lower part of the shell was corseted into a sort of waist. The upper half had both a chased flower and leaf design as well as a hammered background. She recognized the fine work in this object. In a flash of awareness, she realized this would be an excellent project for recovering soldiers. She opened her dictionary to how and pointed to the phrase how much and held it out to the chemist. "Combien?" he said delightedly. "Deux francs."

Lorena remembered that she still had no French money so she reached into her pocket and drew out her American coins. The chemist looked at them carefully before selecting a quarter and a dime. Lorena felt she had a real bargain.

The shell vase became a heavy burden by the time she carried it the five miles back to Base 117. However, she displayed it with pride to the other re-aides. She knew that this vase would provide an example of work on materials that were readily available. The re-aides passed it around and discussed how they could get some shell casings to begin to make some other examples for the patients. Lorena decided she would ask Private Pollard for some shell casings at the earliest opportunity.

The re-aides that had gone with Miss Henderson to the barracks for the shell-shocked men recounted their experiences. On this first visit, the re-aides had not taken any craft materials with them; rather, they planned to simply see what the men were like and what they might need.

Miriam reported that she had talked to five different men during the two hours the re-aides were in that building. Several of the men had actually been physically injured; however, most of them were simply full of the jitters from the explosions of the bullets near the trenches. Mable had talked with a man from a few towns away from where she had grown up in Pennsylvania. The conversation whetted Lorena appetite for her work in the morning. The five-mile walk had made her ready for bed, which she did go to as soon as she returned to the tent after supper. She did not awaken until the reveille awoke her at 5:00 a.m. There was just enough time to get breakfast before the 6 a.m. shift.

She followed Miriam, who had agreed to lead the morning shift to the barracks for the shell-shocked and to introduce them to the men there. The women were realizing that despite their assignment to shifts, they would find plenty of work to occupy them in their time off. Doing double duty as she was gave Miriam much personal gratification. She suggested to the other re-aides that each of them choose two men to talk to, as there were twenty-four beds in each barracks. The first person to enter would take the men in the first two beds to talk to. The second person in would take the next two and so on. That way, the re-aide could stand between the two beds and hold a conversation with both men at once. With their plans firmly in place, the women quietly tread the duck-boards.

Lorena's view from the door into the barracks was of two lines of hospital beds, with their metal heads against each wall and the metal bed feet framing the center aisle. Most of the men lay upon their beds however; a few men sat on wooden supply boxes places at the foot of their bed. As a whole, they looked like a listless lot. The entrance of the re-aides seemed to perk them up somewhat. It was rather intimidating even to Lorena with her experience at Kankakee, to face a whole barracks of men's eyes on her. She was somewhat calmed knowing that there were eleven other aides with her. After the first moment of self-consciousness, Lorena brought her eyes to focus on each man she could see in the first few beds. She and the other re-aides followed Miriam and began to reach out to shake the hands that the men offered. Because Lorena was first inside the door after Martha, she took her place between the beds of the first two men on her left. One of the men jumped up and dragged his supply box between the beds for her to sit upon. She asked both men where they were from, a harmless question. It was not long before the men began to question her about her own background. The first tensions dissipated. The barracks became a noisy place with a dozen different conversations going on all at once.

Part of the re-aides' plan was to subtly lead the men into conversations about their hobbies and vocational skills. They had been charged by the Army to retrain these men for skills that they could use after the war, if possible. Lorena found them rather easy to guide in this way. Neither man had finished high school.

Henry Page was a farm boy of only 18 years. The other, Gilbert Hyde, was a 26-year-old fisherman from a New England coastal city who had sold his boat to his brother for the duration of the war. Lorena was unable to get either man to talk about his experience at the Front. Eventually, she gave up on this effort and began to describe the brass vases made of artillery shells, which she had seen yesterday. By the end of the visit, she had convinced both men to come to the curative workshop next morning.

As the re-aides said goodbye to the men with whom they had been conversing, Lorena suddenly realized she was looking at Irwin Segal on the bed furthest from the door. A sudden look of recognition crossed his face at the same moment. Despite the push of re-aides waiting for her to go out the barracks door, Lorena went against the current and reached out her hand to Irwin. She grasped his hand in both of hers as she nearly wept to see a familiar face. His eyes sprung tears as he looked wordlessly at her. She said "Irwin, you must come to the curative workshop tomorrow. Now, I must return with the other reconstruction aides." She loosened her hand from his desperate grasp and went on "Tomorrow we will have plenty of time to talk."

She looked back over her shoulder as she walked the gauntlet between the beds of the men. All the re-aides had disappeared out the door. She hurried to catch up with them, turning to wave at Irwin as she closed the door.

CHAPTER 34

PATIENTS IN THE WORKSHOP

The next morning, Irwin and several other men from the barracks for the shell-shocked were waiting at the door of the curative workshop when Lorena and the other morning re-aides arrived. The young farmer whom Lorena had met the day before was there. Miriam had the keys to the door of the barracks. All the re-aides had felt it important to keep the curative workshop locked at night. There were so many strange men from different places in this base hospital as workers or as patients.

This was their fourth morning at Base 117, July 3. Already they felt they had accomplished much and had done a lot of work. None-the-less, it was exciting to anticipate having the first patients come to the workshop. The morning shift had taken the opportunity last evening to discuss what they would do with the patients when they came. They had decided to ask each patient about their previous experience with leatherwork, metal work, woodwork, twine or cord. Fortunately, there were enough patients for each re-aide to have one patient to work with. Lorena had wished that she might work with Irwin but she had a feeling that perhaps she was not the best one for that. She knew him too well. She felt another re-aide could probably teach him things he did not already know. Lorena felt that she had already probably taught Irwin as much as she could. She told Miriam, whom Miss Henderson had named as the "head re-aide" for the morning shift. Miriam said that she would try to assign another re-aide to work with Irwin Segal. And now, she did indeed assign Martha to work with him. Lorena was assigned to work with the 17-year-old farmer, Henry Page.

As there was no good place to sit, Lorena led the young man to one of the upturned wooden supply boxes. He did not appear to have any physical injury; none-the-less, she asked him to sit. He motioned for her to sit first, but Lorena realized that would put the two of them facing away from each other if they both sat on the box. "How important manners must be to this humble farmer," she thought as she seated herself and looked up at him. She explained again, the purpose for the curative workshop and the offered the various craft options. She went to the windowsill and took the brass artillery shell vase and handed it to him. His first reaction seemed repulsion. So Lorena retrieved it from his grasp and turned it to show him the beautiful design.

After a moment, he reached out for it again and said "This is what they should have done with all the shells. A shell just like this landed in our trench and killed Gerald from our platoon. Every time I see these shells, I remember how his head was torn from his body."

Just at that moment, Private Pollard came into the workshop and said, "Look what I've got" as he held out an arm full of empty 75 mm. shell cases. "I've got a whole wheelbarrow full of them outside. I didn't really steal them. We are supposed to turn in all the empty ones for rearming. But I thought they would be more useful here." With that he dropped the five empty casings on the wooden crate near Lorena and turned out the door.

Lorena followed him. Indeed, he had twenty more in the wheelbarrow. Lorena stuck her head back in the door and called out to Henry to come and help. Private Pollack loaded Henry's arms with the brass casings and gave several to Lorena, then filled his own arms with the remaining shells. Inside, they made a row against the wall under the window of this treasure trove of workable metal. Lorena thanked Private Pollard profusely. He seemed embarrassed by her gratefulness. Lorena thought to herself "Men are such strange creatures. They crave praise just as I do but cannot accept it when it is given."

After his departure, she took up one of the empty shell cases and looked at it carefully. She glanced toward Henry who was watching her. "I believe the first thing we must do is to make a pattern." She went to the upturned crate upon which they had put the stack of white writing paper and took a sheet. She carried the sheet to Henry and showed him how to wrap the paper around the shell, to mark it for the circumference and then asked him to draw a design he might like.

"Mam, I ain't no artist," he said hanging his head.

Lorena had encountered this response often enough that she then proposed that they find a tree leaf outside that they could use as a pattern for the design. Private Page was glad to find this alternative. The two of them walked outside the barracks and looked for a tree or bush. It took them five minutes just to walk beyond all the tents and barracks buildings. Nearby the road to Neufchateau, there was a tree that Lorena was unable to name as she was unfamiliar with European trees. The tree had small oblong shaped leaves. Private Page chose several and they trudged back to the workshop. The summer weather was so pleasant; Lorena wished they could stay outside to work. However, she felt being with the other men and re-aides was probably the best thing for him. She helped him trace the leaves and apply the design to the shell. Then she realized they would need some carbon paper in order to trace the design. Since there was no carbon paper in the workshop yet, she asked him if he could just draw around the leaves to mimic on the brass what he already traced upon the paper. The young man took the metal tracing awl and with a very steady hand, began to trace the leaves again, straight onto the metal.

Next she helped him shape a piece of wood to put inside the shell to hammer and press against in planishing the background of the design. As he worked, he told of how he came to be in the Army. However, if she actually brought up his time in the trench at the Front, Henry changed the subject. It became obvious that Henry did not want to discuss his battle experience. Lorena allowed him to lead their conversation while he progressed on his shell design.

When it came time to clean up for the afternoon and evening shift, Lorena found Irwin had stopped near where she was working with Henry. He asked if there was a time when he might visit with her. Miss Upham had lectured on "fraternizing" when the OT Workshop time was over. She said it would lead to complications and the reconstruction aides should avoid getting involved with their patients outside workshop hours. Despite the memory of this admonition, Lorena thought it would be too cruel for Irwin to deny him a harmless conversation. She thought for a moment and then proposed that on the next afternoon; perhaps she and Martha might be able to go out walking with some of the patients who came to the morning curative workshop. "I will discuss it with Martha and Miriam" she responded.

This answer seemed to satisfy Irwin and he left the workshop smiling.

Chapter 35

Irwin Again

The summer weather continued balmy. It was hard to remember that there was a vicious war being conducted only 35 miles away. Because it was July 4th, the anniversary of the signing of the Declaration of Independence, the re-aides asked the patients to think of the best way to observe this national holiday. The patients suggested singing some patriotic songs. All agreed that this would be a good way to observe the day. In the evening, there was a performance group scheduled through the YMCA that would put on a patriotic show. After lunch, the group who had planned to take a walk assembled. Rather than repeat their walk on the Neufchateau road, Lorena suggested that this time the four re-aides and three patients take the road south back toward Chaumont. Martha and Alice led the group as they scuffed along the dusty trench, which was called a road. Next came the three male patients, Irwin, Henry and the fisherman named Gilbert. Lorena and Mable brought up the rear. It was not long before they met a supply caravan heading for Base 117. The loaded wagons were visible at some distance. The walkers found a dip along the grassy side of the road trough and stepped out unto the July vegetation. After the dusty caravan passed, they stayed on the grass. Here on the grassy ledge by the road, one would hardly know there was a war going on and that there was an Army hospital so close by. They continued to parallel the road, just feeling safer knowing they were not straying too far from the sure route back to base. When they left the road, Irwin made it his goal to find a place by the side of Lorena. The constellation of the walkers continued to change except

Irwin stayed by Lorena's side until they were nearly back to Base 117. She had not realized how tall he had become as his 6-foot 3-inch frame strode beside her. He appeared eager to have Lorena know what had happened to him since they said goodbye in summer 1916. She did not interrupt.

"After I graduated from the Jewish Training School, I began to look for a job. For someone with a high school education, there were teaching jobs out West but as soon as they received my letter and discovered from my name Segal, that I was Jewish, I received a letter saying the job was taken. One of the letters even said they did not hire Hebrews. After the third time this happened, I decided I must find some other form of work. I went back to The Jewish Training School and talked to my science teacher Mr. Cohen. He encouraged me to try to go to the University of Chicago but I could not afford the tuition. All during these months, I also worked in the butcher shop and lived with my uncle. My step-mother tried to persuade me to get a factory job, but Mr. Cohen encouraged me to wait. He said it would kill my spirit and I would never go to college. They had an Army recruitment poster hanging up in the hallway at the high school. I asked Mr. Cohen about it and he said they hung it to prove they were patriotic. He discouraged me from enlisting, but I felt like I should enlist. Some of my classmates from high school got together and we all decided to enlist together. We went to Camp Custer in Battle Creek, Michigan for our training. We were all on the same trains and troop ship together. We became really good friends. The train took us from Le Havre to Rouen. We marched together from Rouen to the Front." He stopped speaking.

Lorena hoped he would continue and asked "What happened then?"

There was a long pause before Irwin started speaking again. Lorena simply waited fearing she would distract him from his thoughts and consequently lose what he might say if she spoke.

"Then we got to the Front just before the battle at Cantigny. We lived in trenches that had been there from the years before. They were often muddy but we did not have long to wait for action. On May 28th early in the morning, we in the 28th Infantry of the First Division were ordered to start shelling the Germans. Nothing can prepare you for the noise and smoke. We were fearful of mustard gas since the Germans had done that before. But our sergeant was a real leader and just kept us firing. By evening, we had captured the village. Three of the boys from the Jewish Institute had been killed. I knew all three of them well after having trained and traveled with them. It was horrible having to drag their bodies back out of the firing."

Lorena could not help but respond, "That must have been like torture." Her commiseration encouraged him to go on.

"Yes, it was horrible. But, it quieted down during the night. The next morning, the Germans started shelling the village again. They kept it up for two days without stopping. But finally on the third night of the battle over Cantigny, the Germans surrendered. By that time, two more of the boys from my class had been killed and another had had an injury to his arm. I helped carry his stretcher to the First Aide Station. He was crying with pain and I could see the bone of his arm. I heard that when he got to the hospital, they cut off his arm. I haven't seen him since. I've been afraid to find him, I guess. After the shelling stopped, and after I carried his stretcher, I just curled up in the trench and put my raincoat over my head. Eventually, one of the infantrymen came looking for me and pulled the coat off. He forced me to get up out of the trench and come back to where the others were camped in a field. I started shaking and couldn't keep my food down. Eventually, the sergeant told the captain I needed to go to the hospital. I was worried that I might have shamed all the other Jewish soldiers. I got here just the same day you did, I believe. I think I am the only Jew in the shell-shocked barracks. And the others don't know I am Jewish. Just when I think I might tell them, one of them will make a joke about Jews and I am too embarrassed to tell them then. Now I don't feel I can tell them or they will be angry because I have duped them."

Just as Irwin finished this story, the group arrived back at the gate of Base 117. They had been walking over an hour. The re-aides wondered after they took the men to their barracks if they had allowed them to exert themselves too much. When the women got back to their tent, they huddled on Lorena and Martha's beds and discussed the stories they had heard during their walk. It seemed that each of the three shell-shocked patients had found that walking encouraged the sharing of their stories. They had all been part of that first horrendous battle that the Americans fought at Cantigny. However, they had not met until they arrived here at Base 117.

Lorena did not feel like telling the other re-aides all that she knew of Irwin. However, she felt it would be all right to share his story of how he came to the hospital. She did not tell them he was Jewish. His discomfort with telling made her feel uncomfortable about it also. By bedtime, around nine o'clock for these women who had to be back at the curative workshop by 6 a.m., they all knew the three stories of the patients who had walked out with them that afternoon. The story sharing felt wonderful to Lorena. In some ways this experience was like living in the nursing dormitory, though it was not nearly so comfortable. The cots were sagging and there was hardly any place to walk without hitting somebody's clothes hanging up. But the camaraderie was wonderful.

CHAPTER 36

READJUSTING

After the first week, the re-aides met together when the afternoon/evening shift returned to the tent. It was nearly ten o'clock, which would make it a short time for the morning shift to get sufficient sleep. But there had been enough discussion between the re-aides on their own shifts and the two head re-aides. Miriam had emerged as a true peacemaker and leader. All the other re-aides had come to respect her decisions. Miss Henderson had become aware of how the re-aides felt about Miriam and the women had reaffirmed her position as the second "head re-aide." On this, their seventh night at Base 117, all 24 re-aides found places to sit on the cots, either on their own or on a friend's. When all were seated with a tin cup of tea in their hands, Miss Henderson stood up and said that there were several things that they needed to talk about together. She said she felt from observing both shifts that the re-aides were capable of serving many more patients than they currently were doing. She then asked the women if they felt they felt capable to working with more patients than they were presently working with. Though some of the morning shift were definitely sleepy since it was an hour past their bedtime, there was a concerted affirmative response.

Miss Henderson explained then that Major Fenwick had told her to prepare for more patients. He had heard from one of the doctors that several of the patients had reported how much improved they felt after working in the curative workshop. The doctor had said he was going to prescribe occupational therapy for more of his patients. Also, the battles were still going on up on the River

Somme and soon more patients would probably be arriving. They were already building some more barracks here at Base 117. Then she turned to where Miriam sat on a cot and said, "Miriam has some suggestions about how she thinks we could serve more patients."

Miriam stood up with her red hair caught back into a snood on her neck. Despite this confinement, it still showed red gold in the light of the kerosene lantern. The re-aides almost always removed their caps as soon as they reached the sleeping tent. The summer heat made them want to wear as little as possible, but the uniforms were expected whenever they left the big sleeping tent. She stood by one of the supporting ten poles and said, "I think if we were to partition off the curative workshop space into sections for the different crafts, we could have several men working on the same craft supervised by only one re-aide. That would mean we could serve more men."

"But there isn't enough room with all those wooden supply crates sitting everywhere," complained Mable.

"We are going to get a shipment of work tables and chairs soon, so we will be able to dismantle the wooden crates and use the materials for wood projects like foot stools and toys, and partitions," reported Miss Henderson from the cot where she had sought a seat. "That is part of the reason we thought we could work with more men. We are getting sixty chairs. The boards in the supply crates we already have are just the right length for partitions."

"That will make the room very crowded, won't it?" commented Mable again.

Miriam looked serene as she replied, "I know we can meet this need. Just think of how miserable life has been for these men living in trenches. We must offer whatever we have for them. I feel sure from observing us work this week, that we can do more. The soldiers are giving all that they have. Surely we can give all that we have, too." The re-aides applauded her short speech.

The next morning, the 24 re-aides were all there, ready to work by 6:30 a.m. Letitia and Alice were sent to the shell shock barracks to tell the men that they would need to wait till tomorrow to come back to the curative workshop. The re-aides had agreed to work assignments the night before after they all agreed to the plan to increase their capacity for patients. The women had stacked their tool kits safely in one corner of the area. The wooden crates were all moved out by the women unto the duck-board walks outside the barracks for disassembling. Lorena and Martha were assigned to work together at this task. Lorena got her claw hammer out of her tools case, as did Martha. Fortunately, the weather was cloudy so the women hoped to avoid sunburns, as there was no shade here by the barracks. They set about their task one crate at a time. They put the nails they removed into a large tin can from the kitchen. The boards from the sides and bottoms of the crates were put into one stack against the wall of the curative workshop. The other connecting boards were placed in another pile. Lorena requested a large tarp to put over the wood to keep it dry enough to work with. Rains would undoubtedly come soon. By noon dinnertime, the two women had dirtied their white aprons almost beyond recognition. The rust from the nails got on their hands and then on the aprons. But the two women felt as if they had accomplished a lot. They had disassembled more than half the crates.

After a short dinner break, they returned to their disassembling work. Miriam came to them and asked if they would like to work inside now since they had been out in the sun all morning. This was an agreeable suggestion so the pair moved inside and began to reassemble some of the crate boards into partitions. The first one was the most difficult because they had to put balance boards at the base and upright boards to which they nailed the crosswise ones. Lorena smashed a thumb while holding a nail on more than one hammer stroke. She was sure she would have a blackened thumbnail. Martha had to go to the surgery and have a large splinter removed from her thumb. Lorena accompanied her there. As soon as they returned to the curative workshop, their work went on. With a bandaged thumb, Martha continued to hold the boards while Lorena went on with the hammering. By evening and suppertime, they had constructed five partitions. It was enough so that they felt they could invite the patients back again the next day after the furniture arrived.

After the last pair or re-aides came back to the sleeping tent, the group had another meeting to plan who would work with which group and for how long. This time, the women decided to draw straws as some of them felt they wanted a different shift. Miss Henderson had found some straws near the barracks where the horses were stabled. She held three straws in her hand. They were of equal height until the re-aide drawing pulled one out to discover if she got the short straw for morning shift or the long straw for the afternoon-evening shift. Lorena felt lucky to have drawn a morning shift straw, as she knew she did her best work early in the day. Those who were unhappy with their draw were placated by Miss Henderson and Miriam who agreed that they could redraw straws weekly. The re-aides were planning to keep the curative workshop open seven days a week between 6 a.m. and 9 p.m. It would require all their energy to do this but if they gave each re-aide one day off per week, they would have to do careful scheduling.

Chapter 37

Curative Work Continues

The workshop had been rearranged last night before the re-aides left off work in the evening. The tables and chairs were to arrive this morning. But as the women had come to expect, the wagons of furniture did not arrive until late afternoon. Most of the re-aides spent the time while waiting by visiting the men who could not get out of bed. Martha and Lorena chose instead, to work in the workshop to prepare their craft areas. Because of Martha's skill in painting, she had been chosen to supervise that section of the curative workshop. Lorena had begun to enjoy converting the shell cases into something beautiful. Somehow, this beating of swords into plowshares fit with some of the ideas she had absorbed from the Quakers at Penn College. She had also thought about how it symbolized the very men she was serving, making warriors into artisans, she hoped. Lorena had chosen an area near the door, so if the weather permitted, the men hammering metal could go outside and sit on the duck boards to avoid annoying the other men with their noise. It was becoming recognized by all the healthcare workers that these men should avoid loud noises that reminded them of the battle field.

After she arranged her area, except for the missing table and chairs, she took a piece of wood and began to shape it into a cylinder, which would just slide into an empty shell case. It would allow a craftsman to hammer the metal against the resistance of the wood in making the pattern on the metal. She planned how she would make more tools for piercing and tracing the metal.

After mid-day dinner, Lorena and Martha invited several of the men who enjoyed walking to join them in their exploration to discover the new YMCA Hut. They had met two women who had come to serve the coffee and ice cream at the hut. The YMCA women had tried to explain how to find the hut but their directions were so confusing, Lorena gave up and said she would try to find it by herself. Martha always seemed eager to join adventures of this sort. They went to the shell shock barracks and asked who would like to join them in their outing. Half the men in the barracks waved their hands to be included.

Lorena realized that the zest shown by the supposedly sick soldiers was undoubtedly due to the opportunity to go out walking with women, never mind that there were two women and a dozen men. She thought that the group should go to the central road which divided the base but Gilbert, the fisherman, reported that he had already seen the YMCA hut and could show them the way. Lorena initially felt a slight challenge to her role as the person in charge of this group, but she quickly rethought and realized it would be a gift to Gilbert to allow him to resume his place as a leader. She smiled and gestured for him to lead on.

As they walked, she suddenly found that Irwin was keeping step with her own stride. Internally, Lorena promised herself she had not sought him out and that she was not "fraternizing" as Miss Upham had termed it. However, she did feel warmly toward Irwin, as their comfort being together had been apparent during the last walk south of Base 117. She saw that Gilbert had engaged Martha in conversation as she followed directly behind him.

Very shortly, they came out into a small space off the road between the barracks and the tents. There a small shed with a hinged half door was flung up and propped open. A small counter was on the inside and behind it, was one of the women Lorena had met the day before. She was serving coffee and cookies. Inside the shed sat a small kerosene stove with a large wooden handled metal coffeepot on it. A ceramic pitcher of cream sat on the counter beside a quart Mason jar of sugar. The ever present tin cups hung on nails behind the woman. A bucket of soapy water sat on the floor by her feet. She said she did not know whether she still had a dozen cups of coffee left but that perhaps if they were willing, she could ration the coffee so each member of the group could have some. Several of the men offered to do without coffee so the re-aides could have full cups, but the counter girl decided to divide whatever coffee was there into 14 cups. By the time she was draining the last coffee off the grounds, each person had half a cup. The cream pitcher was soon empty and the counter girl had to refill it from a metal milk can.

There were no seats to sit on while drinking the bittersweet beverage. Lorena smoothed her skirt under her and sat down on the nearby duck board walk. Irwin sat beside her and picked up their conversation. He asked about her experiences on the troop ship, at Le Havre and Chaumont. Previously their relationship had allowed him to be the center of attention but today he was slowly turning the focus on her. She felt conflicted about how appropriate it was for her to be telling a patient about herself. When at Kankakee State Hospital she had seldom been confronted with this kind of dilemma. Mrs. Radicky was ever present at Kankakee. Lorena struggled during the remainder of their outing to the YMCA hut to keep their conversation on a level of an acquaintance rather than a close friend. She wanted to be more open but did not know if she would be making it more difficult for herself or Irwin later.

Gradually, Lorena became aware that most of the other men had stood or seated themselves around Martha where she sat on the duck-board walk to drink her coffee. Lorena realized that the men rather obviously were leaving her and Irwin by themselves. This thought gave her a jolt as she wondered if they saw something she had not. It was not obvious enough for her to comment to Irwin about it, but she decided she must keep more distance from him.

During the walk back to the barracks, Lorena made an effort to keep other men involved in the conversation despite the necessity to walk single file on the duck-board walkway. At the road, they found the wagon convoy of furniture for the curative workshop. It was parked on the roadway close to the easiest route to the curative barracks. Soldiers were unloading the tabletops, legs and chairs and maneuvering them between the buildings. Martha and Lorena walked with the men back to the barracks before rushing to the workshop to view the new furniture. Several soldiers were fitting legs into tables. The tables were square. The re-aides had not known exactly what kind of furniture to expect since they were to receive what was described as regulation Army issue furniture. The chairs looked like adult versions of chairs for school children, sturdy oak.

Lorena stood out of the way as the soldiers moved the square table top into her "metal working space". She felt impatience as she stood aside and watched the soldiers attach the legs and turn the table right side up. The varnished top would soon have some scars on it from the slip of tools during craftwork, Lorena thought to herself. After all the tables had been assembled and placed within their spaces between the wooden partitions, the soldiers began to bring the rest of the chairs. The few partitions that had not been finished the day before would be given to willing patients to complete, now that the pattern for their construction was fixed.

Chapter 38

The Mail Arrives

Lorena's days began at last, to have a pattern. Awake at 5 a.m. Go to the latrine. Wash her face and brush her teeth. Breakfast at 5:30 a.m. with whomever of the other re-aides was ready for breakfast. Get the key for the curative workshop, which hung from a nail on their tent pole. Unlock the curative workshop if she arrived first. And often, she was the first. Miriam Wentworth was not as early a riser as Lorena, and often did not arrive at the curative workshop until seven o'clock.

The men who could walk, would begin to arrive almost immediately. If they were working with the empty shell cases, Lorena immediately set to work to demonstrate the tools, the design processes of pattern making, repousse', chasing and hammering. Some men, who felt unable to create a pattern, she set to making more wooden cylinders to fit inside the shell during tooling or to work on assembling more partitions. Her small section of the curative workshop was lucky to be near the door, so the extra men could spill outside where there was more room to sit on the duckboards to work. They had almost used up the supply of empty shell cases that Private Pollard had brought. Some men sought to persuade Lorena that she need not ask Private Pollard to get more shell casing. They knew of the place near the ammunition depot where they could get them themselves.

In the midst of this discussion, a soldier stuck his head into the curative workshop and yelled "Mail call." It seemed such a long time without letters, that most of the women had lost their expectation of getting mail. However, this announcement caused excitement in the workshop. Miriam almost immediately said that she expected everyone to wait until noontime break to get his or her letters. An audible sigh of resignation went through the workshop. The men were as eager for the letters as the re-aides. The curative workshop had no wall clock yet, so the women who had wristwatches, began to watch the hand slowly move toward noon. There was a mad dash to clean up for the afternoon shift of re-aides and workers. Then another rush was made to their own tent to ask where they should go to find their mail. Stepping inside the tent flap, they saw that their letters had already been sorted and laid on their cots. Lorena had three letters; one from Mrs. Radicky, one from Edna May and one from Colin.

She just sat for a moment and looked at the three envelopes, wondering which she should open first. The one from Edna May would undoubtedly be the most fun to read she thought so she reached for it first.

June 20, 1918

Dear Lorena,

I was so glad to receive your letter telling me how to send a letter to you. Since I last saw you, so much has happened. After a brief Army training at Fort Sheridan, I was assigned to the hospital in Fort McPherson, Georgia. I was very disappointed not to be sent over to France. But in the Army, they do not give us choices. The weather here is so hot. I wonder how the patients will stand it in August. We work twelve-hour shifts. I love working with the injured men. They try to be so brave. I cannot complain even though I am often so tired. These men often have horrible injuries, burns or disfigurements. I work hard to keep up their spirits. We have two whole barracks full of patients with that new disease, influenza. I wonder if you have had any cases in your hospital? There is a group of reconstruction aides here and one of them is an occupational therapist. I have not met her yet. The barracks where the nurses sleep is not nearly so comfortable as our room at Kankakee. Please write and tell me what it is like in France.

Your old friend,

Edna May Fagan

Lorena put down this letter and closed her eyes for a moment to bring Edna May's face into her mind. She missed the camaraderie of the Nursing Dorm, however, her friendship with the re-aides, especially Martha was beginning to replace the warm memories of friendship with Edna May. She felt a little like a traitor even having these feelings. But she had two other letters to read so she put away these thoughts of unfaithful friendship, at least for now. When she answered the letters she could think about loyalty and friendship.

She decided Mrs. Radicky's letter should come next, as she feared that Colin's letter would contain feelings for which she was unprepared as had happened in the past. Mrs. Radicky had written on hospital stationary with the picture of the Clock Tower at Kankakee. Mrs. Radicky must be trying to remind her of home, she decided as she unfolded the single sheet with small regular handwriting.

June 17, 1918

My dear Lorena,

We do miss you so much here in the hospital and especially in occupational therapy. I do hope you are keeping safe. We have many of the same patients that were here when you were. The hospital has hired another girl to take your place. She is a nurse who just finished her training at the Henry B. Favill School of Occupations in Chicago. They renamed the school, you may remember. Her name is Ramona Berwith. She is from Evanston, Illinois. No one could really replace you, but she is working hard to try to fill your shoes. I hope you can meet her when you return. There will always be a job for you here when you come back if you wish. I need to have someone trained to take my place since I may not be able to work so hard sometime soon. I have been having a little rheumatism in my lower limbs.

We have one cottage here dedicated to the care of people with influenza. After you had it in March, we thought the epidemic was over. But now, we have a number of new cases. I have taken to wearing my influenza mask while working in the OT Shop. Are there influenza cases at your hospital?

Please write and let me know how you are.

Affectionately,

Madeline Radicky

Lorena felt sure she had heard Mrs. Radicky's given name before but if she had, she had forgotten it because she had never called her by any but her Christian name. It as nice to know she would have a job to go back to when the war was over but right now, she could only think of her work here at Base 117. She folded the letter and put it back into the envelope. Before taking up the one from Colin, she paused a moment and promised herself she would not be upset by anything the young man wrote. His early life had left him with no one he really respected to teach him manners. Almost any of his impulsive behaviors had to be excused, she thought.

July 1, 1918

My dearest Lorena,

It seems a long time since our last correspondence. It took two weeks for your letter to arrive from Washington D.C. I was so pleased to know that we would be on the same continent again. Since my last letter to you, we have seen several fierce battles. I will be getting leave soon. I wondered if I could come to visit where you are working.

Affectionately,

Colin Donnell

She closed her eyes again, this time to try to control her feelings about what was in the letter. She was so fond of the young man, but the idea of him coming to visit could be an inconvenience since all the re-aides were working seven days per week, except when there was a special performance, or a church service. She had not been here long enough to ask for a leave. Besides, it would not be proper for her to be alone with Colin except if other people were around.

Suddenly from the nearby cot, Martha asked, "What is the matter? Did somebody die?"

Lorena realized that she must look strange sitting here with her eyes closed. In a few brief sentences, she explained to Martha about Colin and her dilemma. Martha was more happy-go-lucky than Lorena and volunteered "You should find a way to meet him. Perhaps if he came to Chaumont, there are hotels there. You could probably get a ride to Chaumont after your shift. Everyday, there are ambulances taking men to the railroad depot to go home."

CHAPTER 39

REPLIES FROM BASE 117

It took a day for Lorena to decide how she would answer Colin. Meanwhile, she did put pen to paper and answer the letters to Mrs. Radicky and Edna May. This time she chose Mrs. Radicky first. Somehow, she thought that by writing to the older woman, she might gain some wisdom about how to answer Colin.

July 12, 1918

Dear Mrs. Radicky,

What a thrill it was to get your letter. I am so glad you found someone to help you with the OT work. I have felt badly leaving you in the lurch that way. I am glad Miss Berwith is working well with you. I do miss you but the work here is so interesting. There was not any regular OT material here when we arrived. We have had to make do with what we can get in the supply depot. The building was not ready so we had to prepare everything ourselves. On the second day here, in a nearby village, I found a lovely chased and hammered vase made from a 75mm shell casing. I brought it back to the hospital and have been teaching some of the men with war neurosis, which is what they call "shell shock" here. Already they have made some lovely vases.

I have not heard of any influenza cases here yet but we are still encouraged to wear our influenza masks, though only a few re-aides as we now call ourselves, do remember to wear them. We are all usually too tired to remember when we go to bed. The weather has been very nice here. The battles are too far away for us to hear the guns so sometimes we almost forget there is a war except for the condition of the patients. Some of the re-aides have been working with the amputees. Then we are really forced to think about the war. The men with war neuroses seldom mention the war to us.

I hope your rheumatism is not too painful, now that it is summer. Please keep writing as I think of you often.

Fondly,

Lorena Longley

She laid down the pen to rest her hand and to try to get closer to the lamp as the summer dusk arrived. She had not garnered any wisdom about how to respond to Colin during the writing of the letter to Mrs. Radicky. After a walk for a drink at the water barrel, which had been installed inside their tent, she took another sheet of the paper supplied to all personnel in the camp and wrote:

July 12, 1918

Dear Edna May,

As far as I know, we do not have influenza here at Base 117. I am glad I have already had it so I need not fear. I shall try to answer your question about "how is France." However, I have not had much chance to leave the army hospital except for a walk to a nearby town and once out unto a meadow. We have little to do with the French citizens because we are too busy. You will be surprised to know that Irwin Segal is a patient here in this hospital. Without asking him, I feel reluctant to tell you more. I work in the OT Curative Workshop eight hours per day and spend several more hours making samples, getting materials or talking with patients. There are 24 occupational therapists here though they call us reconstruction aides. We call ourselves re-aides. Only half of us work in the Curative Workshop at one time to keep from being too crowded. I work the early shift. Please tell me more about the reconstruction aide at Fort McPherson. When this is all over, we must have an old-fashioned gabfest.

With love,

Lorena Longley

As she signed the letter, she knew that Edna May would agree with Martha that she should go to meet Colin in Chaumont. If she hitched a ride on an ambulance going to Chaumont immediately after her shift finished, she would be able to be in Chaumont by five or six o'clock. She could meet Colin for dinner in a hotel and then hitch another ride back to La Fauche and be in the barracks by midnight. That way she would not compromise herself by being alone with Colin except in a restaurant with other people. His letters were so fervent, she feared he might assume all kinds of wrong things unless she kept her distance from him. Also, all re-aides were committed to proper and clean living. There would be no opportunity for Colin to get wrong ideas.

With these thoughts, she decided to sleep on it and write to him tomorrow afternoon. Meanwhile, there was the need to launder her underwear and polish her shoes. The laundress laundered the uniforms but Lorena did not trust her underwear being handled by the French peasant woman who did much of the staff's laundry. She went to the water tank and drew a basin of cold rinse water. Then she took a kettle and some hot wash water from the cook in the kitchen. After wringing out her underwear and hanging them on the clothesline strung inside the tent, she emptied her two basins of water into the grass under the nearest trees. By this time, it was completely dark and nearly ten o'clock. It was time to sleep. In the morning she would ask some of the soldiers or nurses about the name of a hotel where she could safely meet Colin.

Next afternoon, she again took pen and paper and wrote to Colin.

July 13, 1918

Dear Colin,

I received your letter yesterday and was so surprised that you were actually able to get a letter to me. I did not know how reliable the mail might be for men at the Front. I will be unable to receive you here at Base 117. However, I have thought of an alternative. Would it be possible for you to meet me for dinner in Chaumont? I have not been here long enough to get any leave time, but I could come to Chaumont and we could have dinner together in the Hotel de Ville. We could have perhaps two hours before I would need to go back to the base in order to be there by midnight. Reconstruction aides are expected to observe all the rules and be good examples for the men. This responsibility will permit me to see you for only a short time. I may bring a friend so that there may be no hint of impropriety. If this seems possible, please respond by the next mail and tell me what date you might be there. I may not be able to be there on the date you would like. If I am unable to come on the date that you indicate, I will send a message to the hotel.

Sincerely,

Lorena Longley

By the time she completed her letter, it was too late to take it to the post office building. So she was unable to mail it until July 14.

Chapter 40

Hotel de Ville

Lorena hardly thought of Colin or her other corespondents. She was too busy working with the shell-shocked soldiers to have time to wonder about those not present at Base 117. She frequently took late afternoon walks in company with other morning shift re-aides and the patients. Irwin was almost always in the group and usually found an opportunity to walk by Lorena.

Lorena received a reply from Colin before she received any others.

July 20, 1918

Dear Lorena,

It took only a week for your reply to reach me here near the River Sommes. I will meet you in La Hotel de Ville in Chaumont on July 30, 1918. That will give us both time to make whatever travel arrangements are needed. I will look for you in the Hotel de Ville at 6 p.m. on July 30. Please wear something pretty. I have so many things to tell you.

I hope you can come alone but if you must bring a friend, I hope she is as pretty as you are.

With anticipation,

Colin Donnell

Her first thought was "Colin doesn't know that I only have uniforms to wear here." But her second thought was "I am going to discuss this with Miriam. Anything could happen if I try to go to this meeting with Colin furtively. I might be unable to get a ride back to Base 117." Responding to these thoughts, she waited for Miriam when the morning shift finished up and cleaned up the curative workshop in preparation for the afternoon re-aides and patients. After all the re-aides except Miriam and Lorena had left, and as the afternoon re-aides arrived, Lorena fell into step beside Miriam on the duck-boards. There was barely enough room for two people to walk abreast so as she explained her dilemma to Miriam, occasionally, she grasped Miriam's hand to keep herself from stepping off into the dirt. She described her previous relationship with Colin, excluding the final encounter in which he had kissed her cheek too fervently. She explained that she had had a letter from him where he was stationed in the Sommes with the Canadian Army. And that he wanted to meet her for dinner in Chaumont on July 30. Then she paused and waited for Miriam's reply.

Miriam was thoughtful for a minute and eventually said, "Lorena, I think you should take someone with you. It just wouldn't seem proper for a woman to be traveling by herself on the ambulance. However, it seems as if this is a reasonable request from the young man. I give my permission and I will mention it to Miss Henderson."

Lorena half hugged her in gratefulness and said "Miriam, you are so helpful. I had thought about taking someone with me but I did not know whether it would be right to take someone away from her work. Do you mind if I ask Martha?"

"I know you and Martha have become great friends. I think it would be a wonderful break for her to accompany you. Martha seems to enjoy excitement. This escapade should fulfill that longing," said Miriam, as they arrived at the re-aide tent.

Lorena made haste to find Martha and officially request her to accompany her on July 30, to Hotel de Ville.

With these plans quite firmly made, Lorena tried to put it from her mind. For the next ten days she worked as hard as she could to begin to teach chair caning to a man that had constructed a chair from the wood of a crate. A spool of twisted craft paper had been found in the supply depot. Lorena remembered that it could be substituted for reed. She also, in the evenings, began making a summer middy blouse from some royal blue polka-dotted cotton cloth she bought during an afternoon walk to Neufchateau. She had seen pictures of the new fashionable middies in a magazine at the YMCA Hut. She spent several evenings seated by the kerosene lamp in the middle of the tent stitching navy piping unto it. By July 29th, she had finished the middy and borrowed a navy blue sateen skirt from Letitia to wear with it. Martha, who had accompanied her to Neufchateau for cloth, made a round-necked green middy, which she embroidered and made a matching straight skirt. Each woman had ingeniously covered a blue organdy re-aide cap with cloth to make an attractive matching hat for her outfit.

Martha had made it a point to become acquainted with the ambulance drives on the route between La Fauche and Chaumont. She had secured the promise that she and Lorena could hitch a ride into Chaumont on the afternoon of July 30.

Nyle Johnson was the ambulance driver who was privileged to be their chauffeur during the three-hour drive to Chaumont. The roads were in no better condition than they had been a month ago when they arrived but it was daylight. There were deep ruts from the frequent ambulance caravans. Dust covered the grass close to the track. This ambulance carried eight stretchers, four above and four below with men on their way home to hospitals in the United States. Despite being dressed in their new middies, the two re-aides got into the back of the ambulance and introduced themselves to these homeward bound warriors. All had lost one or both legs. There was one orderly and he sat in the front with the driver. At first there was conversation, but as the ride progressed, the men were obviously in so much pain that they did not care to interact with the two women in pretty outfits. Lorena and Martha sat on a bench crowded between the stretchers, which swung with each bump. Low moaning came from one man. The two women wondered together whether or not they should alert the driver and ask him to stop. But the moaning stopped. They hoped the man had fallen asleep rather than unconscious.

After an hour and a half, the rhythmic bump and sway of the wagon lulled both women into s somnolent state. Because of their position in facing the back of the ambulance, they did not realize they were in Chaumont until they saw the abbey walls.

Soon, the driver stopped to let the two women out at the corner of the Hotel de Ville. He promised to pick them up in the same place at nine o'clock. They entered the lobby together. Immediately Lorena recognized a taller, more mature Colin hurrying toward her. He came to within a few feet of her and stopped short and held out his hand to Lorena. She realized that Martha's presence beside her had placed some restraint on Colin's greeting. She was glad of this apparent calming effect on his ardor. Turning to Martha, she introduced her to Colin. Then she realized that another soldier in a Canadian uniform was slightly behind him in a position that obviously meant they were together. As he introduced his friend Alex Mullieaux, Lorena came to the realization that Colin had brought a companion for Martha. Either this was extremely thoughtful or it was a ploy to distract Martha from Colin's intent to have Lorena to himself. Time would tell, Lorena thought to herself.

Colin reported that he had made a reservation for the four of them to have dinner in the hotel dining room at 7 p.m. That would give them time so that they could easily meet the ambulance at 9 p.m. and get back to La Fauche by midnight.

The table for the party of four was a pleasant change from the mess hall. A white tablecloth covered a square oak table in an alcove shielded by a carved wooden screen. It did indeed seem very private compared to the tent and barracks living to which they had all become accustomed. A small porcelain vase held some sprigs of fern and a wild primrose. Martha gestured for Lorena to slip behind the table and then for Colin to sit on Lorena's left. Then she took the seat across from Lorena and indicated that Alex should sit on Lorena' right, which was Martha's left. Lorena was surprised at the skill with which Martha quickly got everyone seated without distress or confusion. She realized Martha must have had many opportunities to act as hostess in her work as a teacher in a girls' school.

The waiter brought a bottle of wine and opened it with a flourish. He poured a small amount and held the glass out to Colin for approval. Lorena was amazed at the sophistication shown by this man that she had perceived of as a youth only two years ago. She was not used to drinking wine either. However, the festivity of this occasion certainly deserved wine. She lifted her glass along with the others as Martha made a toast to the Allied Armies. Alex gallantly followed this with a toast to the women who supported the soldiers. Lorena tried to think of an appropriate toast as Colin raised his glass to these two beautiful women. Though his flattery embarrassed her, she was able to respond with a toast to friends, both old and new. This seemed to appropriately cap off the toasts. The mustachioed gray-headed waiter arrived to take their order for plate de jour, the only item on the menu. Wartime had made a full menu impossible. Martha then smoothly and intimately engaged Alex in conversation about his hometown of Quebec City, Canada. He had a slight accent, which Lorena judged to be French. Martha leaned toward Alex, obviously making their conversation a twosome so that Colin and Lorena could have an equally private conversation. Lorena took her cue and began to ask Colin about his adventures since she last saw him in Chicago. When he ceased talking, she prompted him with questions gleaned from bits of information she remembered from his letters. Finally the soup course arrived and the table was silent as they relished the small bowls of onion soup with cheese on top. A long loaf of hard crusted bread was laid on the tablecloth. Martha picked it up and with effort broke off three inches of the end that she offered to anyone. After each person had a piece of the bread with a soft center, the two conversations continued. After twenty minutes of Lorena questioning Colin about his times in the Canadian Army, he turned the conversational tables on her and asked about how she decided to join the Army Medical Corp. Lorena then had to explain that they were not in the Army, but rather civilian workers. With occasional cueing questions from Colin, she reported the trip to the dance at Fort Sheridan, her bout with influenza, Edna May's departure, the trip to Chicago where she first heard of reconstruction aides, her interview with the colonel, her trip to Washington, the short time at Walter Reed Hospital, Ellis Island, Le Havre and Base 117. Colin seemed avid to hear everything that she had done since he last saw her.

Martha and Alex appeared to be enjoying each other's company as a scalloped potato and bacon casserole dish arrived. It was passed first to the women and then the men emptied the serving dish unto their own plates. Colin continued to question Lorena about their sleeping arrangements at La Fauche, about her work, about the soldiers she had met there. She took an opportunity in a small gap in the conversation to tell him about the letters she had received from Mrs. Radicky and Edna May. A dish with 'coq o vin' arrived and was passed. The final course of a bread pudding and brandy peach sauce was served as the clock in the other end of the dining room struck eight o'clock. After eating her desert, Martha stood and excused herself to go to the ladies room. Alex followed her example and excused himself as well. Lorena realized that Martha had contrived to leave her alone with Colin. She had not seen or heard Martha give instructions to Alex but she knew it must have happened. It was just too convenient. Or, Lorena thought to herself, perhaps Colin had persuaded Alex to cooperate so he could have a few moments alone with Lorena.

Colin immediately took this opportunity to reach over and take Lorena's hand in both his. "Lorena, I have missed you every day. Thoughts of you have kept me from throwing myself in harm's way in every battle. I mean throwing myself more obviously in harm's way that I was required to do as a soldier. I want very much to have your promise that you will not get romantically involved with any of those soldiers at the base. I want you to wait for me." He stopped and waited expectantly.

Lorena felt like she had been ambushed. She certainly was not ready for such a commitment seemingly on the spur of the moment. She took her free hand and laid it over Colin's two hands that held her other hand. "Please Colin, I am not ready to make such a decision without thinking it through carefully. You know I have cared for you like a brother. I need time to think over what you have proposed to me. I am older than you are by at least six years. At Base 117, I cannot get into a romantic relationship anyway. There is no time and also it would not be fair to the other men I teach. So be assured that I will not be getting romantically involved with the patients there. But you must not pressure me to make promises. I have not thought of you romantically so I must have time to even consider such a thought. You can understand that surely?" she said.

Her response had not caused his face to become crestfallen. That was a good sign. He still leaned hopefully toward her. "You'll think about it then?" She nodded in the affirmative as Martha and Alex resumed their seats. They had obviously found each other on the return trip from the lady's and gent's rooms. They acted as if nothing had interrupted their conversation thus leaving Lorena and Colin in the slightly embarrassed position of not knowing where to take up a neutral conversation.

Lorena struggled to resume a conversation by asking Colin "What are your reading these days?"

This was just the opening Colin needed to begin to tell her how he had found Tolstoy's *War and Peace,* in one of the boxes of books at the Y Hut near Amiens. Lorena wondered how he could enjoy reading about war while involved in fighting one, but she herself had never read the novel. She asked him to tell her the plot. This took up the last few minutes before the gentlemen paid the bill and walked them to the corner. They waited with them until Nyle Johnson arrived with the empty ambulance. Colin, who hugged Lorena before he assisted her up, helped the two women into the back of the ambulance. Alex and Martha promised to write letters to each other. Lorena sat on one empty stretcher and Martha sat immediately across from her. The men jumped down from the ambulance and off they went. The horses were fresh so they moved more quickly than the ones that had pulled the loaded ambulance. The wine had made the two re-aides sleepy and before they had left Chaumont, the women had lain down and gone to sleep on empty stretchers.

Chapter 41

August 1918

Men began to arrive at Base 117 Hospital from the battles on the Vesle River, from Fisme, and from Fismette. In order to make room for them, some of the men in the "war neurosis" barracks were given orders to be sent back to their units. One of those receiving his orders was Irwin Segal. He immediately went as soon as he got his orders to find Lorena working in the curative workshop. Tomorrow, he reported, he would be driven into Chaumont with other able bodied men who were deemed sufficiently recovered from shell shock. His unit was near Chalons-sur-Marne. He felt he must speak to Lorena privately before leaving as others always accompanied them on their walks. He needed to have her to himself for a short time. "Miss Longley," he formally addressed her in order to camouflage any intimacy that could be inferred from their conversation being overheard. "I have been given my orders to report back to First Battalion of the 28th Infantry Brigade at Annaye d'Igny. I leave tomorrow evening. Is there a time when I might talk to you in order to give you my address?"

Lorena looked up from where she continued to work with the man on caning the homemade chair with twisted craft paper. She realized he was asking to speak to her alone. A moment of reflection allowed her to decide that it would be proper for her to be alone with Irwin, as long as his leaving was imminent and there was no danger of a rumor about the two of them starting. "I will be finishing up here at 2:30 p.m. this afternoon. Perhaps if you are feeling like taking a walk then, you could meet me at the YMCA Hut. We could have some iced coffee before we start." With a nod he ended the conversation and left the workshop to prepare his clothing and equipment.

She felt saddened that Irwin must return to the Front. He had made so much progress here toward not jumping at every loud noise. His skills in decorating shell casings had complimented the intricate flower designs he had drawn. Lorena had thoroughly enjoyed the times when he, along with several other men, had sat tapping out their designs together at the table. She heard their stories of the Front as she assisted them. However, they had become skilled enough to hardly need her guidance. She was now supervising both the metal work and the chair caning areas, occasionally assisting other re-aides as the need arose for her skills. Rolls of copper had been discovered in the supply depot and copper tooling was becoming the new craft of interest for several of the men. They had learned how to make their own tools for inscribing designs.

At two thirty, Irwin awaited her outside the curative workshop. She realized she did not look her freshest self since her apron was soiled from wiping her hands on it. She removed it and hung it on a hook near the door. It had her name embroidered on the back so she could be sure no other re-aide would mistake it for hers. Her uniform dress was not too soiled though it was not fresh either. She ran her hands along the edge of her cap and swept any stray strands behind her ears. Then she stepped out unto the duck-boards to join him. They walked in silence until they arrived at the Y Hut. Irwin ordered two iced coffees. The woman behind the counter liberally added milk and sugar to the glasses of coffee and ice. For an August afternoon, it was welcome refreshment. Because they could not carry the glasses away, they stood under the nearby tree to savor this treat.

Irwin handed her a paper upon which he had written his name, rank, the company, battalion and brigade numbers. Between sips, he said, "Lorena, I would very much appreciate keeping in contact with you. I realize that relationships between the patients with the re-aides and nurses are discouraged. However, I will no longer be a patient when I leave tomorrow. Besides, we have known each other several years by now."

Lorena was prepared for this conversation as she had been unprepared for Colin's more ardent approach. Irwin's maturity and thoughtfulness were easier to deal with. "I believe it would be perfectly permissible for us to correspond. Besides, I shall be interested in how resilient you will be when you again hear gunfire. Please tell me what you discover about you ability to withstand the harshness of battle. The horror stories the men have been telling as we worked in the curative workshop have showed me how difficult it is on the Front. Besides, if we write, I will continue to know you are safe."

Irwin waited while she finished this long speech before smiling and saying, "Oh, Miss Longley, I will feel I am able to withstand much more if I can look forward to your letters."

They finished their coffee and walked toward the edge of the Base where there were a few trees demarcating the meadow and the hospital grounds.

How handsome he looked in his khaki uniform. The color was just right for his olive skin and dark brown hair. Lorena was surprised by her thoughts about his appearance. She had seen some harsh sights of injured patients. She thought she was immune to the men's looks. The message from Mrs. Slagle as well as Mrs. Upham had been that personal feelings about patients must be suppressed or they would interfere with the cure of occupations. She had felt she had successfully avoided overly warm feelings for any of her patients. But now it occurred to her that she was indeed taking pleasure in Irwin's good looks. At that moment, he handed her a photograph of himself. Since inviting her this morning, he had found a photographer who was willing to take his picture in uniform and develop it immediately. She looked at the sepia photo in admiration. He was indeed a handsome man. Sensing her approval of gift of the photograph, he continued, "If you'll just keep this picture, it will mean a great deal. Somehow, you having a photograph of me in uniform means a great deal" He paused, "I've also had the photographer make a picture to send to my sisters at home." When he tacked on this last sentence, it softened the intimate message of the previous one. Lorena was grateful, as she knew she should not allow any patient to receive special treatment. But if Irwin were to think of her having the photo as if she were another family member, it would seem permissible.

The mid-afternoon sun was warm despite frequent clouds covering it. As they walked the edge of the meadow, a log from a fallen tree lay in their path. When they actually got to the log, Irwin took her hand to assist her to step over it. The actual touching of hands communicated an intimacy that Lorena had not previously felt or perceived from Irwin. She quickly released her hand from his when she had regained her balance. No words were spoken until they had traversed another one hundred feet. The grass here was well trodden, as it was one of the few places to find some personal privacy away from tent or barracks mates. However, at this moment, they were the only ones in the meadow. Shortly, the meadow ended at a creek-bed. Again, Irwin offered his hand to her in descending the 45-degree slope. Together they stumbled into the dry bottom. August had dried up any water though there were dark spots where water had sat in the not too distant past. Irwin found a shallow ascent to the other side of the creek and reached down to pull Lorena up to the other bank. She stumbled slightly as she reached the top and he caught her in his arms. Flustered, that's what she felt as she attempted to free herself. However, apparently Irwin's maleness overwhelmed him and he kept his arms around her and turned her toward his face. Lorena found herself looking up into his brown eyes. She thought he was going to kiss her but instead he stopped and asked, "May I kiss you?"

Many issues passed through Lorena's mind in the moment before she gave her permission. She shouldn't be allowing this. But Irwin would be gone tomorrow evening. They were far enough away from the perimeter of Base 117 that no one could see him kiss her. Would allowing him to kiss her make him return to his previous neurotic state? None of these thoughts could impede the meeting of male and female emotional needs and physical attraction. His lips were generously wide and warm. They felt good and healthy. She allowed herself to relax in his arms and began to enjoy his tongue exploring hers.

When eventually they pulled their mouths apart, Lorena expressed all the doubting thoughts she had had before the kiss. "I should not have allowed you to kiss me. But you will be gone tomorrow evening and there could be no harm I thought. We are far enough away from the hospital that I felt sure nobody could see us. But I am afraid that this might cause you to have neurotic fears again." She used the words that the doctor had used when discussing the patients with war neuroses.

Irwin looked tenderly at her with her re-aide cap slightly askew and said, "There's nothing but good that could come from kissing you. I've thought about it since I first met you at Kankakee but my position as a patient there and here, always made me feel somehow inferior. But since I have recovered sufficiently to go back to my unit, I felt confident enough to act like a man. I know the rules forbid co-mingling of patients and staff, but those rules are not human rules. They are the rules of war." With this, he embraced her again and again kissed her lips.

Lorena was quite at a loss at how to react. Her body told her to enjoy this intimate contact. Her mind continued to repeat the cautionary rules against closeness between male patients and female staff. After several minutes of this extremely pleasurable conflict, she pulled away and grasped his hand and led him on away from the creek-bed. She began to chatter to push away her embarrassment at her own response and pleasure in the kisses.

Irwin apparently perceived her state of conflict and began to speak in a calming voice. "I will not tell anyone that we have been out here alone. I will just keep this happy memory when I return to the Front. I may die this time rather than just becoming neurotically paralyzed. Thinking of these moments will give me strength to fight. Please don't be ashamed of giving a man the strength to fight for his country."

These patriotic words released Lorena from the guilt she was already starting to feel. The couple retraced their steps toward the hospital boundary stopping only to sit on the log for a moment where Irwin put his arm around her waist and pulled her toward him and kissed her cheek and hair. She stroked his hand and said she would miss his presence here in camp but that he was fortunate to have recovered so well. They both knew that some shell-shocked men never recovered. They had seen them everyday either in the barracks or the curative workshop, men who flattened on the floor or hid under the table at the sound of the hammer on wood or metal.

Irwin stood up and pulled her up beside him, straightened her re-aide cap and they returned to the edge of the hospital where they separated. They hoped to avoid critical comments. He went to his barracks, she to the curative workshop to recover her dirty apron.

Chapter 42

September 1918

The rains alternated with sunny days. Lorena received mail from all her corespondents, including her sister Margaret, who in her poor grammar, reported that Charles, her older brother had died of the influenza. Grief gripped her momentarily. However, there was so much to do to keep the soldiers who were her patients busy working on their craft projects that she could not take more time to feel sad. Also, the influenza had arrived at Base 117. Several barracks had been assigned to caring for the infected. Lorena had not had time to even pay attention to all the deliveries of coffins, an everyday occurrence. The morgue here at the base was overwhelmed with the bodies which daily piled up.

One of the re-aides, Mable Perkins, had become sick and been removed to one of the influenza barracks. At first, they thought she was just doing her usual complaining. After three hours, she was delirious and talking nonsense from where she lay on her cot. She burned with fever, then shivered with chills and had begun to cough up bloody mucus. Miss Henderson immediately ordered all re-aides to wear their influenza masks. Then she had Letitia run to the doctor's tent to ask for orderlies to be sent with a stretcher to carry Mable to the influenza barracks. Meanwhile, Miss Henderson shooed all the masked re-aides outside the tent until the orderlies wearing masks came. After they left carrying a thrashing Mable on the stretcher, the re-aides opened the tent flap and fanned as much fresh air into the tent as they could before re-entering.

Several of the war neurosis patients had become sick and ceased coming to the curative workshop as they too had been moved to the quarantine barracks. The nurses that Lorena had met her first day here in Base 117 had been assigned to care for patients in the influenza barracks. When they returned to the nearby tent from their twelve-hour shifts, the re-aides would ask them for news of the epidemic. At first the re-aides had not known it was an epidemic despite having had their influenza masks for three months. Since no epidemic appeared when they were first issued the masks, they had forgotten the warnings given then. It was not an uncommon sight to see a soldier or two wearing influenza masks if they had to walk toward the end of the base where the two barracks were located. However, wearing of the masks was not done consistently. People forgot or did not believe they could prevent infection.

Miss Henderson called a meeting that night after the remaining re-aides all returned from the curative workshop and others from visiting the orthopedic patients. After all had found a place on the cots so they could see the face of Miss Henderson as she stood near the lone kerosene lamp, she began to speak. "We need to keep in contact with Mable. She was so sick when they took her to the influenza barracks. I feel it is important for us to help her in any way were can. However, I know that some people a fearful of being near people sick with the flu. I am asking for a volunteer to go to visit her." She stopped and looked at them expectantly.

It was quiet several moments as the group came to understand what Miss Henderson was asking of them, in fact to risk their lives by going into the barracks with all the sick people. They had all recognized the risks of working so near the War Front. However, stepping into an infection hospital ward made the risk of sickness and death even more imminent. Lorena reviewed what she knew of immunity. One of the evening lecturers at Hull House had spoken about the work of Emil von Behring on the antibodies to diphtheria and tetanus. She raised her hand slowly. "I have already had the flu last March and April. I am probably immune. Let me go to visit Mable."

All the re-aides turned to look at her in the dim circle of the lantern. There were looks of incredulity and admiration on their faces. Miss Henderson who was usually rather unemotional, reached out and embraced her saying, "I was fearful no one would volunteer and I would have to assign someone to go. You have made it easier for all of us." Then other re-aides also embraced her and ask if she truly was willing to be their representative.

Lorena was not experienced with speech making so she simply said "Look, girls, I have already had influenza last March. I am probably immune to the germ or whatever it is that is causing the sickness. It is unlikely that I will catch it again. But I would like to get some sleep before I go. Also, I do not think I could find my way through the base to the influenza barracks in the dark." So with that statement which absolved the guilt of her tent-mates for not volunteering, they all prepared for bed.

Early next morning, Lorena donned her usual clean re-aide uniform and apron and joined Martha for breakfast in the mess tent. They enjoyed the fried cornmeal mush with maple syrup and coffee. The noise of the voice in the tent seemed singularly subdued on this day. Martha walked with Lorena as far as the curative workshop. They discussed how Lorena should launder her clothes as soon as she came back to protect the other re-aides. Martha gave Lorena a quick hug before sending her on her way. Martha pulled her influenza mask out of her pocket and put it on, even though she thought she was immune. It could not hurt to be careful.

As Martha neared the influenza barracks, she began to smell an unpleasant odor through her mask. Was it feces, dead bodies or just unbathed bodies? She was the only person outside the two barracks sitting side by side. There was a sign over each barracks door saying in block letters INFLUENZA WARD. The door to the ward opened inward with a screen door on the outside preventing flies from entering. Lorena knocked and peered through the screen. In the dimness inside, she could see two nurses moving between beds at the other end of the ward. The smell became more distinguished. It was not feces. Later, Lorena came to recognize it as the smell of dead bodies. Rather than wait for the busy nurses to leave their work to invite her in, she opened the door and saw three half clothed bodies stacked on the floor by the wall closest to the door. The horror of the realization impelled her steps onward toward the nurses as she tried to absorb this reality. Despite the influenza mask, she could see that the first nurse was one of the ones who slept in the tent near the re-aide tent. She looked completely fatigued. Her white uniform was covered with smudges. Her mask had a damp circle over her mouth. She carried a bundle of soiled sheets to a large bin near the back door. Meanwhile she looked over her shoulder at Lorena and asked, "Whatever are you doing here?"

Lorena explained her mission, "Mable Perkins, one of the re-aides came down with the influenza yesterday. I volunteered to come and check on her. I had influenza last March in the hospital at Kankakee. I hope I am immune to the disease here. Do you know how I can find Mable?"

The nurse explained that the three women who had become infected were in a small screened off section of the front of the other barracks. The back part of the other barracks had become a morgue. Big blocks of ice had been drug in to keep that part of the barracks cool until they could put the bodies in coffins and ship them to the train siding and then on for burial. The other two women with influenza were nurses. While she explained this, Lorena could see that most of the men in the iron beds were shivering, crying out or coughing. They were not even aware of her presence.

Lorena gave the nurse a wave of thank you and went out toward the other barracks. This time she did not knock since she knew the nurse inside would be too busy to bother with her. Inside the door, she stopped to adjust to the dimness since the wall built across the middle to divide the morgue from the patient beds diminished much of the light that the other barracks had. She then saw the wooden screens, which shielded the sick women from the sick men. She also recognized the nurse on duty even with her influenza mask. She explained her mission in a soft voice fearing to disturb the patients. The nurse merely motioned her toward the wooden screens. It was with a sort of dread that Lorena moved around to look down on the faces in the three women's bed, finally finding Mable in the third. None of the women opened their eyes to look at her as she stood over them. Mable's honey brown hair looked black, as it lay plastered to her feverish head. Lorena picked up Mable's damp cold hand and squeezed it. Slowly Mable opened and focused her eyes on Lorena. She started to speak and instead coughed so hard that bloody phlegm flew onto the white sheet. Martha said to her, "Don't try to talk. I came to check on you for Miss Henderson and Miriam Wentworth. We want to make sure you are as comfortable as possible." Mable gripped her hand a moment before she went off again into a paroxysm of coughing. Lorena looked around for the nurse and finally saw her as she rose from where she had been stooped between the beds wiping up spittle from one of the patient. Lorena asked her for a wet cloth to lay on Mable's forehead. The busy nurse swung her head to indicate where the wash clothes were stacked. A barrel of water laid on its side on some wooden supports had a spigot and was labeled clean water. Lorena took an white enamel basin from a nail on the wall, half-filled it with water and grasped several wash clothes. She carried the basin and sat it down on the floor between Mable's bed and the nurse beside her. Then she put one of the cloths into the basin and wrung out the cold water. She placed the wet cloth on Mable's forehand. Then she realized that it was rather unfair for the re-aide to get all her attention. She dipped the other washcloths in the water one at a time and put them on the foreheads of the two sick nurses.

Mable's labored breathing somewhat quieted as Lorena simply held her hand and looked into her face. After a few minutes, Lorena felt of the washcloth and realized it was no longer cool, so she dipped it again into the basin and wrung it out before placing it back on Mable's forehead. She repeated the exercise with the two nurses. She wondered whether someone had done this for her in the Kankakee State Hospital Infirmary but could not remember. After more than an hour of this activity, she seated herself on the foot of Mable's bed to save her tired feet. She heard someone come in the front door of the barracks followed by clanging of metal on metal. Peeping around the screen, she saw that an orderly had brought on a large covered kettle with a metal ladle hooked to the handle. He set it on the floor and put a stack of enamel bowls and enamel spoons on the small desk that the nurse used in the few moments she had between crises. Lorena asked the nurse if she could help by serving the soup to the sick nurses and Mable and Lorena perhaps could feed them if necessary. The nurse gave her a grateful look as she mumbled under the influenza mask.

None of the three sick women wanted food, but Lorena used her best persuasion to get them to take some soup. She reminded them of how much they were needed to give succor to the heroes from the war front. It was their duty to try to take nourishment so they could get back to their duties. She had some level of success with each of the three she had undertaken to assist. The nurse on duty showed her gratefulness by laying a hand on Lorena's uniformed arm and mumbling through the mask a thank you. Eventually, Lorena asked the nurse where she should go to the toilet here on this end of the base. The nurse motioned outside and to the left around the building. Despite the rain, Lorena found the newly constructed outhouse, which had no designation for male or female. She saw a stack of coffins and two orderlies carrying empty ones into the morgue and occupied ones out to a wagon that had several layers of the wooden containers. The depth of the epidemic became apparent to her as she closed the outhouse door and dropped the hook into the eyehole.

At suppertime, she returned through the rain to the re-aide tent to discuss with Miriam the advisability of taking some of her things to the influenza barracks and sleeping there until Mable could return. She described the hard work the influenza nurses were doing. Her plea was that Mable would recover faster if she had Lorena there to feed her, to cool her when she was feverish and cover her warmly when she had chills. Miriam was easily persuaded but encouraged her to be careful and be sure to eat enough to keep her from getting to tired or worse yet, sick herself.

Lorena took one valise containing her pajamas, some underclothing, and another re-aide summer uniform. For the next week, Lorena slept on an empty cot that was brought into the influenza barracks. She spent 18 hours per day nursing the three women and assisting the nurse in the barracks whenever she had free time. She helped with bathing feverish bodies, with reapplying bandages to wounds and holding cloths for coughing patients to catch their bloody sputum. Finally, Mable was able to return to her cot in the tent. It was two more weeks before she could return to her re-aide work.

CHAPTER 43

OCTOBER 1918

The Battle of the Argonne Forest brought many new patients to La Fauche Base 117. The rain continued. Some nights, artillery could be heard. One morning, a German observation balloon was visible in the sky north of the hospital. They could hear artillery shooting toward it but it was too high. Mud was everywhere. Even the duck-boards had spots where the mud squeezed up between the slats with each step.

When Lorena finally caught up with her sleep, after returning to the re-aide tent, she got back to work in the curative workshop. There seemed to be more and more shell-shocked men coming to Base 117. The dreary weather did not help in cheering them up. All the re-aides except Mable were working longer hours everyday. Mable was gradually regaining her strength after her bout of influenza.

Lorena received letters from both Colin and Irwin in the same batch of mail. Both men wrote as if she had promised to be "their girl". However, she recognized that she felt emotionally paralyzed with two men both thinking she was "theirs". And she thought she belonged to neither. It was quite a tortuous feeling. Mentally, she writhed about several days before answering. Lorena responded with letters that were as low keyed as possible about a possible long-term relationship. Instead, she described her recent stint of caring for Mable and the two nurses and about the influenza epidemic generally. Since this seemed to be her total experience for the recent past, her letter consisted almost wholly of influenza stories; how many men had become infected, how many had died here at Base 117 and anything she had been able to read in the newspaper. The Y Hut almost always had an English language newspaper, usually from England.

Lorena came to the realization that she needed to discuss her dilemma with another person. Martha was the logical confidant since they had become such close friends here. She made it a point to ask Martha if they could take a walk tomorrow afternoon. Martha eagerly agreed and asked to walk toward Neufchateau, as she had not visited it yet. Lorena thought that would be a good idea. They needed new tapestry needles, which they had been unable to get in the supply depot.

Next afternoon, fortunately, the rain had stopped, though the roads and paths were very muddy. With the October wind, their Ulster capes felt good. Soon their shoes were quite muddy. They decided to do as they had in July, walk on the grass beside the road; what was left of it which was not much. They could wipe their muddy boots there. When they had been walking and talking small talk for perhaps a mile, Lorena began to describe her situation for Martha. An empathetic listener, Martha encouraged Lorena to tell anything she did not already know about her past relationships with the two suitors. Lorena knew she would not be able to tell most of the re-aides about closeness with an orphan six years her junior or a Jew who had been her patient twice. Most of the re-aides were quite proper and would have been scandalized even if they tried to hide that fact from her. Martha, on the other hand, had been there when she saw Colin in Chaumont. And Martha had also worked with Irwin on crafts and knew what a talented and thoughtful man he was. Because this was the first time Martha had worked with psychiatric patients, she did not have the negative feelings toward the men with war neurosis that often stigmatized them. Perhaps she could give a truer response to Lorena's self-questioning.

"Martha, I am in a fix", Lorena started. "Both Colin, whom you met and Irwin Segal have been writing to me as if I had agreed to be their girlfriend. And I suppose I did in both cases act in a way that allowed them to think I was their girlfriend," she confessed hesitantly. "However, I don't feel it's fair to tell both men that I am their girlfriend. It should be either one or the other. But especially during war, when they both need everything they can to cheer them up, I would really hate to write to either one and disappoint them about being their girlfriend. I am just bumfuzzeled about what to do."

Martha hummed sympathetically before speaking, "Is there any harm in letting them both think you're their girl until after the war is over? Then maybe you could make arrangements to spend enough time with both of them, separately, of course, until you decide if you want either one?" She gave Lorena a thoughtful look while she awaited her answer. Obviously, her attitude toward life was more carefree and less guilt ridden than Lorena's.

Lorena groaned, "I was really hopeful that you would help me figure this out. I am tired of feeling miserable about it."

"Well, I am helping you think about it" she said as she stepped over a log which hid the remains of a dead campfire. "I'm telling you to not worry about it until you have to. That's what I'd do. By the way, I have had a very nice letter from Alex Mullieaux. He wants me to meet him in Paris when the war is over. He thinks it will be over soon. The Boche have been dropping ridiculous pamphlets telling the Allied troops to surrender rather than die. He wrote that he couldn't tell me anymore but to plan to meet in Paris after the peace treaty is signed. You could join me and meet Colin in Paris, too."

"Yes, I could do that but just thinking about it makes me feel a little sorry, as I know I'd enjoy it so much more with Irwin because he is so much more mature and sophisticated. He is also more sympathetic to other people than Colin is. But meeting in Paris would be great fun if we went together, wouldn't it? Also, if we went together, nobody could gossip about us not having chaperons," Lorena responded as she sorted through her complex feelings about herself and the two men.

Soon, the two women walked into the Market Square of Neufchateau. It was again too late for the market. There they saw a woman walk up to an American doughboy and put her hand on his uniform shirt and rub up and down on his upper arm. Then she slipped her hand through his arm and guided him inside a door that closed behind them. The two re-aides could not help gaping at what they had just witnessed. They had listened to discussions in the re-aide tent of the problems the doctors were having with men becoming infected with syphilis. Prostitution in its various reincarnations had been a topic of interest to almost all the women, including Miss Henderson, who used the opportunity to warn the re-aides away from soldiers.

Martha had a small map drawn for her by one of the nurses, which showed how to find the shop for tapestry supplies. She held the map in front of her as she led Lorena out of the square and down a side street. The shop held few supplies, as the war had taken its toll on such non-essentials as art goods, in which tapestry was definitely included. However, there were several small cylinders with a few needles in each. Martha was able to purchase two of the proper size for the patriotic flag tapestry her patient was working on.

On the walk back to La Fauche, the rain began to fall and the two women we glad of their Ulster capes. It made having a conversation difficult. The mud made it necessary to concentrate on not slipping. However, Lorena mulled over the discussion she and Martha had had on the way to Neufchateau and also the prostitute she had seen in the square. She wondered if either Irwin or Colin had gone to a prostitute while here in France. Her own virginity was of some concern to her as she was no longer a youth. Neither was she middle aged, but she was definitely mature mentally without the knowledge of what sexual fulfillment was. One of the things Irwin had written about in his last letter was how difficult it was to be back in his unit. Most of the men he had joined up with in Chicago had been killed either when they were in Cantigny or while he was away in the hospital. He was pretty much the only Jew. He had added a question about how Lorena felt about him being a Jew. Lorena knew that this was something she could write to him about. She might not feel like committing herself to being his "girl" but she certainly could tell him that his Jewishness affected her very little. She vowed to begin a letter to him when she got dry back in the re-aide tent.

CHAPTER 44

ARMISTICE

The Armistice was signed on German General Foch's train on November 11, 1918. It took two days for the news to get to La Fauche. Lorena could hear the wild cheering as each barracks received the news. From her spot in the metal crafting section near the front door, she stepped outside to ask a passing nurse if what she suspected was true, that the war was over. The nurse confirmed her speculation. She immediately went back into the curative workshop and shared the good news. The dozen men and dozen re-aides made the wooden sides of this barracks shake with their hurrahs. In fact, that ended the reconstructive work for that day. The hospital immediately arranged for a celebration show near the Y Hut. The wooden platform was quickly prepared again and musicians who had given a show the night before were again pressed into service. They led the nurses, orderlies, dieticians and re-aides, and any patients who could walk or get themselves there, in singing patriotic songs and some of the favorites from the last few years. They sang "Pack Up Your Troubles in Your Old Kit Bag", "Tipperary", "There's a Long, Long Trail A-Winding", "Madelon" and "The Star Spangled Banner". Such joy had not been heard in this place since it had opened. But the work must still go on. Though the flow of men from the Front had diminished to a trickle, there were still plenty of men to care for. Until they got their orders to be shipped home, there was work here for the re-aides to do.

In the beginning of November, two re-aides at a time had been given leave just as the doughboys had. After four months of straight service, they were allowed one week of leave. The first pair to go had been Letitia Johnson and Helen Vander Gaast. By the time they had returned, Mable Watkins was sufficiently recovered from the influenza to travel with Alice Simpson. These two were away when the armistice was declared. Pairs of re-aides continued to take their turn at leave, some going to Paris and some to the beautiful spa at Aix-les-Bains in the French Alps. Miriam Wentworth told Lorena and Martha that they were eighth on the list of pairs of re-aides. The two did not mind waiting as that meant they could spend Christmas in Paris. Lorena decided tow write to Irwin and tell him of her good fortune, forgetting that he probably did not celebrate Christmas. And she decided not to write Colin of this impending adventure. Realizing that by this act she had indeed made a decision about the two men, she wallowed in guilt for the hurt she would have to eventually deal to Colin. But that could be postponed until they were all back on American soil. And she was by no means committed to a firm future with Irwin, but he was mature, more sophisticated, more educated, and certainly a more skilled kisser. Also, she felt she had grown to know him more deeply through their common history at Kankakee and again here at Base 117. She had enjoyed her conversations with him since she met him in 1915. When he felt good, he was fun. His letters had been clever and descriptive without exploiting the ugliness of his situation near Verdun. She hoped he would be able to get leave to meet her in Paris. But even if he did not, she knew she would enjoy Paris with Martha. Though she had had little time to learn French, she felt confident she could learn enough between the time of learning of their leave and the actual event. The little dictionary had been hidden away in the valise under her cot most of the time.

After the Armistice, many more men in the hospital who could travel were sent on their way. A barracks, which had been a patient unit, became free and was offered to the re-aides instead of the nurses because there were fewer re-aides. This development was welcomed as the weather was making tent living very uncomfortable.

Letters arrived during the first week in December from both Irwin and Colin. It seemed natural to open Irwin's letter first even though guilt about future disappointment for Colin clouded her mind.

November 15, 1918

Dear Lorena,

The men have been celebrating ever since the news of the Armistice arrived two days ago. They have billeted us in a former German camp. The mess hall is hardly a building, more like a shed. Tables have been set up on sawhorses so we eat our meals outside. The barracks are like sheds, too. Those poor German soldiers must be glad to go home. But they left their cooties here. It has been a long time since I had a good hot bath. This brings up the topic of possibly meeting you in Paris. We have not had any orders to head for home. The Armistice is still too new for the big brass to have made any decisions about transport home. Anyway, I have been scheduled to go to musketry school. And Jews usually do not celebrate Christmas. But in your next letter, tell me where to look for you, in case I should be able to come when you are in Paris.

Our time together made it possible for me to dream of you when the noise of the artillery got terrible. I had worried about how I would be able to stand the shelling since the last time I got kind of paralyzed. But it just didn't affect me as badly. Being able to remember our last afternoon together helped me shut out the din. I hope I will be able to get to Paris, but do not count on me. If I cannot come, beware of all those hungry doughboys that will be there. Don't forget me.

Yours,

Irwin Segal

Lorena felt disappointed that she probably would not see him in Paris. It was with reluctance that she reached for Colin's letter, as each seemed more fervent than the last. It was just one small sheet of onion skin paper.

November 20, 1918

Dearest Lorena,

The war is over. Isn't that grand? How long will you stay in France? We are being sent back to England within the month. I will be there until they assign us a ship to take us back to Canada. I do not know how long before they will discharge us. Please tell me your plans. This barracks is too noisy for me to write more now.

Love,

Colin

Lorena was aware that this was the first time Colin had closed by using the word "Love". Heaviness settled in her chest as she considered this. It was not brotherly love she felt sure. She decided to wait until tomorrow to answer these letters since she was feeling quite upset now.

Next afternoon, before going to visit men in the amputee barracks, Lorena sat down to write to Irwin first. She had had an opportunity to ask some of the nurses in the mess-hall who had been to Paris about where she should tell someone to look for her. They had advised her to say that she would leave the name of her hotel or lodgings at the YMCA Center nearest the Gard du Nord railway station. It was a common thing for people to leave messages at the Y and Red Cross stations for comrades.

December 5, 1918

Dear Irwin,

We celebrated the end of the war too. There was a band here from the YMCA Expeditionary Army entertainment. They had given a concert the night before so when we got the news of the Armistice on the 14th, they led us in another performance where we all sang together. But now it is three weeks later and we are all eager to learn when we can go home. The patients here are especially eager to be on home soil for their care. We know we cannot leave until the patients have gone. I will leave a message for you at the YMCA Center near Gard du Nord railway station to tell you where Martha and I will be staying in Paris. I do hope you can manage to get there. Martha is writing to a man she met from Quebec, Canada and he may meet her there as well. I am sorry that I forgot that you do not celebrate Christmas. It would still be wonderful to see you in Paris. We could visit the museum together and drink coffee on the boulevard.

Sincerely,

Lorena Longley

She caught Martha before she had an opportunity to write to Alex Mullieaux. Lorena made her promise to tell Alex not to tell Colin that she was going to Paris. She hoped that Martha could be persuasive enough to keep Alex from telling his best friend he was going to Paris without him. She hated this deception, but she just did not want to have to fend off Colin's advances in a romantic place like Paris. Even though Paris had experienced the difficulties of four years of war, it was still an exciting place.

December 5, 1918

Dear Colin,

What wonderful news it is that the war is over! And we are fortunate to have survived it since so many men died in battle and also many others died from the influenza. You are especially lucky since you were here so much longer than most other American soldiers were.

We have had no information about when we will be able to go home, as there are still many men here to take care of. Some men have been sent home though because we were able to move into an empty barracks. It is getting so cold here now, that we are very grateful not to be in the tent any longer. Keep writing and I wish you a speedy trip home.

Merry Christmas,

Lorena Longley

CHAPTER 45

PARIS

Gard du Nord station in December was cold, cold. Lorena and Martha had arrived late in the afternoon. The train had been full of soldiers of all nationalities. There were American doughboys, French poilus, and English Tommies. They were either on their way home or on furlough for the Christmas week. Many of them were drunk or drinking. The two women, along with several nurses from Base 117, had found themselves a corner of a passenger car and barricaded themselves with their luggage to avoid unwanted advances from drunken soldiers. The trip had taken all day from Chaumont, where they had stayed the night before in the hotel so they could board the early train to Paris. They had instructions from the re-aides that had already visited Paris, that the best thing to do was to go immediately to the Red Cross Center and ask about lodging. Following the instructions, the re-aides and nurses were directed to a hotel that had been rented by the Red Cross just for women. Lorena and Martha went to the nearby YMCA Hut, which was enormous compared to the one at Base 117, to leave messages for Irwin and Alex. The volunteer in the Y Hut also offered them hot chocolate, which was just the thing after the long train ride. The toilet in the Y Hut was much better than the one on the train. By the time they had walked nearly a mile, carrying their valises, they were ready for a rest.

Their hotel, La Petite Fleur, was a narrow building squeezed between two other narrow buildings. They were assigned a room together on the fourth floor. By the time they had lugged their valises up four flights, they thought they were done in for the day. However, after a short rest, the excitement of being in Paris motivated them to find the bathroom in the hallway, take a hot bath in the zinc tub and by 10 p.m., they were out enjoying watching the Paris nightlife. There were so many soldiers around who wanted to buy drinks for them. They had difficulty declining these offers as many of the men were drinking or drunk already and did not want to take "no" for an answer. Finally, they went into a building with a CAFÉ sign over the door. Obviously, the proprietor was used to Americans. He asked, "What you want?" The two women ordered coffee and pointed to an empty corner table. They hoped this would put them out of the way of the horde of soldiers. The feeling of celebration was electric in the air, despite the fact that the city was recovering from four long years of deprivation. Christmas spirit was evident, even though there were few obvious symbols of the season. They could hear familiar Christmas songs being sung in a few cafes. After midnight, the two re-aides found their way back to their hotel. Despite the coffee, they both fell asleep immediately. Lorena thought it must be the deserving sleep of exhausted hospital workers who never seemed to feel they had had enough sleep.

They were still sleeping when the concierge knocked on their door next morning to say in tolerable English, that a gentleman was waiting for them downstairs. She did not say his name.

Both women scrambled to get ready to go down. Toileting, dressing in some borrowed dresses rather than uniforms, hair combing, and teeth brushing before out the door they went. Lorena led down the narrow staircase. As she almost lunged into the small room that served as a parlor and reception, she saw the back of a Canadian uniform and knew that it was not Irwin. He turned around just as Martha saw him and threw herself into his arms. Lorena wondered how Martha had come to feel so comfortably familiar with Alex to be so forward but at this moment, she pushed that thought aside. Her own disappointment was overshadowed by the pleasure she saw in the faces of Martha and Alex. After Martha loosened her embrace upon him, he reached out to shake Lorena's hand. Then he invited the two women for breakfast.

He found a taxicab and the road to the center of the city. They walked along the Rue Lafayette enjoying being away from the hospital environment. Alex told them that he was on his way home via England. He must be in Calais in two more days. Eventually, Alex led them to a small café on a side street. It was late morning already so the trio ordered some of the soup that they could see bubbling on an ancient stove behind the counter. With it, the waiter brought a 14-inch loaf of bread and a small plate with creamy cheese to spread on the bread. The soup was thick vegetable with tiny shreds of some sort of meat. The flavor was delicious. Perhaps it was just the Parisian air that made it so tasty as they had had similar soup in the mess hall at Base 117 quite often. Alex sat between the women at the small round café table. He tried to be equal in dividing his conversation but Martha not so subtly drew his attention to her as often as she could. Lorena did not mind, though she realized she herself was somewhat superfluous. She did make an opportunity to query Alex about whether he had told Colin that she was in Paris. She watched him closely as he promised that he had kept her secret. He seemed to be telling the truth. She wondered if he thought her a bad woman to be playing so loosely with Colin's feelings. But the couple did not seem to have much interest in her concerns.

As soon as they all finished eating, she explained that she would like to purchase some souvenirs of Paris to take home with her whenever they were able to return to America. She did not think she would have another opportunity to come to Paris. The other two did not make any attempt to dissuade her from that errand. She left them sitting at the table and went back to Rue Lafayette. She walked and did find a small shop where she could buy some French soap. She also bought a French newspaper, determined to try to read it with the help of her small dictionary. Then she hailed a taxicab and directed the elderly driver back to La Petite Fleur Hotel. He seemed to know exactly where it was. His pronunciation of the English language charmed her but she limited her conversation for fear he might get the wrong idea about her. She did not want to be away from the hotel when and if Irwin tried to find her.

She experienced some pride in her success in getting back to the hotel alone with her meager French. As she walked into the small reception parlor, she saw Irwin sitting in one of the spindly-legged chairs reading an English language newspaper. He looked up just as she recognized him. He rose and dropped the paper as she moved toward him. As their hello embrace ended, they heard the door behind the reservation desk open. The voice of the concierge was clear despite her French accent. "May I remind you of the Red Cross rule that there will be no men above the ground floor."

Both Irwin and Lorena reacted with surprise as they were simply so glad to see each other that they had not thought about attempting to subvert the rules of the women's hotel. After a moment of being flustered, Lorena responded, "Of course, Mademoiselle, we would not think of breaking the rule." She asked Irwin to be seated while she took her purchases up stairs. While she was in the room, she re-combed her hair and put on the small, smart, brimmed hat she had forgotten when Alex was announced. It was unfortunate that she had only her Ulster cape for a wrap, as it did not do justice to her hat, she thought. However, Irwin did not seem to even notice that she had added this fashionable touch to her costume. She asked the concierge to please inform Martha that her friend Irwin had arrived and she would hopefully meet them for dinner. Irwin took her arm and led her out into the street. They did not speak for several blocks as the feelings between them were non-verbally expressed by a tightening of the grips on each other's arms. The day was spent just wandering on different streets, pointing out to each other novel sights and events. Occasionally, they would sit on a park bench or convenient short wall. They were more aware of each other than they were of the sights.

Eventually, Irwin told her how he had manipulated to get a pass to come to Paris to meet her. They were not yet ready to be sent home until the German prisoners of war were all repatriated. But they hoped to be sent home sometime soon. He had volunteered to accompany a trainload of coffins with bodies to be shipped to the cemetery. After he delivered the coffins, he had a four-day pass and he immediately took the train for Paris. He would only be able to stay two days before he would have to start back to their camp at Pagny-La-Blanche-Cote.

Lorena was disappointed that he would be in Paris for such a short time, but she determined to enjoy the time they had together. She realized that these short encounters were a certainty peculiar to wartime. People seized on whatever enjoyment they could squeeze out of life.

CHAPTER 46

CHRISTMAS EVE 1918

Five hours of sleep per night was all that could be spared from the time Lorena and Martha had to spend with their men. The couples did not spend time as a foursome but rather two twosomes. The men slept in accommodations provided for men by the Red Cross. This hotel was half a mile away from La Petite Fleur Hotel.

Lorena and Irwin were familiar with the Chicago "L" so they felt comfortable using the Metro. Using the small dictionary and pointing to their destination to the conductor, they were able to find their way. They visited as many of the famous sites as they could squeeze into their time together. They walked across the Pont Neuf Bridge to the Ile de La Cite. They viewed the grandeur of Notre Dame Cathedral. Lorena asked Irwin if it bothered him to be in a Catholic Church. He replied that beauty was not the possession of only one group of people. Perhaps they should see if they could find a Jewish temple. Instead, they found Jewish gravestones in the Montmartre Cemetery. They saw some buildings that had been damaged by the German bombs.

During their walks and rides these two days, Lorena shared her own background and learned much more about Irwin's. His paternal grandparents had immigrated to the United States from Germany in the 1880s. His grandfather had come first to New York, later sending for his wife and three children, the oldest of whom was Irwin's father. His mother's parents had come from Poland in 1890. She was also the oldest child. They had met in the temple in New York.

Both of them had been doing factory work in New York before they married. A matchmaker arranged their marriage, though the two young people had already met each other. They moved almost immediately to live near relatives in Chicago where there was more opportunity. Irwin was born the following year, followed by his five brothers and sisters. Lorena already knew much of Irwin's story, about his father's death, Irwin's suicide attempt and his stepmother.

As the time for Irwin's departure to Pagny-La-Blanche-Cote approached, their feelings of having to leave too many things unsaid overwhelmed them. Lorena questioned herself about how much of her ardent feeling toward him was inspired by the Paris atmosphere since the war was over. However, her answer to herself was that Irwin was a kind and loving man, well educated compared to others and probably had many prospects when he returned to the United States. He had expressed his wish to continue his education when he got home. He felt sure that Mr. Cohen, his teacher, would help him decide how to go to college. In fact, Mr. Cohen had answered his letter from France, and had discussed his future in Chicago.

Lorena accompanied Irwin to the railway station and stood with him on the platform as passengers loaded. He put his grip in the luggage carrier and come back outside to stand with her. He took both her gloved hands in his and tipped her face up toward him. He lifted the veil from her hat where it covered her forehead. He kissed the tip of her nose, her forehead and finally brushed her lips. Their behavior was not unlike that of many other couples saying goodbye on the platform. However, most of the other couples had known each other a much shorter time than Lorena and Irwin. "I will write to you as long as I am here in France and hopefully I can let you know before I ship out for home. But even if I am unable to notify you of when I leave, I'll write you as soon as I get home. Will you do the same for me?" She simply nodded, as she feared she would cry if she spoke. "It has meant so much to me," he went on. "You have helped me restore my faith in myself. First there was the hospital in Kankakee and then the shell-shocked barracks at La Fauche. I feared that I would always be a neurotic person. You have helped me see that my reactions both times were normal for the circumstances. War is abnormal, something to hate. Lorena, we haven't really talked about our future, but I want to ask you to think of spending the rest of your life with me." He put his finger on her lips before she could speak. "Don't answer me now. I realize that my being Jewish may make you hesitate. But many people marry out of their religion. Being Jewish is important to me, but the religion part is not as much. I've never been very religious. You haven't said much about what you believe, anyway. Just take time to think about it and we can discuss it when we are both safe in Chicago again." Lorena realized he automatically assumed she would be returning to Chicago before she had even confirmed it to herself.

The conductor called "Tout au loin." Irwin hugged her and kissed her on the mouth one last time before swinging aboard. He found a window and opened it to speak to her until the train got underway. She ran along side the car for a few steps and threw him a kiss.

The trip back to La Petite Fleur was rather bleak despite many offers to buy her drinks. She clutched her cape about her and strode forward looking intently ahead to discourage unwanted attentions. Martha had not yet returned. Lorena was so concentrated on her own relationship with Irwin that she had nearly forgotten that Martha was also saying goodbye to Alex this evening. She lay on the bed in her cape since the room was quite cold and hugged her memories of the last two days to her. After some time, her growling stomach made her get up and go out looking for food. She found the little CAFÉ that she and Martha had had coffee in their first evening in Paris. As she sat there eating onion soup with bread and cheese, she remembered that it was Christmas Eve and she was here alone. Irwin had said nothing about Christmas because he did not celebrate it. If she was serious about him, she would need to realize that there could be other Christmas Eves in which she felt lonely because he did not have any particular feeling about Christmas. She wondered why she felt anything in particular because she had not ever had a fervent religious experience. The Quakers seemed so private about their religious feelings. Whatever others around her were worshiping did not seem to matter to her. But still Christmas and the warmth of the Christmas stories and pageants were things she looked forward to each year. The café had no decoration to symbolize the season except a large red ribbon bow on the simple four-socket chandelier. She finished her soup and bread and geared herself up to discourage revelers on her way back to La Petite Fleur.

When she got there, she found Martha in the room wrapped up in her cape. Her breath smelled of wine. She was delighted to see Lorena. The rest of Christmas Eve was spent telling each other how they had spent the last two days. Tomorrow, Christmas, they could sleep in.

Chapter 47

Christmas in Paris

When the two women awoke about 10 o'clock on Christmas morning, they surprised each other by giving each other presents. Martha had made a small wood carving of an ambulance. The wheels had wooden spokes though the windows were simply a suggestion of indentation. She had carried it in the bottom of her valise all the way to Paris to surprise Lorena on this holiday. Lorena had made an elaborate white collar to be worn over a dress or waist. It was made of ribbed cotton with tatted edging. Lorena had made the tatted edge while she was in the influenza barracks. She had carefully washed it before hand stitching it into the collar. The collar tied in the back with a ribbon. They both admired each other's handiwork and knew that they would always remember this special Christmas in Paris.

After grooming themselves carefully, they agreed to find some breakfast and then go to mass in one of Paris's big churches. The concierge told them of a small shop on a nearby street that usually sold Christmas bread and coffee. They felt lucky when they found that the shop was indeed open. They felt even more fortunate when they were able to hail a passing horse-cab outside the shop. It was near 12 noon. They asked the driver for Notre Dame Cathedral. He drove them there and stopped in the square in front of the church. The service was already underway when they entered the carved doors. They were surprised at the distance of the ceiling in the nave. They did not realize that they would need to stand during the mass as the seats were all occupied by the choir. It was a Lorena's first Catholic mass. She had heard that it was in Latin but it did not register until she realized she could not understand a word. However, she had developed a keen interest in observing the behavior of others. Martha also had attended few Catholic services. They kept themselves toward the back of the huge nave. They could hardly see the priest and his helpers as they moved near the altar. But the women were entranced by the music of the choir and the organ. There were candles in the side altars as well as in the candelabra at the front. The incense was a faint smell. It was such an exotic experience for a woman who had spent seven years with Quakers who did not approve of such popish things. The two women were not the only ones who did not know when to kneel and when to stand. Because they were in the back they simply stood and observed.

After the mass finished, they clutched their capes about them and went out and walked around the building straining their necks to look up at the gargoyles. They learned that that they could climb the towers. After the crowd thinned, they did climb the tower closest to the river and enjoyed the view of others out enjoying a peaceful Paris on Christmas. The view gave them the opportunity to orient themselves to the River Seine and nearby monuments.

Soon they were on the ground wearing their feet and legs out enjoying the famous city, knowing that it would probably be their only chance. The museums were closed on Christmas so walking and talking was the best pleasure. They found, on their own, a small elegant restaurant where they were able to have some beef Burgundy over wide noodles for early supper. Burgundy wine filled their glasses as well. This alcohol imbibing in Paris was the most Lorena could ever remember drinking. She had had to study hard for so much of her life that she had not taken time to discover wine. Martha seemed more sophisticated about food and drink than her friend. Lorena put her trust in Martha about these matters. Even in the small restaurant, there were three American soldiers who sent a bottle of wine to their table. Martha knew that it was expected that they invite the men to their table. So they did. Soon the waiter had pulled another small table up to the one at which Lorena and Martha sat. He gestured and three doughboys from a table across the room rose and walked over. One was obviously already somewhat drunk. It was hard to tell about the other two. The tallest one was a man from Nebraska who easily began the conversation by asking where the two women hailed from. Each of the people sitting at the two tables shared this information. The blond man from New Jersey refilled the wine glasses. The man from Massachusetts, who seemed drunk when he sat down, continued to sink lower and lower toward the table, offering little in the way of conversation. The men wanted to know how two such upright American women were here in Paris at Christmas. Martha told them that they were on leave from Base 117, neglecting to say they had both come here to meet special male friends. Lorena realized she could not explain about Irwin without forcing Martha to tell why she was here so she held her tongue, though she feared it was not fair to withhold this information. When the bottle was empty, the two men who were still upright asked the two re-aides if they would like to walk out on the Champs-Eylees despite the nearing dark. They insisted on paying for the women's supper. When they got outside the restaurant, the men assisted their drunken friend into a horse-cab and paid his fair to their hotel. Then the tall man from Nebraska seized Lorena's arm as the New Jersey man did Martha's. Off they walked at a brisk pace to fend off the cold wind. Because of the nearing darkness and the cold temperature, there were few people strolling on the famous street. Those that were out, walked briskly. Lorena could feel that the tall Nebraskan was not fully sober by the occasional stumble over a brick paving. She could see that Martha was enjoying the attentions of these men so she did not follow her impulse to ask to be excused. Additionally, she knew that it was not a good idea for a lone woman her age to be out walking in Paris on Christmas night. She did her best to seem cheerful, rather than fearful. But when the New Jersey doughboy saw another café and suggested going in for more wine, Lorena said firmly, "I have had enough wine and I think you have, too. I am going back to the hotel. Will you come with me Martha?" She waited a moment while Martha hovered uncertainly between Lorena and the New Jersey man. Then Martha disengaged herself from his arm and walked up beside Lorena. Without a moment wasted, the two women walked quickly across the sidewalk toward the street. They crossed quickly before the men knew quite what had happened. When on the other side, Lorena saw a free horse-cab and waved him toward the curb. He seemed to quickly comprehend the situation as the men came hurrying across the street as fast as their alcohol impaired legs would allow them. The horse-cab drove off as the men were about twenty feet away. The two looked angry and as if they had been duped. Lorena thought that yes, indeed they had been duped as they had paid for the women's Christmas supper. She had a small feeling of guilt but also triumph at their escape.

Once on their way, Martha said, "Even though it seems early to go back to the hotel in Paris, I am glad we escaped from those drunks. I did not realize what we were getting into, did you?"

Lorena explained, "We put ourselves in a compromising position with those fellows. We should not have allowed them to buy our supper. I would feel better going back to the hotel now. I'm fearful of meeting them again. They are probably pretty mad. I want to go back to the hotel where it is safe." Martha nodded in agreement.

When they got up to their fourth floor room, they tucked themselves under their fluffy feather comforters and discussed their adventures and how they planned to spend their last full day in Paris tomorrow. At last, the wine seemed to put Martha to sleep.

Lorena, unable to sleep, thought with dread of the letter she would have to write to Colin when she got back to La Fauche. She tried several times in the dark cold room to formulate in her mind what she would say. It was too cold to get up and try to find paper to capture her thoughts. Soon she too slept a somewhat disturbed sleep.

CHAPTER 48

MUSTERING OUT

At the end of February, Lorena received a letter full of bitter recrimination from Colin in Toronto, Canada. His unit had mustered out in Quebec City. Her letter telling him of her sisterly feelings for him and that she was in love with someone else was awaiting him there. After drowning his sorrow with some of his dough-boy buddies, he had boarded another boat to Toronto. In Toronto he had decided to try to get a job rather than returning to Chicago where he might meet her. He was sarcastic about her "sisterly" feelings toward him. He wrote a few choice names for women that she had never heard him use before. Lorena surmised he must have learned them from other soldiers. Then she remembered that his young life had been spent sleeping in a bordello. He had known these words all along but did not think they applied to her. She could not bring herself to show the letter to Martha though she knew Martha would console her and tell her it showed she was too good for Colin. Lorena felt badly about disappointing his young dreams. He was not yet twenty years old.

Lorena waited a few days before answering his letter assuring Colin that she would always think of him as an important person in her life and if he ever returned to Chicago, she would like to see him again. Then she tucked his letter away in the bottom of her valise under her cot.

By March, Base 117 was beginning to empty out. Gradually one barracks after another was closed. Those with influenza either died or got better and were sent home. Major Fenworth told Miss Henderson that when the re-aides went home, there were places for some of them at Walter Reed Hospital in Washington and in some other military hospitals. Lorena quickly told Miss Henderson that she intended to return to Chicago. Her time there as a student at Hull House had been the most exciting she could remember, with the exception of her work here with the shell-shocked doughboys. Also, Chicago was the place where Irwin had already returned. His letters had become more ardent after he was home in his native city again. She answered with equal ardor.

Martha invited Lorena to visit her in Lexington, Massachusetts before returning to Chicago. Lorena decided this would offer a good opportunity to visit Boston as she had never been in the New England States. The trip to France, especially to Paris had whetted her appetite for seeing and knowing more about the world. Martha had expounded on the various places of interest that Lorena might like to visit in Massachusetts. This little hiatus before returning to Chicago would offer her an opportunity to think about the rest of her life before she arrived in Chicago and had to make decisions about work and about Irwin. She had saved most of the money she had received as salary.

The last letter she received from Irwin before her departure from Base 117 explained that he had decided he would like to study the subject of education. Mr. Cohen from the Jewish Training School had arranged for him to have a scholarship to the University of Chicago. He was looking forward to taking classes there. He wrote that he was reading John Dewey's book *School and Society* and found it so interesting. He wished Dr. Dewey was still teaching at Chicago, but he could not attend Columbia University in New York where Dr. Dewey was now. Irwin's scholarship was for the University of Chicago.

Lorena thought Irwin's educational plans sounded very enterprising. She wrote to him of her support for his educational endeavors. She also wrote that she had considered his question about sharing the rest of their lives. She wanted to say yes, but he must get his education before they could marry. She had heard from other re-aides about Margaret Sanger's arrest for the publicizing of birth control in New York. She knew that when a woman married, she could expect to become pregnant soon after as birth control was not readily available. As the re-aides had come to know each other better, such topics as sex and birth control had been common topics of conversation in the tent after the lamp was blown out. Lorena also realized that Irwin's scholarship to the University of Chicago would not support a wife. She would need to work when she got to Chicago. Married women were not allowed to work in most places. She hoped that her straightforward letter writing did not shock him as they had never discussed sex. They had just felt their feelings.

The re-aides were ordered to close up the curative workshop before Lorena received a reply from Irwin. They packed up whatever craft materials could be used at home in the US in military hospitals. They would be shipped home on a separate ship with other recovered goods. Many of the re-aides had made new tools to use with the patients or to replace ones that were broken. These were packed in their kits along with the ones they had brought with them. They left the curative workshop in a much cleaner and more orderly state than they had found it.

The night before they left Base 117, Lorena took out Colin's last letter and burned it rather than make the mistake of forgetting it and having Irwin find it someday.

Retracing their steps and the ride from Base 117 to Le Havre was much more enjoyable than the trip toward the war zone. The train was less crowded and there were other people who had worked at La Fauche and in Chaumont on board with them. The re-aides felt less fearful of having soldiers make inappropriate advances. In their ten months, they had encountered all kinds of men and all kinds of advances. Fending off proposals, honorable or dishonorable, had become a habitual practice. The re-aides had highly developed their skills in solving almost any problem. This confidence allowed them to enjoy the French countryside despite the occasional bomb or shell crater. Lorena shared these thoughts with Martha and the small group of nearby re-aides as their train approached Le Havre. The concierge at Hotel Canard Blanc welcomed them like old friends. Nothing was too good for the American women who had served and helped France win this war.

On board the troop ship from Le Havre, she had plenty of time to write letters to Irwin, Mrs. Radicky and Edna May telling them of her plan to go with Martha to her home in Lexington to visit for a few weeks before returning to Chicago. She told them of wanting to visit the Boston School of Occupational Therapy and to see other sights in that famous city. To Edna May she directed a question about how long she would continue as an Army nurse. To Mrs. Radicky, she confessed that she, Lorena would be very pleased to have a job again at Kankakee. She neglected to tell Mrs. Radicky that she now considered herself engaged to Irwin Segal. She knew that Mrs. Radicky would not think this a good idea. Since she and Irwin could not marry for at least four years, she would have lots of time to let Mrs. Radicky discover their relationship for herself.

Lastly, she explained to Irwin why she planned to stop to visit Martha, as she might not have another such chance before taking up work in or near Chicago. Though she was eager to see him, she did not want to miss this opportunity.

Then she went on to tell him that she had written to Mrs. Radicky asking for her old job back. She realized it was a generous train ride away from the University of Chicago, but that this way she would not interfere with his studies. She left unwritten her thought that it would also help both of them keep their urges under control. In Paris, she had sensed how easy it would be to let their emotions take over. The Red Cross rule about no men in the hotel rooms or women on furlough saved them from impulsively giving in to their urges. She saved the letters to mail when they got to New York. The troop ship, though crowded with soldiers as it had been on their initial crossing, was less intimidating as the re-aides knew they had survived much and could survive more. They continued with their usual cautions as groups of men could be rough and dangerous. They continued to go in pairs whenever they were out of their cabin.

One thing Lorena realized was that she had become less of a loner during her service for the Expeditionary Army. Most of what she had achieved before she went to France, she had achieved by herself; her education, her choice of the new career, and her job at Kankakee. But the experience in France could not have been lived without the support of the other re-aides. The parting with these women in New York was poignant. They knew they had been pioneers and probably would not see each other again. There had been occasional differences but they had been solved with the welfare of the group and their patients in mind. Now they would be going off to try to share their experiences with others. Would others think their work had been important? Or would the soldiers be the only ones to receive honor? These thoughts were unstated but felt as the women went down the gangplank carrying their valises.

0-595-28723-9

LaVergne, TN USA
08 January 2010
169254LV00003B/35/A